THE CARETAKER

ALSO BY SHAWN MCGUIRE

THE WITCHES OF BLACKWOOD GROVE Mystery Series

HEARTH & CAULDRON Mystery Series

WHISPERING PINES Mystery Series

GEMI KITTREDGE Mystery Series

THE WISH MAKERS Fantasy Series

THE CARETAKER

A WITCHES OF BLACKWOOD GROVE MYSTERY

SHAWN MCGUIRE

CHAPTER 1

*C*ricket's life was in danger.

Who would want to hurt my four-year-old granddaughter? Why?

I lost everything in last night's fire. Except for her, my backpack, her favorite blanket, the clothes on our backs, and the shoes on our feet. And whatever was in my car. That was it. Everything else was gone, so I'd had no choice but to ask for their help. It was embarrassing to have to do it again, but it wasn't just me this time. I'd do whatever was necessary to keep my granddaughter safe.

After a mostly sleepless night in the most secure hotel in town, I buckled my little bug into her booster seat.

"Where are we going?" Cricket asked.

"To the park."

"Yay, the park!"

This child was always happy, despite the tragedies that had struck her young life recently. Probably because she was too young to really understand.

Including red lights, it took less than five minutes to get

there. Which gave me time to wonder what had started the fire. Or more accurately, what had started the *fires*? There were two of them. One in my bedroom at the back of the house and another in the garage at the front of the house.

"Who is that?" Cricket asked as we crossed the expanse of lush green grass at the park. She stretched her hand and pointed at the gray-haired man in the forest-green anorak.

"His name is Jasper."

He looked so old. His hair was white gray now, his back hunched, and he looked smaller than I remembered. When had that happened? I couldn't help but smile when I spotted the binoculars hanging from his neck. No surprise there. It also wasn't a surprise to see him holding an open book in one hand —surely a guide to the birds of southwestern Wisconsin—while patting his jacket pockets, pants pockets, and then the side of his head with his free hand.

In three, two, one, I counted down to myself.

On cue, he gave up the hunt and held out his hand. A pen appeared on his palm. Or more likely a pencil so any errors in note-taking could be erased and corrected.

"Jasper is my father." I tapped Cricket's little button nose. "Which means he's your great-grandfather."

Dad saw us nearing him and leaned forward as though trying to bring us into focus. "Dusty?"

As he shuffled toward us, he slid the pencil behind his ear. I almost laughed when it dropped onto the grass behind him. We used to find pencils all over the place—every room in the house, on the floor in the garage, scattered around the yard. My father was a constant note jotter so always had a notebook or two in a pocket, but he was forever losing his pencils. How many times had I told him his ears stuck out too far to hold them in place? Fortunately for him, he could summon a fresh one at will so was never *really* without.

A tsunami of emotions rose higher and higher inside me as

we closed the gap. We'd talked for a literal couple of minutes every six months, give or take, but hadn't seen each other face to face in twenty-nine years. Shortly before my son, Micah, was born.

"Look at you both." His smile made deep wrinkles appear around the corners of his beard-and-mustache framed mouth. Crinkles like quotation marks punctuated his tired brown eyes. "I like your hair short."

I absently touched my choppy blond bob. It had been this way for decades. "Thanks."

He reached out and trailed a finger down my granddaughter's forearm. "Who are you?"

Not liking to be touched by strangers, she pulled her arm away. "I'm Cricket."

He looked at me in question.

"Her given name is Alice, but we call her Cricket because she never stops chirping." I blew a raspberry on one of her still pudgy cheeks. The nickname Chipmunk would have fit, too, but we figured she'd grow out of her cheeks. They had gotten smaller but were still as adorable as the day she was born.

I set her down on her sandaled feet. "I need to talk to Great-grandpa. Can you go play for a few minutes?"

She frowned and hugged *baba*, her pink-and-white striped blanket with the yellow and purple flowers she pretended smelled so pretty. Right now, they smelled like smoke. "I don't have anything to play with."

My heart ached. As soon as we were settled, a toy store run was high on our to-do list. So was a bath for baba. Meanwhile, the park Dad chose didn't have a playground, and we were the only people here. Which was probably exactly why he chose this location. For privacy.

He held out his hand again, and a pair of child-sized bubblegum-pink opera glasses appeared. "Have you ever looked through binoculars before?"

Her frown intensified, and she shook her head. "What are they?"

Interesting that their sudden, out-of-nowhere appearance didn't faze her.

He pressed the handle into her little hand and told her to hold on tight. "See how there are small circles on one side and bigger circles on the other?"

Cricket inspected the binoculars-on-a-stick closely. "Uh-huh."

"Look through the small circles." He showed her how by raising his non-handled pair to his eyes.

She shoved baba at me, held hers up, and Dad adjusted them until they were the perfect width for her face.

"Everything is huge!" she declared. "Is it magic?"

"There are a set of lenses that—"

I cleared my throat. If left unchecked, we'd stand there for an hour listening to a lecture on how binoculars functioned.

"They're like glasses," he amended and tapped the round pair on his rectangular face. "Do you know what glasses are for?"

"Yep. They make things look not blurry."

He chuckled. "Right. Instead of making things not blurry, binoculars make things look bigger and closer."

She shifted on her feet with excitement. "What can I look at?"

"Absolutely anything you want." He pointed up. "The clouds in the sky." He pointed down. "The grass on the ground." He pointed into a tree. "I use mine to look at birds. That way I don't have to get too close and scare them. I love birds."

"I love birds too."

That was the first time I'd heard her say that. Looked like my granddaughter and father had bonded.

"I'm gonna go look at . . . everything." She threw her arms out wide and spun in a circle. Without falling down this time.

"And then you can tell me all about it later," I replied. "Don't go too far away. Make sure you can see me and hear my voice."

We watched as she wandered off, the tulle skirt of her pink ballerina dress bouncing with each skip.

The wrinkles of amusement on my father's face smoothed away. Creases of concern furrowed his forehead and the spot between his gray eyebrows. "How are you doing, Dusty?"

I'd texted him about the fire last night. "We both made it out alive, so I'm fine."

"Let's sit." He indicated a small picnic table that hadn't been there seconds earlier. Once we were settled, he said, "I know this isn't easy for you. Catch me up on everything."

By *everything*, he surely meant my life since the last time we saw each other. I'd left home thirty-two years ago when I was eighteen. That was the first time I asked him for help. Or rather, approached The Council for help. Dad was my liaison. The second time, twenty-nine years ago, I was terrified because I was penniless and pregnant. At least this time, my desperate situation wasn't because I'd made a stupid decision.

Still, humiliation, like toxic sludge, flowed through my veins over having to approach them a third time. But as I decided last night, I had no better option.

"Life had honestly been normal," I replied. "Until about a month ago."

"What happened a month ago?"

"Cricket's mother, Josie, went missing. I don't know what so-called *evidence* they have, but they decided that my son is responsible. They arrested my Micah."

A notebook, labeled *Dusty* on the cover, and a fresh pencil appeared on the table in front of him. He flipped to about the midpoint. Seemed he'd been keeping notes on me all along. Probably every two-minute phone call we'd had over the decades was documented in there.

"You *know* he's innocent?" Dad asked.

"Yes. I had a dream."

When I was about Cricket's age, I started having dreams that were far from standard. I came from a family of witches, and we each had a power. Some of us had more than one. For me, if I had a dream that woke me with a start—heart pounding, covered in a cold sweat, gasping for breath—it was a prophetic dream. They *always* indicated the truth behind something that had already happened. If I was ever going about my day and froze in the middle of whatever I was doing, that meant my second power had just kicked in. Premonitions were about events that would happen in the future. How far into the future was rarely indicated, but like with the dreams, they were always accurate.

That had to be what happened last night. I had pulled into the driveway like usual, stopped, and decided it would be better to park on the street. I *never* parked on the street. If I had parked in the garage, I would have lost my little twelve-year-old hatchback too.

The problem was, unlike my father's ability to produce items at will, my dreams and premonitions were not on demand. I'd had my powers for forty-five of my fifty years and had never been able to willfully bring on either. This meant that while I couldn't see where Josie—or goddess forbid her body—was, I knew my son was innocent because of that dream.

"Okay," Dad replied with a firm nod. "If you dreamt it, it's true, but that doesn't bring home the bacon, does it?"

He meant that didn't provide the proof I needed to get Micah out of prison.

"No, it doesn't. He seems to be safe enough where he is, so my concern right now is Cricket."

I glanced across the field to see my blessing of a grandchild looking at wildflowers through her opera glasses. She looked through them, then pulled them away. Looked through and pulled them away. What an amazingly thoughtful and educational gift.

I opened the main compartment of my backpack and then the interior zippered pocket. "I found this tucked beneath my windshield wiper last night."

Dad took the folded piece of paper from me. His mouth dropped open as he read the message.

HER MOTHER WAS FIRST. THEN HER FATHER.
IT WOULD BE A SHAME IF SHE LOST HER ENTIRE FAMILY.
THEN WHO WILL TAKE CARE OF HER?

"You're right. Sounds like a threat but not just against Cricket." His now worried gaze fixed on me. "Sounds like you're in danger too."

Staring across the field at my tiny ballerina, I answered, "I know."

He refolded the paper and handed it back to me. Then he reached into his jacket and pulled out a folder that could not possibly have fit in an inside pocket. "After our discussion last night, I immediately approached The Council with everything you told me, and I believe the solution we've come up with will take care of your problem."

I blew out a breath of relief. "You're giving me enough that we can get far away, right?"

He shook his head. "We're not giving you money this time, Dusty."

The first time, The Council gave me enough to cover tuition and expenses for four years of college. The second loan allowed me to set up a good home for myself and the baby who had been a surprise. That infusion lasted until after Micah was born, at which time I managed to secure a decent job. *This time*, apparently, was strike three. Was I out?

"We came up with an alternative." There was a *not sure you're going to like this* quality to his voice. "Basically, we'll scratch your back if you scratch ours. *Quid pro quo*, I believe it's called."

I froze. "What do you want me to do?"

He opened the folder and revealed a contract typed on familiar letterhead. The first two I'd signed simply stated I had to pay back every penny they lent me. No timeframe and no interest. I still owed The Council ten thousand dollars. An embarrassingly large amount after more than three decades. But kids are expensive. So are rent, car payments, and college tuition. And bank loans came with both payment schedules and hefty interest rates, so I paid off those debts first.

"We want you to return to Blackwood Grove." Dad spun the contract around so I could read it. "Look it over."

The Council's solution to my problem was for me to return to the town I left days after graduating high school. If I agreed to return to my family's farm, Cricket and I would be protected by the enchanted property my family had lived on for two hundred years.

I had to admit, there was no place in the world safer for us than Applewood Farm. No stranger could enter the property without at least one witch being present. As long as Cricket stayed on our side of the hedge or with me if we went into town, she would be absolutely safe. There was one big problem with The Council's solution, however.

Pushing the contract back across the table, I shook my head. "I can't go back."

"Whyever not?"

"The curse."

"What curse?"

"You must remember the accident."

He appeared to scroll back through his memory. "You mean the boat?"

I nodded. Along with the dreams and premonitions, I had a

third power. One that gave me the ability to do wrong things for the right reasons. On the day in question, I had reacted to what would have been a horrific accident. I held out a hand, almost like preparing to catch a ball, and unintentionally used this power I had not fully developed. As a result, ten people's lives were forever changed. Mine too; I hadn't cast a single spell since.

"They told me to leave town."

"Who did?"

"The parents of one of my victims. I think."

"They weren't your victims, Dusty. You cast a spell that didn't go as intended." He said that as though saying, *you made toast for breakfast, and it burned.*

Talk about a one-eighty turn. I vividly remembered overhearing him and my mother talking about me in their bedroom the night of the accident. I'd gone to them hoping for guidance on how to fix the awful thing I'd done.

". . . was wrong," Mom was saying as I reached their door. "I'm not surprised this happened. She shouldn't have tried. She's not ready."

"No," Dad agreed, "and she may never be. To think of where you were at her age—"

"She's far too unpredictable."

The disgust I heard in their voices, especially hers, was like a knife to my heart.

I stared at my father now, leery of this supportive attitude. "I cast a gray spell that went horribly wrong. I stepped in on something that wasn't my concern."

"You prevented—"

"There are consequences for gray magic, Dad. You know that better than anyone. Unintentional as it was, I altered people's lives."

He waited for me to calm down. "Because of that incident, you lived the last thirty-two years away from your family and without the protection of Blackwood Grove. I'd say that's a pretty big consequence and you've paid your dues."

Sure hoped so, because while living away from everyone had been agony at times, it was only part of my punishment. I also got conned out of all my money by my slimy ex-husband. I was barely able to care for my child after becoming a single parent at age twenty-one. Josie disappeared. Micah was incarcerated. I'd lost my job yesterday morning and my house last night. I couldn't handle much more.

"I can't go back."

He stared at me like I'd just dropped in from another planet. "Why do you believe this so vehemently?"

"This parent told me to leave, which nullified my protection. They told me that if I ever returned, all my troubles would be cast onto the family." I glanced at Cricket. She was included in that threat.

He smacked his palm to his forehead. "This is what happens when you don't finish your training and then live in an Ordinary town for thirty years. Our family was given Applewood Farm, our parcel of land, to live on two hundred years ago. Blackwood Grove developed around the farm and was deemed a safe town. One of many across the world. It's been a couple of decades, but you must remember that witches are protected inside safe towns."

"I know." His explanation was unnecessary. I was fully, painfully aware of the differences between safe towns and Ordinary towns.

"This is true for any witch inside any safe town. These towns are where we're allowed to perform magic at will. Everyone, witch and Ordinary alike, knows and accepts this. You remember that as well, correct?"

"I do." *Ordinary* was our term for non-magical people. Also *Ords*, *Ordy*, or *Ordies*.

"You must also know that you're not a prisoner of the town. You can come and go as you choose."

"Yes, but if I come back to—"

He reached across the table and took my hands in his. "If you're a witch in a safe town, you're protected no matter how many times you leave and reenter. The only thing that can remove, alter, or nullify the enchantment from a family's parcel and the safe town around it is for the family to sell that parcel or for the wards to be taken down. We aren't selling, and Blackwood Grove's wards are securely in place."

I sat in embarrassed silence, eventually whispering, "So I *can* return?"

"You can. You'll be protected instantly and completely. So will Cricket. You're only vulnerable when outside a safe town."

My face grew hot as I thought of Micah sitting in a jail cell. "I could have returned long ago."

"You *should* have. We would have welcomed you with open arms." He squeezed my hands and waited for me to meet his eyes. "You went through a lot since you left, but you always figured a way out of your troubles. Being a young single parent was surely a struggle, but you *did* care for Micah, and he's become a fine young man. You made a comfortable life for the two of you. Last night, you got yourself and that beautiful little girl out of a burning house, and then you contacted us for help, which is a strength, not a weakness. You, my dear, are a survivor."

He released my hands and pushed the contract back to me. Then he held up his hand again and manifested a quill and pot of ink. When I reached for the implements, he asked, "Did you read everything? Do you agree to the conditions?"

"Mm-hmm," I hummed as I dipped the quill into the pot. Cricket would be safe. That was all that mattered. As I signed my name, *Dusty Hotte*, on the line at the bottom, red ink flowed from the nib. "Tell me that's not blood."

"This contract doesn't require a blood oath."

"Wait, did you say conditions? What conditions?" As my signature absorbed into the parchment and the ink dried, I saw a line of small print above my signature. Literal fine print that I had *not* read.

I dug in my backpack for my reading glasses, which I only needed if a font was tiny or the ink faint. These were both. "What does that say? What did I just agree to, Dad?"

He closed his eyes and groaned. "I asked if you read it all."

I thought I had, but then we started talking about curses and how I could have returned home years or even decades ago. He distracted me. No, that wasn't fair. I was hyper-focused on Cricket being safe. I shoved my glasses on my face and still had to practically press my nose to the parchment to see the lines clearly. My spine straightened. "Are you kidding me?"

He cleared his throat. "You will receive room and board for both you and Cricket for as long as you wish, and your remaining debt to The Council will be forgiven if you agree to become the witches' caretaker. Your signature states that you do."

"Caretaker?"

"They're getting up there in age, and you know how some folks get when they reach their seventies and eighties. They no longer care what anyone thinks and become a little free and loose. Their magic has gone a bit . . . wonky. They sometimes forget that their underwear should go on before their clothes. Although they might have been messing with me that day."

"Dad? You're one of them, you know." He turned seventy-seven on his last birthday. His magic appeared on point, however. Based on what I'd seen over the last few minutes.

"Indeed, I am. On the bright side for you, I'm so busy with The Council I don't stay at the house very often anymore." He patted his binoculars next to him on the table. "And there are my birds."

I hesitated to ask, "What about Mom?"

His hand fluttered in the air like the wings of one of his birds. "Oh, Griselle is around."

I paused, not sure I wanted to hear the answer to my next question. "Causing problems?"

His mouth opened, and a few unintelligible hemming and hawing noises came out. Finally, he settled on, "She means well."

Oh, dear lord. "You said witch*es*. How many of them are living in the house?" Last I knew, there were six. Aunt Comfort and her husband, Maks, although he wasn't a witch. Aunt Gwynne and her husband, Filip. And my parents. Granny Sadie had passed a few years ago. That made six, but Dad said he wasn't around much. So, five?

He counted on his fingers. All of them. "Nine? Ten?"

"There are ten witches living in that house?"

"The number fluctuates, but the house is bigger now. It added a few rooms. Some of the witches are ghosts, so they're on their own. Sometimes there's a visiting witch or two from another parcel."

I leaned back, remembered I was sitting at a picnic table—no back rest—and caught myself before I fell backward. "There are nine or ten witches with varying levels of magical stability plus visitors."

"See why we need your help?"

I was almost afraid to ask, "What about Carly?"

"She's overwhelmed but will be there to help you."

If she'd even talk to me. I'd ruined our plans so wouldn't be surprised if my cousin never forgave me for leaving.

"And Brenda?"

"We have no idea where your sister is. The last time you saw her was the last time we saw her."

There was a trend with us Warren girls. I left home at eighteen. I was ten when my big sister also left at eighteen years of age. How different would my life have been if I'd had her by my side during my teen years? Because my parents were never around.

I gazed at my hopeful father and sighed. "Caretaker, huh?"

"We need you, sweetheart."

What had I gotten myself into? I glanced at Cricket, who was looking at the sandals on her feet through the wrong end of her opera glasses, and smiled. It would all be fine. I had survived a house fire. That, however, might prove to be a far easier task than surviving the witches of Blackwood Grove.

CHAPTER 2

*R*oadside signs ten, five, and then two miles outside of town beckoned people to come to *The Blackwood Grove Mall* for shopping and food. What mall? The "shopping district," as we called it when I was growing up here, was comprised of ten stores that honestly weren't much to get excited about. Certainly not a mall or worthy of billboards.

Once I got into town, smaller signs led me down Ambrosia Road, the town's main street, and indicated I was to take a right. I sat at the intersection of Ambrosia and River Road, which formed a T, and stared at the Mississippi River.

The view of the wide, deep-blue water and the tree-covered green bluffs of Minnesota in the distance was exactly as I remembered and took my breath away. This was the Driftless Area, a large swath of land spreading through the four corners of Wisconsin, Minnesota, Iowa, and Illinois left untouched by glaciers. Where other areas had gotten scraped and flattened by the ice, this region was all bluffs, coulees or valleys, streams, and lakes. Absolutely gorgeous. And more than a little magical.

A car behind me honked.

"Sorry." I stuck my hand out the open window and waved.

I turned right, as the sign to the mall directed. This was conveniently the way to Applewood Farm as well. Thankfully, the other car had turned left because I was driving a good ten miles below the speed limit. And there it was. I shivered. Blackwood Grove's shopping district had tripled in size. It now took up three blocks, two of which used to be peoples' houses if I remembered correctly. I couldn't see much from the road but did see people buzzing about. I got a clear look at my family's diner, however, as it was the only building with a front door facing the river, and it was smack in the middle of the others.

The mall's three blocks extended from Ambrosia to the hedge that delineated our property from the town. At the hedge, I turned right and followed the driveway straight for twenty-five yards to where it curved to the left. There we came to a gateway sign hanging overhead that welcomed us to Applewood Farm. I paused with the nose of my Prius right below the sign, like a sprinter waiting for the starter's pistol to go off. I wasn't ready to start this race. What was this feeling inside me? Apprehension? Embarrassment? Shame? Until this moment, coming here felt like the right decision. The *only* decision for keeping Cricket safe. Now, I wasn't so sure. The town felt different somehow and not just because of the new mall.

Get on with it, girl.

Right. The damage, so to speak, was done. My signature was on the contract. I had committed.

"Why are we sitting here?" Cricket asked.

"I'm looking at everything." Like with the town, much of the farm appeared to be the same, but some things were different. I pointed out the big red barn on our right. It had a large white sign that read *The Apple Barn* in apple-red letters.

"Apples!" Cricket declared from the backseat and pointed at the overflowing basket of them painted on the barn's sign. "I love apples. 'Specially applesauce."

"I know you do. An apple orchard surrounds the farm, and

my aunties make all sorts of food out of apples." And products, some of a more magical variety, but that was more than the four-year-old needed to know right now.

"They're my aunties too," she reminded me. Good to know she was listening while I described our family tree.

"Yes, your aunties too. And a few uncles." And cousins and witches from other families that were always welcome at the farm. Again, more than she needed to know at the moment.

"That barn used to be white like the house," I murmured mostly to myself and indicated the structure across the driveway from the barn. The house used to be smaller.

"Look! A kitty."

A black cat had strolled from the house to the middle of the driveway where it sat and stared directly at us. After a minute, it turned back toward the house, paused to look at us again, and continued along its route.

"I think she wants me to play with her," Cricket decided and unbuckled the harness holding her in her booster seat.

"The car is still running, little miss. Do not get out of your seat."

She settled back and hugged baba.

It did look like the cat wanted us to follow, so I pushed back my shoulders, stepped on the gas, and entered the property.

My dad had told me we'd be staying in the carriage house. I'd made a face. "That old cobwebby building where we kept the garden supplies?"

"It's been renovated," he'd promised. "Two bedrooms, bathroom, living room, and kitchenette on the second floor. Half of the ground floor is a garage where you can park your car. The other half is for the garden tools. It's nice. You'll like it."

I drove past the house to a detached three-car garage, which wasn't here thirty-two years ago, and the admittedly cute carriage house. It was painted white to match the main house, had an apple-green door, and a covered patio ran along two sides.

"What does that say?" Cricket pointed at the sign hanging off the patio roof.

I smiled. "It says Apple Blossom Cottage." Cute.

"Is that where we're going to live?"

"I guess so. Should we take a look?"

"Yes!" She slid out of the harness straps and waited for me to come let her out.

With the keys my father had given me in hand, we went to the door beneath the sign. A peek through the mullioned window showed a small entry, a bench with a built-in coatrack, and a shoe rack. Perfect. I'd taught Cricket that shoes came off at the front door and either stayed on the shoe tray or went directly to her bedroom closet. Stairs led to the apartment above.

Cricket bounced up and down. "What's in there? I want to see."

"Okay, hang on."

The key ring held two keys. Green for the carriage house and red for the main house. I stuck the key in the lock and turned it. Or attempted to. The key fell to the ground.

"Oopsie daisy," Cricket chirped.

My breath caught at her declaration. That was what my son used to say to her while playing *disappear* as he called it. He'd throw a bath towel or her baba over her and chant, "Oopsie daisy where's the baby?" Then he'd pull it off her again, cry out "There she is," and act so surprised that she'd been underneath it. Cricket would laugh and laugh. I couldn't believe she remembered that.

She handed me the key, I inserted it again, and it fell to the ground again. And a third time.

"Something must be wrong with this key. Or the lock." A

lump formed in my gut as I said, "Guess we'll have to go to the main house."

I was hoping to have a few more minutes to collect myself before dealing with my family.

We turned, paused, and then Cricket let out a squeal of glee. "Look!"

Three cats—the black one, a black-and-white one, and a gray —sat on a short stone wall and stared at us. Familiars, I assumed. Dad told me there were nine or ten witches in residence here. Did they all have familiars? Were the other six or seven animals also cats? That seemed awfully cliché.

"What are their names?"

"I have no idea, honey. We'll have to ask the aunties and uncles."

We crossed the courtyard to the house's back door, and I checked the knob. It was locked. Dad said the red key would work on both the front and back doors, so I inserted it in the lock, and it fell to the ground.

"Are you kidding me?" What was going on? I tried it twice more with the same results, but the third time it spit out the key, it also spit a notecard beneath the door.

Go to the diner.

"What does that say?" Cricket reached for the card with grabby hands.

"It says we have to go to the diner. That's the restaurant that Auntie Comfort runs."

"Why do we have to go there?"

"I'm not sure. That's what the card says, so I guess that's what we should do. It's not far, so we'll walk."

I got my backpack from the Prius.

"Don't forget baba."

I grabbed her blanket from the back and handed it to her. "I would never forget baba."

She "folded it," which meant scrunching it into a ball she could carry without it touching the ground, and we headed back down the driveway. I glanced up at the house as we passed by and could have sworn something moved in one of the top-floor windows. Either someone was in there and didn't want to let us in, or it was Granny Sadie's ghost checking to see who was outside. The entire property, all one hundred acres, was enchanted so only family members or those given permission could enter.

"Which way?" Cricket asked when we got to the curve in the driveway.

"There's only one way." I started for the main road.

"No, that way too."

I looked where she pointed and saw that an opening had appeared in the thick black wood hedge. The opening lined up precisely with the mall. Very convenient. I didn't like the idea of walking along that busy road.

"Straight ahead, captain," I told her.

"Aye-aye, matey," Cricket answered in her best four-year-old pirate voice, mimicking a particular spongy cartoon character she especially loved.

The first shop on our right was Silver Moon Apothecary. The emerald-green building could have been plucked from a bayou in Louisiana. It appeared to have a history, rather than being staged to look that way, and gave off a distinct witchy vibe. Richly colored scarves, gourds, strings of beads, and intricately carved iron lanterns hung all around the small front porch. Big floor pillows were tossed casually about, summoning passersby to come sit for a spell. Despite its ancient appearance, the hut couldn't have been more than thirty-two years old, because it hadn't been there when I left. It took all my willpower to not go inside. Another time. We needed to get to the diner. That directive suddenly felt urgent.

The town had closed off most of what used to be Crispin Street, leaving the houses, now stores, on either side. What had been the street was now a park, and it was packed with people. Three sidewalks, one on each side of the park and one down the center, were connected with random short walkways that led shoppers to the different businesses. Picnic tables and benches were scattered about so folks could stop to eat or rest a bit. A playground near the middle of the mall caught Cricket's eye. She threw baba over her head when I told her she couldn't play now, indicating a rare meltdown was coming. To fend it off, I said she could have a snack at the diner. I understood. Not only was she tired and hungry from the long drive, but she missed her mommy and daddy.

I carried her the rest of the way, looking around as I walked. The whole area was really nice and clearly popular, but something felt off. I felt it as we drove through town too. A sort of unsettled vibe or heaviness. I held my little bug closer.

The diner had been around since well before I'd been born. In fact, it was the first business here. Or maybe the general store was first. The two always argued over who could claim those rights. Regardless, being right along the Mississippi, the diner was a popular spot back in the day for anyone floating by on a boat to stop and grab a bite to eat.

Unable to decide between Comfort's Food—a twist on comfort food, which was what my aunt specialized in—and the more traditional Comfort's Diner, Aunt Comfort blended the two into Comfort's Food Diner. Most people, as far as I could recall, just called it the diner.

The name changed depending on which witch was running it as did the menu, but that was up to the diner itself. We never knew what the enchanted building would choose. Now and then it changed the exterior too. Once it opted for the nostalgic silver train car look. Another time it looked like a simple rectangular roadside building with two big signs on the flat roof proclaiming "Diner" and "Eat." One rendition looked so much like someone's house the only way people knew it was still a restaurant was by the sign declaring *World's Best Pie* in blinking pink neon. As far as I knew, that declaration was the absolute truth. I'd never had better pie than Aunt Comfort's, and I tried slices everywhere I went.

The interior always maintained a classic 1950s theme, but the colors changed. I recalled a teal, brown, beige, and green scheme that created a soothing atmosphere. One day I walked in to find it had turned white, red, and black with a black-and-white checkerboard floor. Unsure what we'd see today, I held my breath as I reached for the handle.

"*Ooh*, pretty!" Cricket declared.

The checkerboard floor was still there. As was the window to the kitchen on the far wall where servers clipped tickets to the order wheel, and the cook placed plates ready for pick up. The refrigerated pie case stood in the same spot near the register. Booths big enough to seat four to six lined the outside wall. Chrome stools bolted to the floor ran along the white Formica counter where folks could eat breakfast or lunch—Comfort's wasn't open for dinner—or grab a slice of pie, which always came served on a metal pie pan. Or used to. I hoped they still used the pie pans. Down the center was a row of square tables set diagonally, each with four chairs. The building must have expanded to accommodate the tables because I didn't remember there being room for that much seating.

Everything was basically as I remembered, except the walls were now a shade of pink somewhere between baby and bubblegum. Bright-turquoise vinyl replaced the teal shade on the bench seats and stool covers. Pink-and-white buffalo plaid tablecloths covered the square tables.

At the far end by the small retail section—which offered

things like packaged food, kitchen wares, and simple items of clothing like T-shirts and sweatshirts—a trio of elderly women were gathered around something on the floor. They had turned as one when the bell over the door jingled and looked at us.

"Dusty?" called the one with long curly gray hair and round glasses. Aunt Gwynne. "What are you doing here?"

"Dad didn't tell you—" What was I doing? My reappearance in town was hardly the point at the moment. Far more urgent was the man lying on the floor with the knife in his chest.

CHAPTER 3

I immediately turned Cricket away from the dead man. Across from the front door was a small alcove with a loveseat and a few mismatched arm chairs. A perfect spot to tuck her.

"Aunt Comfort makes the best pie. She has really good ice cream too. Would you like that for a snack?"

She fixed a suspicious look on me. Snack time meant a piece of fruit, carrot sticks, or cheese cubes. Dessert was only for if she ate all her dinner.

"Ice cream," she declared before I realized my mistake. "Vanilla with chocolate syrup and sprinkles."

"Okay. You stay right here, and I'll get it for you."

I turned and found one of the women standing behind me. Not an aunt, she had wrinkly medium-brown skin and wore a deep orange and navy blue patterned headwrap that matched her long tunic dress. Her voice held a slight Cajun accent as she said, "The girls tell me you're Dusty."

"I am. Who are you?"

"Pepper Boudreaux. Gwynne and I have been friends for more than fifty years. I've been living on the farm with her and the others for the last twenty-five." She held a small white ceramic bowl of vanilla ice cream with chocolate syrup out to me. "This is for your little one."

I blinked at the delivery of the order that had literally been requested a heartbeat before Pepper appeared with it. "Are those sprinkles shaped like toe shoes?"

"And tutus." She smiled at my granddaughter, clad in her ballerina dress. "I thought she would like them."

Nodding toward the scene at the opposite end of the diner, I asked, "Am I really seeing what I think I'm seeing?"

She frowned. "Unfortunately, yes."

"Any idea what happened?"

"None at all. We were all helping in the kitchen and suddenly this." She shook her head, visibly upset. "You go talk to Gwynne and Comfort. I will keep the little beauty away from all that. We'll color some pictures." Pepper held up a coloring book and crayons that I was fairly sure hadn't been in her hand seconds ago.

First Dad, now Pepper. I'd been away from magic for so long, it would take a bit for the shock of seeing it performed out in the open to feel natural again. While it wasn't illegal to be a witch, it was illegal to practice witchcraft outside a safe town. When I left here, I went to an Ordinary town where magic was forbidden even inside a witch's own home. For the last three decades, I'd completely denied my witch self.

"Go on now," Pepper urged. "They're waiting."

"I'll be on the other side of the diner," I told Cricket.

"Okay."

I could have told her I'd be jetting off to the moon and would have gotten the same, uninterested response. Her focus was on the ice cream.

Rounding the corner, I found Gwynne and Comfort looking my way. My mother's sisters. Two women who had been more like mothers to me than she had. My heart raced as I got closer to the waiting women. They'd aged so much.

Gwynne was my healer, earthy aunt. She dressed in all linen —loose-fitting pants, tunics, and knee-length vests. Her long curly hair still held the tiniest bit of her natural blond but was mostly gray and wilder than I remembered. A collection of necklaces hung from her neck, and round tortoiseshell glasses perched on her nose. As much as she was the same, something was also different about her. The spark I remembered wasn't there.

Comfort, the oldest of the three sisters, was the leader. She still dressed as I remembered in wide-legged jeans with a belt, tucked-in blouses or T-shirts, and Converse sneakers. The addition of the red bandana folded into a headband was new. As were the fully gray hair and soft wrinkles creasing her face. She had a smile that made you feel hugged and welcome. Right now, however, she was glaring at me.

"You're back." Gwynne's statement felt more like an accusation.

"What are you doing here?" Comfort's question was full of icy chill.

Not sure what I'd expected. I left without notice and hadn't contacted them once in all these years. Also, there was a man lying on the floor with a rather large knife protruding from his abdomen. A valid reason for not being chipper, but this wasn't about that.

I let their harsh greetings pass. "What happened? Other than the obvious."

"Couldn't tell you," Comfort began with the same tight attitude. "Gwynne and Pepper came for lunch and stayed to help when we closed at two. We normally let the diner take care of clean-up, but since we had volunteers today, we gave it a break. Besides, Carly likes to put things away. She says the diner tends to hide things or put them where they fit rather than where they belong."

My heart fluttered at my cousin's name. We'd been best friends since birth, I was six months older, but I destroyed our dream when I left. How much did she hate me?

"Is Carly here?" My mouth had gone dry.

Comfort's glare intensified, as though I had no right to speak her daughter's name. Gwynne nodded toward the kitchen. "She's calling the police."

"Do you know who he is?" I asked of the dead man.

"His name is Ludo Beck," Comfort said.

"A townie?"

They shook their heads in unison.

"Come away from him, Gwynnie." Comfort took her sister's arm and wouldn't look at me as she spoke. "All I know about him is that he wanted to open a store in the mall. I don't know what kind and don't know the status of it. He asked me a few weeks ago if I would sell this building to him." She shook her head. "Never."

Gwynne went to the closest table and sat heavily, her back to the scene. Comfort stood close with a protective hand on her sister's shoulder.

"What exactly happened?" I checked the time on the clock hanging over the front door. Two thirty. "I assume your hours are still six to two." Closed on Sundays and Mondays. "Sounds like you closed at your normal time. Walk me through the last half hour. When did you discover him?"

Irritation at my request flashed in Gwynne's eyes, and her words were crisp. "Comfort was in the office totaling the day's tickets. I tidied behind the counter. Pepper ran the dishes through the washer. Carly cleared tables, brought dirty dishes to the kitchen, and put things away."

"We stop taking orders at one forty," Comfort took over.

"Not that we'd deny anyone who wandered in shortly after that. We were busy today, especially for a Thursday."

"Grilled cheese and tomato soup was the special. The diner hasn't put that on the menu for months," Gwynne reasoned numbly. "Not a lot of people want soup in the middle of summer."

"It's the middle of August," Comfort reminded her. "The closer we get to Labor Day, the more people start thinking about fall."

"True. Good move on the diner's part."

They were getting off topic. "Okay, the diner closed at two. When did the last customer leave? When did you find this poor guy?"

Comfort sat next to Gwynne with a groan. "We announced last call at ten to two like always. That means final top offs of coffee or soda refills. No more orders are taken, and we turn off the *Open* sign. Everyone pretty much cleared out ten minutes later."

She looked toward the serving window behind the counter as though someone was there and gave a short shake of her head.

I turned to look but saw no one. "Is Carly okay back there? Should we check on her?"

"She's fine," Comfort snapped. End of discussion.

"Mr. Beck, the dead man, was sitting there." Gwynne pointed behind her at the first stool on the right side of the counter. Then she pointed toward the door at the opposite end of the diner. "There were six shoppers sitting between two booths. A man and woman at one. Four friends at the other."

"Did you know any of them?" I asked.

"No, they were shoppers, not townies."

"Like Gwynne said," Comfort added, "I was in the office. I closed out the till a couple of minutes before two and saw him sitting there. I told him we were closing shortly, so he needed to leave."

"The others left when I came out to lock the door," Gwynne recalled, "but he was still here. I said we were closed. He promised to go as soon as he finished his coffee, so I went in back to help Pepper. A few minutes later, Carly came out to do a final dining room check and lock the door. I heard her yell, 'You need to leave now.' I assume she was talking to Mr. Beck."

"And?" I pressed when neither of them said more.

Gwynne rolled her eyes, annoyed with my questions. "Carly returned to the kitchen. Once we were done back there, we came out to leave through the front door and . . ." She pointed behind herself at Beck.

Past his body, in the retail area, a stack of T-shirts fell off the shelf and two boxes of cookie mix exploded getting flour everywhere. Comfort barely reacted to that, only gave a small sigh, as though this was a normal thing. Gwynne was telekinetic on top of being a healer. For as long as I could remember, she'd been able to move things with the simple flick of a finger. Was her power on the fritz? Was this what Dad meant by their magic was going wonky? Could Gwynne have accidentally sent that knife flying at Beck?

"All four of you were in the kitchen?" I tried to not be obvious about keeping an eye on her hands.

"Yes," Comfort hissed.

"And none of you heard anything going on out here? No arguing? No scuffling?"

Before they could reply, the bell over the door jingled, and a police officer walked in. Comfort stood and my breath caught. This wasn't just any police officer. Beauregard "Beau" Balinski was the classmate I'd unintentionally injured thirty-two years ago. He was the main reason I left town. My gaze shot to his right leg, the one he'd lost above the knee in the accident, and back to his face. Beau had always been a good-looking kid, and now he was a handsome man. His face had a weathered, rugged look. His dark-blond hair was cut in a standard, high-and-tight police style. Shockingly, even though I was the reason he had a prosthetic leg, he seemed happy to see me.

"Dusty? When did you get back to town?" He had a great smile. I remembered that now.

"About forty-five minutes ago."

"And this is what you return to." He frowned at the grizzly scene. "A murder. The first one in . . . I'm not sure there's ever been a murder here. Not in the last fifty-some years, at least."

He looked at my aunts. They shook their heads, confirming his statement.

Maybe I'd been right about being cursed.

Another officer entered the diner then. A pretty younger woman with her hair pulled into a massive corkscrew-curly ponytail.

"This is Officer Leeza Chapman," Beau introduced. "She just started at the station and will be assisting me." He crossed the diner to where Ludo Beck lay, a slight sway to his stride. "We'll need to question all of you. Dusty, I know you just got here, but I'll want a statement from you, too, since you're here. We're going to check over the scene before they come and take the body away, and then, Ms. Warren—"

Both aunts responded with, "Yes?"

"Sorry. Ms. Gwynne, you can stay where you are. Ms. Comfort, would you take a seat at a different table, please? Who else is here?"

"Carly's in the kitchen," Comfort answered. "Avery had to leave early today. No one else worked today."

I indicated the corner in the back. "Pepper is over there with my granddaughter."

His eyes lit up. "You've got a grand little? Nice. Congratulations."

Not at all the attitude I expected from him. "Thanks."

"Would you ask Ms. Pepper to also choose a table? I'll come chat with her in a bit. Officer Chapman, would you tell Carly to stay in the kitchen and that I'll be there shortly? Come back and sit in on the interview with Ms. Gwynne and then you can interview Comfort."

"Yes, sir." The rookie cop gave a crisp nod and scampered off to the kitchen.

I relayed his request to Pepper, then sat next to Cricket on the loveseat. She had a smear of chocolate sauce on her chin.

"I like Pepper." She chose a teal crayon from the box. "She likes to cook and is gonna make me chocolate chip pancakes for breakfast tomorrow."

Cricket chattered on and on about the ice cream, the next picture she planned to color, and all the different options for pancakes she and Pepper discussed. I murmured *mm-hmm* and *wow* and *really* as she talked, but my mind was on Ludo Beck. None of them heard anything? Really? That bell over the door jangles whenever someone comes in. Granted, it isn't very loud, more for atmosphere than function, so maybe they couldn't hear it in the kitchen. Or maybe my aunts were hiding something.

Could Gwynne have accidentally killed this man? She didn't seem to have any idea of the mess she'd made in the retail area a few minutes ago. She said she came out and told him it was time to leave. Could she have unintentionally . . . No. She and Comfort agreed Carly came out later and yelled at Beck to leave. Then they found the body.

Could Carly have killed a man? I'd already seen a lot that had changed around here in thirty-plus years, but I couldn't for one moment fathom my cousin doing such a thing. My aunt either.

A good hour passed before Beau finally came over to talk to me. Thankfully, the medical examiner or coroner or whoever had come during that time and taken Mr. Beck away, so I didn't have to see that disturbing scene again or worry about

Cricket seeing it. How would I have explained that to a four-year-old?

We took seats at the breakfast counter. Officer Chapman was standing by the order window, spinning the ticket wheel. Beau cleared his throat and flicked his fingers for her to come stand closer.

I repeated to Beau everything Gwynne and Comfort had told me. "That's all I know. I literally walked in to find them and Pepper standing over the body. As though in shock. You know what I mean." I hoped. Did that sound incriminating? Should I mention Gwynne's magical mishap?

"Your statement matches theirs." He reviewed his notes, more serious now than when he first entered the diner. "Any questions for her, Officer Chapman?"

"No, sir. Ms. Comfort told me the same thing."

He closed his notepad and slid it in his pocket. "I think that's it. You'll be at the farm? In case I have more questions."

An image of last night's fire flashed in my mind. "Yes, Cricket and I will be staying in the carriage house."

The bell jingled again, and a third police officer entered the building. The officers had a short discussion and then went into the kitchen.

Minutes later, the three older witches and I stood near the door and watched in open-mouthed shock as they escorted Carly out of the kitchen. She was thinner than I remembered. Her medium-brown hair was tied up in a messy bun. She looked tired but good. Except her hands were handcuffed behind her back.

"I didn't do this," Carly insisted. When she saw me standing there, she froze in her tracks and stared, her expression undecipherable. A heartbeat later, she was as angry as Comfort had been. "You're back? Well that explains a few things. You waltz in and everything goes to hell."

My heart sank. Dad told me it was fine for me to return to

Blackwood Grove, that the enchantment would remain securely in place, and no one in my family would be at risk. Yet here I stood watching my cousin being hauled away for murder not even two hours after I got here.

"We'll figure this out," Comfort promised her daughter as the third officer led her away. "We'll have you out of jail in no time."

Carly glared at me as she passed. As soon as the door had shut behind her, Comfort covered her face with her hands. Gwynne and Pepper wrapped her in a hug and murmured soothing words.

"Ladies," Beau began after a few seconds, "Officer Chapman and I need to investigate the scene now, so you'll have to leave."

"How could you?" Comfort spun on him. "How could you think Carly did this?"

"We're only bringing her in for further questioning—"

"In handcuffs?" Gwynne demanded.

"You all agreed," Beau began, "she was the last one to interact with the victim. None of you heard anyone else enter the diner, and a few minutes after she hollered at him, he was found dead."

"She didn't do this," Pepper muttered.

Beau spoke gently. "And when the evidence proves that, I'll release her."

That settled them for the moment.

"Will we be able to open tomorrow?" Comfort asked.

"I don't see why not." Beau scanned the dining room. "If that changes, I'll let you know immediately. You'll want to come back later to clean up and lock the doors."

Comfort shook her head. "The diner will take care of that."

As if confirming, the lights flickered.

After collecting Cricket, her baba, her coloring supplies, and my backpack from the loveseat, I turned to find the aunts were gone. They left without us.

Dad knew all along that I was alive, well, and had a son. He must have kept them informed about me. Didn't he? For sure he would have told Mom, and she would have said something to her sisters. Right?

I should have called or sent a letter. Something. I had a lot of making up to do, and regardless of how any of us felt about me being back, we had plenty of time to heal our wounds. That contract with my signature on it meant I was now responsible for their wellbeing. Lordy, what had I gotten myself into?

While Cricket and I walked back to the house through the mall's park, her chattering about everything that caught her eye, something caught *my* eye. Or rather, someone.

A couple dozen yards away were two men and a tough-looking black-and-white dog. One man was sitting on a blanket in the middle of the grassy area and appeared to be a bit down and out. The dog seemed to be with the second man who knelt on the grass next to the blanket. It was the kneeling man who caught my attention. He dressed in jeans and a short-sleeve medical-uniform shirt. A doctor or dentist? His head was completely bald, and while I was too far away to see them clearly, he was covered in tattoos. His arms, hands, neck, and even the back of his head. He must have sensed me watching them because he looked over his shoulder at me.

Embarrassed to be caught staring, I turned away.

This guy seemed familiar. This area of Wisconsin was full of lifers, so even though I'd been gone far longer than I'd lived here, I was pretty sure I'd seen him before. Who was he?

CHAPTER 4

"Do we get to go inside now?" Cricket asked as we stood outside the door on the house's covered front porch.

"Let's see." I wasn't sure if I should ring the bell or just walk in so started by reaching for the knob. This time the door opened a few inches before I even touched it. I looked down at my granddaughter, whose eyes sparkled with excitement. "I'd say, yes, we get to go in now. Stay with me, though. Don't go running off."

"Okay."

Like the diner did, the house changed its interior whenever the mood struck. I remember antique, Victorian furniture being everywhere when I'd leave for school in the morning and when I came home in the afternoon, it would be wall to wall mid-century modern. I didn't mind when the main areas of the house changed, but I hated it when Carly and I got our bedroom just the way we wanted it and then next thing we knew it looked like a 1970s disco.

As Cricket and I stood in the entryway, it appeared that the interior finally matched the exterior. Farmhouse décor filled the dining room on our left and sitting room on our right. I was pleased to see the fireplaces were still in their original spots. That was one of the many details I loved about this house. Being well over two hundred years old, every room had a fireplace in lieu of central heating. And while the house usually kept every room at the occupant's desired comfort level, the ambiance of a fire crackling away in the hearth always made doing homework more enjoyable.

"Hello?" Cricket called out. "Anybody here?"

Apparently she wasn't interested in the furnishings or waiting while I harkened back to the olden days.

"We're in the kitchen," someone answered.

"Where is the kitchen?" Cricket asked.

Good question. "Last I knew, it was ahead and to the left."

Her little lips pursed. "Left is that way?" She pointed right.

"That's your right hand. Left is the other one. Remember."

She held her hands in front of her so she could see her fingernails. Then she lowered her thumbs. She was good with her letters so knew what an *L* looked like. She grabbed my hand and pulled me through the foyer, into the family room, and then took a left at the stairs. Sure enough, the kitchen was right where it had always been. It was even grander and more beautiful than I remembered. Or maybe I simply appreciated kitchens more than when I was eighteen.

Taking up the middle of the room was a twelve-foot-square island that provided plenty of room for kitchen work, spellwork, and spots for diners or visitors to sit. The island acted as the room divider. One side for cooking. The other, eating. In the cooking section, a three-bowl sink sat beneath a window that looked out at the river. To the right of the sink was a pantry cabinet. To the left, a doorway led to a butler's pantry and the formal dining room. Then came an industrial chef's range with two ovens, six burners, and a griddle. On the eating side of the room, a fireplace and a long wooden table surrounded by Windsor chairs created a comfortable space where the entire family could gather.

"What a great room," I murmured. "Good job, house."

A puff of ice-cold air chilled my face . . . in thanks? Seemed the house was mad at me too.

"About time you finally got here," Comfort snapped when she saw us. As though we'd been an hour behind them instead of only a minute or two. She hollered, "Lucia!"

"What does that mean?" Cricket leaned against my leg. Comfort was scaring her.

"It's someone's name," I replied. "But I don't know who the person is."

A woman with gray hair the exact color of her business suit appeared from the butler's pantry. She was "pleasantly plump" as my grandmother would have said, had flawless skin, and a no-nonsense air about her.

She looked at me and gave a small nod. "Good, you made it. Lucia Valentina, Council member and attorney for the witches." She held a hand out for me to shake. Then she bent forward to look Cricket in the eye. "You must be Cricket. Pleasure to meet you."

The girl giggled and held out her tiny hand.

"Glad they made it?" Gwynne repeated. "You knew they were coming? Why didn't anyone tell us?"

"It all happened this morning." Lucia waved a dismissive hand. "Jasper and I were completing the details until a few hours ago. Then I had some phone calls to return. No clue where Jasper is now."

She looked at me like I might know something about my father's comings and goings. "Couldn't tell you."

"Anyway, Dusty can explain all that later. What did you need me for?"

Before the three began their retelling, four others arrived. I knew two of them—Granny Sadie was a ghost, and Comfort's husband, Maks, was an Ordy who'd lived with witches for sixty-some years. No idea who the other two were.

Tears stung my eyes when my grandmother floated over to me. She wasn't clearly visible like the living but not see-through either. It was like looking at her through heavy fog or a sheer curtain. And she couldn't speak, at least not so I could hear her. She raised a hand and held it up to my cheek. I expected to feel cold, like a blast from a freezer or an open door in the middle of winter. Instead, I sensed that her hand was there but couldn't feel it. Then she crossed her arms and scowled hard at me.

"I'm sorry." I had no idea if she could hear me. "I should have come back sooner."

She spun away, and we all listened intently as Comfort, Gwynne, and Pepper filled Lucia in on the events at Comfort's Food Diner. Amazingly, even though they switched narrators with each sentence, the recounting came out perfectly understandable.

"And you're sure Carly didn't do it?" Lucia asked.

"Of course she didn't," they objected like a perfectly timed chorus.

"But do you have *proof?*" Lucia clarified. "We'll need indisputable evidence to prove innocence. Were at least one of you with her the entire time the murder occurred?"

Oh shizzle.

"There were those few minutes," Pepper began.

"When she was doing the final dining room check," Gwynne supplied.

"And Ludo Beck was still out there," Comfort concluded.

Lucia arched an eyebrow. "That's a problem. Okay, I'll get to work. If you could do a little legwork and find more details for me, that would be great."

This last bit was said to the room in general, but she looked straight at me. Seeing as I was the caretaker and all. Regardless of that contract, I would do anything to get my innocent cousin out of jail.

"I'm on it," I promised, and she disappeared into the butler's pantry again. Must be a portal of some kind in there.

"Is anyone hungry?" Pepper asked once Lucia left.

"I'm starving," I told her. "Cricket? Do you want something to eat, honey?"

Despite that dish of ice cream, she had to be hungry. She ate a cheese stick on our drive here, but that and the ice cream at the diner were all since breakfast. I hadn't had anything except the cup of coffee I grabbed at the gas station when I stopped to fill up on gas halfway here. I felt like the world's worst grandma right now.

Three pies—apple, banana cream, and peach—appeared on the table near the fireplace.

"Yummy!" Cricket bounced up and down.

"I was thinking something more along the lines of a late lunch." I checked my watch. Four thirty already. "Or an early dinner."

The pies vanished from the table and reappeared on the kitchen island. A big platter filled with pot roast and roasted vegetables took their place.

Cricket frowned. "Where did the pies go?"

I wondered when she'd acknowledge the magic. "Remember I told you the house could do tricks?"

"Yeah."

"That's one of the tricks. Let's have some dinner and you can have a little pie later."

Uncle Maks kissed my cheek before he sat next to Comfort. "Don't know where you've been, but I'm sure glad you're back, darlin'."

Maks was adorable. They say long-term partners start to look like each other. This was true with Comfort and Maks. Their smiles were almost identical. Their hair was the exact same color. And they were equal amounts of cute. Well, Comfort was cute when she wasn't scowling.

Being a ghost, Granny Sadie didn't need to eat, but she did sit at the table with us. I could feel her staring at Cricket and me. It seemed everyone else could see her, too, but I wasn't sure if Cricket could. Maybe she didn't realize the tiny old lady with the playful, mischievous personality wasn't actually alive.

"We haven't met," I began, addressing the other two folks I didn't know. "I'm Dusty. Who are you?"

The woman had short silver hair that reminded me of a Mohawk growing out. She wore the long middle part like bangs that swooped off to one side. She looked younger than the others, so late sixties?

"Oh, sorry." The woman wiped a napkin across her mouth and, with a Scottish lilt, said, "I'm Jett MacGregor, and he's my husband, Freddie."

Like Granny Sadie, Freddie appeared foggy or filtered. He had black-and-gray hair that fell a couple of inches past his shoulders and a full beard and moustache. He looked like a Santa Claus who rode a motorcycle. In a kilt. Was that even possible?

"We've been here for ten years," Jett continued. "Freddie died five years ago but isn't ready to move on yet. He used to run the saloon, and I tend the gardens, goats, bees, and chickens."

"Goats and chickens?" Cricket repeated through a mouthful of carrots.

"Swallow your food first," I reminded. Gwynne grinned at her. Comfort watched her and looked away. Pepper already adored her from their time together at the diner.

"Do you like goats and chickens?" Jett asked her.

"Mm-hmm." Cricket chewed her carrots extra fast. "So much. Can I see them?"

"Sure. You can help me with them tomorrow."

She stared up at me like she'd just been given the best gift ever. Maybe moving back here wasn't such a bad idea.

Comfort stared at me as she said, "We need to discuss Carly." She'd barely touched her food. She appeared, understandably, to be in shock. "Any ideas?"

Why ask the person who'd only been back a few hours? "We should probably start by finding out more about the victim."

"What's a victim?" Cricket asked and shoved a potato chunk into her mouth.

She did not need to hear this discussion. Coloring entertained her nicely at the diner. I stood to get the book and crayons from my backpack when two of the cats we'd seen on the wall outside earlier—the black one, and the white-and-black one—and an ancient-looking hound dog strode into the room.

Cricket squeaked and pointed at them.

Perfect distraction. "Are you done eating?"

She nodded, chewed, and swallowed.

"You can go play with them then."

"What are their names?" Cricket mumbled through potato.

We learned the black cat was Comfort's. "Her name is Wednesday, like from *The Addams Family*, because she keeps bringing me beheaded critters."

I gave her a warning glance to not scare my granddaughter. She pointedly arched an eyebrow at me in return.

The other cat, named Oreo, was Jett's, and the dog, Gumbo, was Pepper's familiar.

After settling Cricket in the family room with the familiars, I returned to the Carly discussion. "It sounds to me like Mr. Beck hung out at the diner for quite a while. Any idea what he was doing there? Gwynne, you mentioned that you told him the diner was closed, but he stayed to finish his coffee. Then Carly had to basically kick him out."

"Maybe he was waiting for someone," Jett suggested. "Can any of you describe him?"

A piece of lined paper and a nubby pencil appeared on the table in front of me. *Was he waiting for someone* was written on the first line in a perfect, blocky font. Guess I was supposed to take notes.

Since I only saw his legs and the knife in his stomach and never looked at his face, I deferred to the aunts. And I included Pepper, Jett, and Maks in that group. It was easier than breaking everyone down by family, friends, or gender.

"Slight pot belly," Gwynne began, touching her hand to her abdomen.

Pepper touched her own face. "Heavy five o'clock beard and moustache."

Freddie waved his hands in the air to get our attention. Then he said something, although I couldn't hear him. But Jett could.

"He says he's seen the guy." To me, she explained, "Freddie likes to wander around town and hangs out at the saloon most nights." He said something else. "'Have to make sure they're not ruining my place. They're bringing in all sorts of frou-frou drinks.'"

"Like margaritas and cosmos?" Two of my favorites.

"Those too," he agreed through his wife. "But he means any sort of mixed drink. Old-fashioneds are okay because they're a Wisconsin thing, but otherwise, he thinks the saloon should stick to beer and distilled spirits."

Granny Sadie said something that made Freddie laugh long and hard. Probably something about them being distilled spirits knowing my grandmother's sense of humor. That's when I noticed the witch's knot brooch on Granny's mustard-yellow sweater.

The knot reminded me of a loopy plus sign—four interconnected, oblong loops with a circle that ran through the center of each loop. It stood for protection, among many other things, and from the day my family settled on this parcel two hundred years ago, each witch wore a piece of jewelry with the symbol on it. Granny preferred a brooch, most of the aunts wore necklaces or earrings, the uncles preferred bracelets or pins attached to their collars. As other witches moved to Blackwood Grove, they adopted the tradition. Every piece was blessed, and it was an honor to wear them. I had one but took it off when I left, so I wouldn't be identified as a witch. Don't remember what I did with it. Now, realizing everyone in the room except me and Cricket had one, I felt practically naked.

Jett told her husband to, "Quit faffing about and tell us what you know about the dead guy." She listened as he spoke. "He wants to know if the man had slicked back hair."

"It looked slicked back," Gwynne recalled, "but that was because he pulled it back in a short ponytail." She held her fingers two inches apart.

Freddie spoke. Jett interpreted, "Says he's seen this Ludo fella around the shops for the last week or so. Swears he saw him go into Comfort's once or twice."

"Maybe he talked to Carly?" I wrote that down along with Beck's description. "Someone should stop in at the jail and ask her about Beck."

All eight of them stared at me without saying a word.

"Fine. I'll ask her about Beck."

"Grand idea." Comfort fixed a look on me that made me feel like a naughty ten-year-old. "She'll have things to say to you."

"Perfect opening." Gwynne scooted forward on her seat. "I have a few questions for you, Dusty."

Pepper placed her hands on the table as though about to push away. "This is a family discussion. Jett, Freddie, and I should go."

"You've been here longer than she was," Comfort snapped. "Jett and Freddie almost as long. You all are as much family as the rest of us. You can stay. Family should know what's going on with other family members."

The double meaning behind that last pointed comment was clear: I should have let them know I was okay.

Pepper settled back in her chair.

In an effort to postpone this discussion as long as possible, I asked, "Can I have a piece of pie first?" Besides, I really wanted some pie.

The dinner plates vanished, and the pies, dessert plates, forks, and coffee cups appeared.

"Questions first," Gwynne ordered, "then pie."

A sighing, make-up-your-mind sound came from the walls of the house as the pie disappeared. The dishes stayed like the promise of the reward I'd get for spilling my truth.

"Could I at least have some coffee?" I reached for one of the mugs. "Decaf please."

Gwynne thought, then agreed. Once my cup was full, she began the grilling.

CHAPTER 5

"We thought you were dead." Gwynne began. "Where have you been all this time? Why did you leave? What kept you so busy that you couldn't even send a note? And I assume because of that precious child in the other room, there's a much older one that goes with her."

Everyone, including me, looked into the family room where Cricket sat in front of the fireplace, talking to the three familiars who sat before her like an attentive audience listening to a lecture. What was she telling them? A lot had happened in her young life in the past few weeks. Most of it upsetting. And now, the last twenty-four hours. Would she sleep soundly tonight or have nightmares again? Maybe they had a sleeping tincture around here somewhere. Then one of Gwynne's questions stood out to me.

"You thought I was dead? Really?" I felt horrible.

Gwynne and Comfort exchanged a look. Comfort jutted her jaw at her younger sister, so Gwynne spoke for them. "You seem surprised by that. Should we have known otherwise?"

I slumped back in my chair. "Dad didn't keep you up to date."

"Was he supposed to?"

"Of course."

"He knew where you were?" Now Comfort's hands fisted on the table. Maks patted her back, trying to soothe her growing anger.

"He knew why I left. I'm not positive he knew where I was. We spoke a couple of times a year but never saw each other." I felt so bad they knew nothing. I asked him to . . . Didn't I? Did I ever specifically say make sure you tell my aunts what's going on? It was important to be specific with my father.

"All right." Gwynne stood and crossed to the refrigerator. She took out the banana cream and brought it to the table, then went back for the apple and peach. "Coffee, please. Two carafes. Creamers and sugar too."

A carafe appeared at each end of the table. Trays followed with a variety of creamers, each half-pint-sized pitcher labeled with the flavor—unsweetened, chai, hazelnut—and a bowl of sugar. Granny Sadie and Freddie looked longingly at the desserts spread out before us.

Once everyone had what they wanted, Gwynne said, "Start at the beginning, with the day you left, and fill us in on the last three decades."

"Before I do that," I began, "please believe that I never intended for you all to be in the dark. Dad knew. I *know* I told him to tell Mom what was going on. I can't remember if I specifically asked him to tell you all too. I wrongly assumed he would."

"You know how your father is," Comfort hissed.

Granny Sadie scowled. She and Dad often butted heads.

"I do know," I said as an apology. "He'll follow every instruction on a list to the T—"

"But if something isn't on the list," Pepper concluded, "he most likely won't do it. I learned that lesson years ago when he went birdwatching in the mountains of China. I mentioned how much I wanted Szechuan pepper and explained that it comes from a tree in that region. Couldn't find it anywhere around here at the time. I didn't specifically say bring me some, that felt pushy, so . . ."

"It didn't make it onto his list, so he didn't bring you any. Again, I'm so sorry I didn't tell him to keep you informed. Mom didn't say anything either?"

Comfort stiffened. "We don't see much of her."

"But she's still here. Right?"

"She's around," Comfort confirmed, saying the same thing Dad had earlier. "Like you, she hasn't interacted with us much."

"Anyway." Gwynne muted her older sister with the single word. "Continue with your story, Dusty. Why did you leave?"

I sighed and gathered my thoughts. I hadn't talked this much about my past in years. Now twice in one day. "I told my son—"

Granny Sadie shot to her feet and didn't need Jett to interpret her question. *I have a great-grandson?*

I offered an apologetic smile. "His name is Micah, and he's part of the reason I'm back. But let me tell this in chronological order or I'll forget parts. I left after the boating accident."

"What accident?" Jett asked. "Sorry, but if we're to know what's going on, might as well know all."

Fair enough. I'd picked at this scab earlier with Dad. Might as well scratch it all the way off.

"It was the day Carly and I graduated from high school. Nash Kramer took a bunch of kids, nine of them, out boating on the river." I could see the moments leading up to the crash as though they were playing out in front of me. "There were too many of them in the boat, and he was showing off by going far too fast. He kept looking back at everyone. Apparently he got some thrill out of scaring people. The boat was headed straight for this half-submerged tree that had floated down river with the spring thaw and got lodged on something."

"I remember that," Gwynne murmured. "People kept saying

what a hazard that tree was, and it needed to be removed before someone got hurt or a boat got damaged."

"They were heading right for it," I repeated. "At that speed, the crash would have been horrendous. I *saw* the boat launch into the air, flip, and—"

"She gets premonitions," Gwynne explained for the others, softening slightly. "That is what happened, right? You had a premonition?"

"Right. I'm clairvoyant," I told Jett, Pepper, and Freddie. "When I was Cricket's age, I started having prophetic dreams that show me the truth about things that have already happened and premonitions of events to come. That day, I saw kids go flying. They all got hurt. Five of them died. Two in ways too awful to describe. The others were badly injured." I blinked, tears stinging my eyes. "I couldn't let it happen. So I stopped the boat."

"You what?" Jett asked with a gasp.

"She's also a gray witch," Comfort said. The whisper of empathy in her words told me she understood I wasn't proud of this power.

"Doing the wrong thing for the right reason," Maks supplied. "That's a very loose definition."

"Three powers?" Jett gasped again.

They waited while I had a bite of banana cream. My eyes closed. The house may serve them, but Comfort makes the pies. I relaxed as the *comfort* she infused into everything she made spread through my body.

After another bite, I returned to my tale. "I don't know how any of this works. I don't know how to use gray magic. I can't bring on helpful dreams that will prevent something bad from happening or premonitions that will bring about justice." Like proving my son innocent in his girlfriend's disappearance. "Far as I'm concerned, there is no benefit to any of it."

"That's because," Gwynne offered quietly, "you never worked on developing them."

"Like any skill," Comfort added, "you need to practice to become proficient."

I shook my head. "The gray magic scares me. Not just because I'm doing the wrong thing, as Maks said, but because there's always a consequence for using it. Even if the spell was unintentional." They exchanged looks with each other, and I didn't even care at that moment what they were about. "When I stopped the boat, it was sudden and jarring. There wasn't time to kill the engine and let the thing float to a stop."

Jett took the hazelnut creamer from the tray. "That's not on you, lass. Altering time is high-level magic."

"Some of the kids got pretty banged up with bumps and bruises," I recalled, mostly to myself. "One hit her head and got a concussion."

"But no one died," Gwynne assured me.

"No one died," I repeated. "But Beau Balinski lost his leg, and Nash Kramer was arrested for reckless endangerment. He surely would have gone pro but lost his college football scholarship because of the accident. Then he served five years in prison."

Jett set the little pitcher back. "Again, not on you. You weren't responsible for his actions."

"That sentence was an absolute slap on the wrist," Comfort insisted. "The Kramer family gets away with everything."

"Because they have deep pockets," Pepper said while spearing a forkful of apple pie, "and will do anything to get what they want."

"I ended up cursed because of that spell," I muttered and told them what I believed to be the truth all these years. "Dad explained the curse wasn't real."

"Back up," Comfort demanded. "Who do you think cursed you? Why did you believe they did?"

"Is this why you disappeared for so long?" Gwynne asked.

Granny Sadie practically glowed red with anger. An emotion we rarely saw in her. Thankfully.

In his calm way, Maks urged, "Tell us what happened, Dusty. Take your time."

I blew out a sigh and had another bite of pie. "It was a few days after the accident. Beau was in the hospital, and Nash in jail awaiting trial. I went for a walk along the river to clear my head, and someone came up to me. They said they knew I'd been there that day and it was all my fault."

"Who was this person?" Pepper asked.

"That's the thing, I don't remember." I closed my eyes and pictured the moment as though it were happening now. "I can see a person but not who they are, not even if they're male or female. Their words are crystal clear, but not their voice. They said I was to blame for everything. When I said the boat was headed for a crash, they insisted I didn't *know* what was going to happen. Anyone could have seen what was coming, no premonition necessary. There simply wasn't enough room for Nash to even turn the boat and avoid the tree, let alone stop it in time." I shook my head. "It was a split-second thing. I saw it, thought it, held out my hand, and the boat stopped. This person refused to listen to me. They said I was responsible for Beau's injuries, destroying Nash's future, and all the minor breaks and bruises the other kids suffered. They said if I didn't leave town, they'd risk all."

"Risk all?" Maks stiffened. "Meaning what?"

"Meaning they'd risk Council punishment and tell everyone I intended to kill my classmates that day."

"Speak out against a witch?" Maks huffed. "In a safe town? That is risky."

Maks wasn't a witch but understood us as though he were one. When he fell in love with Comfort more than fifty years ago, she told him all about the family. That being able to be her true self meant never leaving Blackwood Grove and always living on the farm. Maks said he didn't care where he lived, he just wanted to be with her. He even took the Warren name, claiming the surname he'd been born with was too hard for Americans to pronounce. Ironically, his first name, Maksim, meant *greatest* in Russian. That's Maks. The greatest.

"Risky," I agreed, "but effective. Most Ordies aren't as accepting of us as you are, Maks. Even though they agree to not torment us anymore, many of them are still afraid of us. That's why magic is illegal in Ordinary towns."

Gwynne scoffed. "Don't get me started."

"Fear and anger," I continued, "can bring about untold problems. If this person had done what they said and got the Ordies to believe I was capable of purposely bringing harm to others by simply thinking it—" I swallowed the emotion rising in me. "I didn't know what they'd do. And then they took their threat even further. They said if I didn't leave, they'd tell the town you all were capable of the same actions."

Granny Sadie slammed her hands on the table, although they went right through, and shouted something.

"Lies!" Jett interpreted.

"Yes, lies, but words once spoken can't be unheard," I quipped. "This person told me that once I left, I could never return. If I did, the protection surrounding the family would be null and void."

"They don't have that kind of power." Gwynne, like her mother, seemed to glow with anger. "This is our parcel. No one but us can take down the protection."

"I know that now. Dad explained it to me this morning. Back then, I didn't know. I'd been positive this person had cursed us all. I understand now they were just trying to scare a naïve eighteen-year-old, and it worked. They made me believe they'd start a smear campaign that would make life miserable for you all. I couldn't let that happen."

The anger and hurt the aunts had been directing at me dropped palpably. I meant what I said. I would do anything to keep my family safe.

"And you have no idea who this person was?" Gwynne asked.

I shook my head. "This is only a guess, but it might have been Henry Kramer."

"Nash's dad," Maks murmured.

I nodded. "Henry was furious that Nash had been so severely punished."

"Even though Nash caused the accident," Jett said.

She wasn't going to let me take the blame. I gave her a grateful smile.

"Where did you go?" Pepper asked me.

"I packed a bag and left town with no destination in mind. Once I figured out my money would be gone in about two weeks, I contacted The Council for help. Dad, of course, was my contact. He presented my situation, and The Council agreed to give me enough financial help to get me through four years of college." I shook my head. "I can't believe he never told you all any of this."

"Not a word," Gwynne said tightly.

"I went to Stevens Point to get a degree in Environmental Ethics or Environmental Science and Management."

Gwynne offered me a genuine smile. "That sounds like you. Always concerned about nature and sustainability."

"I had big plans and then—"

"Micah," Jett guessed.

"Not right away. Micah's father was the first speed bump in my plans. We met early in my freshman year. He wooed me and convinced me to move in with him. We got married, and then he conned me."

"He what?" Maks was angry now.

This part was humiliating but better out than in as the saying goes. "We were struggling financially, so he came up with a *plan*. He decided it made more sense for him to finish his certification program since he only had a year left and I still had three to go. I could work full-time, and once he graduated, I could return to school."

"What's the punchline?" Maks looked like he'd literally punch the jerk if he was here.

I could barely look at them. "Since we were married, we kept all our funds in a joint account. He transferred all the money The Council gave me into a separate account and then disappeared with everything. He left me with two hundred dollars in the bank, rent due on an apartment I couldn't afford, and a loan on a car that was falling apart."

"Oh, Dusty," Gwynne moaned.

"The day after he left, I found out I was pregnant."

More groans and moans.

"And then someone from the court contacted me. My marriage wasn't valid because he was already married. I thought he was in his twenties like me. He was really a young-looking thirty-four." I laughed at the looks on their faces and held my right hand in the air. "I swear it's all true. I kept his last name, Hotte, because I'd already changed it and figured it would help disguise me in case whoever cursed me came looking for me."

"What did you do at that point?" Pepper asked. "You said you were pregnant."

"I had a job as an administrative assistant, which didn't pay anywhere near enough to cover my expenses and debts, so I found a cheap apartment and picked up a second job working nights at a restaurant. Around my eighth month, the restaurant let me go. They claimed it had nothing to do with me being pregnant, that they were cutting expenses, and I was the last one hired. Total shizzle." They chuckled at the only swear word I ever used. Except for the day I found out all my money was gone. I let loose with a blue stream that day. "That's when I went to The Council again. They agreed to give me a second loan that would get me through until I was on my feet again, but now I had two Council loans to pay back. Fortunately, the office where I was an admin was happy with my performance and gave me regular raises along with higher-level responsibilities. Once Micah was born, they gave me a promotion to office manager. I stayed there for a few years, then got another managerial job with better pay. Eventually, I worked my way up to an income that was enough for us to live off of without so much stress."

"Unbelievable," Gwynne breathed. "It sounds like things were going well for you. Why are you here, then?"

I nodded toward the family room where Cricket was still chatting up the familiars. Whatever she was saying must have been interesting, because the three appeared enthralled. "Cricket is in danger."

"Cricket is?" Pepper blurted.

"Micah's girlfriend, Cricket's mother, is Josie Santos. We don't know where she is. Micah thought she was going to the Philippines for a family emergency. Or she was meeting a family member somewhere, Green Bay maybe, regarding a family emergency in the Philippines. He said she was really upset when she called him at work and was speaking too fast for him to fully understand her. He told her to go and take care of the problem and call as soon as she could. She never called. This happened about a month ago. Three weeks ago, he was arrested on suspicion of being involved with her disappearance. They don't have a body, so can't charge him with murder, so instead pressed kidnapping charges even though they have no proof she was kidnapped."

"Who said he did it?" Maks wanted to know.

"One of Josie's family members, I think. They claim she never arrived at the meeting. Or in the Philippines. Wherever it was she was planning to go."

"And why is Cricket in danger?" Pepper asked.

I shoved a huge forkful of pie into my mouth, waited for the magic to help me relax again, and followed it up with a big swig of coffee. "Yesterday, I lost my job. No clue why, although I suspect the woman they hired six months ago wanted my position. Last night, early evening, my house caught fire. I barely got out with Cricket."

I'd stunned them into silence.

"It was a complete loss. I literally have nothing but the clothes on my back, my backpack, my car, and my granddaughter." What else? Was that really it? "A few thousand dollars in the bank. A meager retirement savings. Health insurance until the end of the month."

When I revealed everything all at once this way, I had to wonder again if maybe I really was cursed.

"You contacted The Council again," Gwynne guessed.

"Right. Dad said they wouldn't give me a third loan. That it was time to come home." We'd deal with the fact I was now their contracted caretaker later. "So, here we are."

For the first time in approximately thirty-six hours, I let my emotions break. I rested my head on my arms on the table and cried. The next thing I knew, there were hands on me. Gwynne pulled me to my feet and wrapped me in a hug.

"Right here," she whispered with a quavering voice, "is your safest place. We will take care of you both."

I wiped my eyes after she pulled away. The short cry released some of the terrible pressure that had been building in me since Josie went missing. Such a lovely girl. Micah was crazy about her, and Cricket missed her horribly. I sure hoped she was okay.

"Let's go back to this supposed curse," Comfort stated. She was still angry at me but not quite as intensely. "Since you can't remember who this person was, they may have put a forgetting spell on you."

They all agreed this was possible.

"It was a witch, then," I concluded.

"But not Henry. He isn't a witch," Comfort pointed out. "He could have convinced one to cast a spell for him."

Witch against witch. We couldn't turn on each other. We had to stick together against those who still hated us.

"Any way to break a spell?" I asked.

A strange look came over Gwynne. "If you can figure out who this person is, we have ways of making them comply."

Aunt Gwynne scared me a little sometimes. I needed more pie so took a small slice of peach. "This tastes like sunshine."

"We've been picking peaches this week." Jett gestured toward the gardens. "There are only a half dozen peach trees, but they produce like crazy. We preserve and keep what we want and sell the rest to the general store."

I finished my pie while they, thankfully, moved on to plans for tomorrow. I checked the time. Somehow, it was almost seven o'clock. "I should get Cricket ready for bed."

Pepper agreed. "You'll need a key."

"I have one. Two, actually." I patted my jeans pocket. "Dad gave me one for the carriage house and one for the main house. Neither worked earlier, though."

"Spit them back out at you, did it?" Pepper chuckled. "The property gets that way sometimes."

"It's probably angry at me. Just like you all are."

"Were," Gwynne corrected and shot a look at her sister.

I inclined my head in a bow of thanks. And relief. "I heard what all of you have planned for tomorrow. I'll need to look for a new job."

"*Look* for a job?" Gwynne stared at me. "You're not serious. Have you forgotten how much work there is to do around this place? On top of tending the orchard, taking care of the gardens and animals, and the diner, we now have The Apple Barn. Our on-premises store."

"Store? Oh, the red barn across the driveway?

"People took such an interest in our apple products," Gwynne explained, "not to mention our many other items, we decided to open a store."

"Didn't the barn used to be white?"

"We moved the original barn and put up a new one," Gwynne said as if moving a barn was the most natural thing in the world. "The white one a little further down the driveway used to sit there. That's where we keep the tools and tractors and such for the farm. To keep them straight, we call the white one the workshop. You'll need to come take a look at the store tomorrow."

I tried to imagine the moving process. Did it vanish from its original spot and reappear? Did it elevate and float down the driveway?

"She can take a look tomorrow afternoon," Comfort insisted. "With Carly in the pokey, I'm going to need help at the diner tomorrow. Bright and early, sunshine, so make sure you get to bed soon."

Exhaustion was setting in from the last couple of days. Falling asleep shouldn't be a problem. "How early?"

"We need to be there by five so I can bake pies and you can prep for breakfast. I'll do the cooking. You can take and serve orders."

"Okay, but who's going to watch Cricket? I can't leave her here alone. And I can't keep an eye on her while dealing with customers."

"The little lass can hang out with me," Jett offered. "She said she wanted to tend the animals."

Jett was new to me but had been here for ten years. Clearly my aunts trusted her, so I would too.

"Cricket? Would you come here, please?"

"Yes, Lola?" She skipped into the room seconds later, the trio of familiars following her. Make that a quartet. A cockatoo had joined the group. It swooped in and landed in front of Gwynne.

Must be her familiar.

"That's what she calls you?" Pepper asked with a grin. "Lola?"

"As I mentioned, her mother is from the Philippines. *Lola* is the Filipino word for grandmother, so that's what Josie taught her to call me. I love it." I nodded at the cockatoo. "Who is this?"

"Tony B." Gwynne stroked his head, and he leaned against her hand. "He's mine but will take attention wherever he can get it. And he's great with little ones, so no need to worry about Cricket's fingers."

Frowning, Cricket held up a hand and wiggled her fingers.

I lowered her hand and tapped her nose. "Auntie Comfort asked if I would help her at the diner in the morning. Would you like to help Jett with the animals while I do that?"

She gasped and turned toward Jett. "Really?"

"Honest and true." The Scottish woman held a hand in the air as though taking a vow. "We'll need to gather eggs from the chickens, then feed them and the goats. We should check on the beehives, but don't worry, they never sting. Then you can help me pick peaches off the trees and beans and tomatoes off the plants. There's loads to do around here."

Cricket turned to me. "I wanna help do all those things."

A farm girl in training. Coming here seemed to be the right decision for her. I had to wonder after finding Ludo Beck. "Okay, but in that case, we need to get ready for bed."

"Can I have a hug before you run off?" Pepper asked, arms wide and ready.

Cricket was always leery of strangers, but it seemed she was okay with this group now. She made her way around the table, ending with her new bestie, Jett.

Jett told me, "If the lass is still sleeping when you leave, let her sleep. I'll check on her."

"How will you know when she wakes up?"

The soft sound of crickets chirping filled the kitchen. Jet pointed at the house in general. "Guess that's the Cricket alarm."

CHAPTER 6

hen I reached out with the key this time, Apple Blossom Cottage's front door popped open.

"Yay," Cricket declared. "I get to see my next new room."

I wasn't nearly as excited over this as she was. Three bedrooms in two weeks didn't exactly scream stability. However, my granddaughter was loved and safe. That's what really mattered.

"Okay, little bug." She giggled as she did every time I called her that. "Same rules as at the other house. Shoes off at the door."

She plopped down on her butt, pulled off her sandals, and set them side-by-side beneath the bench on a little rug covered with apple trees. The words *You're the apple of my eye* arched over the trees like a rainbow. The tiny apples on the trees all had big eyes and smiles. Cute.

"Can I go up?"

"Yes, ma'am." I hitched my backpack over my shoulder, waited for her to grab the handrail like I had, and then followed her up. I groaned when we got to the top. "Really?"

The stairway led directly into a small living

room/kitchenette area . . . decorated in 1950s bubblegum pink and apple green. Of all the schemes the house had presented over my eighteen years, this particular pink and green combo was the one I hated the most. Even more than its psychedelic tie-dye phase.

"Ooh." Cricket clasped her hands beneath her chin. "It's so pretty. Isn't it pretty, Lola?"

Ugh. "Sure, honey. I know how much you like pink."

"But purple is my favorite."

Dear lord, child, don't say things like that out loud. Who knows what we'll walk into next time.

"Are those the bedrooms?" She pointed at the two closed doors on the far end of the apartment.

Far being a relative term. The whole space was about twice the size of the hotel room we shared last night.

I set my backpack down and smiled. "They must be. See the sign on the door on the right?"

Picking her up so she could point to each letter. "C-R-I-C-K-E-T." She looked at me and whispered, "That says me, doesn't it?"

Oh, this child. "It does. It says Cricket, so that must be your bedroom."

She squirmed for me to put her down, and with both hands, she twisted the knob. I held my breath, half in fear of what we'd find on the other side. Then my heart swelled to near bursting.

Even though there was no doubt about the outcome, the courts took two days to declare me her guardian after Micah was arrested. She had to stay with a foster family during those days—which meant she'd actually had four bedrooms in two weeks—but doing so gave me time to prepare a room for her. I'd wanted to paint the walls her favorite shade of pinky lavender but didn't think two days would be enough time for the paint fumes to dissipate.

I was beyond excited when I found a bedspread with tiny

ballerinas dancing their way across the hem. It came with two ballerina-shaped pillows Cricket loved to hug and dance around her room with. The store displayed the set with framed illustrated pictures of animals in tutus and toe shoes in various ballet poses, so I bought those too. Once I got everything home, it took me an hour to put her room together. I had planned to do even more but never got the chance.

Somehow, when she opened that door in the apartment, there was the room I had envisioned. Pinky-lavender walls. The same bedspread and pillows I'd bought her. Even the same pictures of animals in tutus. There was also the four-poster bed I'd planned to buy. A canopy in a pastel rainbow of tulle was a fun touch. The matching tulle bed skirt was so thick it looked like the bed was wearing a tutu. And the toys! She'd never be bored in this room.

She looked around with wide eyes, baba clutched in a hug, and for the first time today was speechless. As she wandered around, touching various things with the tip of her finger, as though they'd *poof* out of existence if she was too forceful, I scanned the rest of the room.

A pair of ballerina pajamas lay on the bed for her. Little pink shorts and a yellow T-shirt with witch kitties lay folded on the dresser, waiting for her to wear them tomorrow.

A quick check of the dresser drawers and the closet showed we needed to go clothes shopping. While the property was clearly capable of providing things Cricket would love, it would be more fun for her to choose her own clothes.

Feeling greatly relieved, I whispered, "Thank you," to the property. This little girl had been through enough lately. "Please, leave it alone until she asks for something different. She needs stability, not variety."

The lights flickered in what I hoped was agreement.

"I know you want to play," I told her, "but how about you

take your bath and get ready for bed first. Then you can play for a few minutes before I read you a story."

She stood in the middle of the room, arms at her sides, and sighed. Not a happy sound. "Okay, Lola."

I sat on the edge of the bed and pulled her into my lap. "What are you feeling?"

"Sad," she admitted after a pause. "We just got here."

"Where do you think we're going?"

"To another new house." She seemed to believe a new room every couple of days was her new normal.

"We're not going anywhere," I promised. "The aunties said we can stay here for as long as we want."

A smile brightened her face, but then a shadow crossed it. "How long do you want to stay?"

A very good question that I couldn't answer yet. Moving back to Blackwood Grove had never been in my plans. I'd spent most of my life as an Ordinary so had completely lost touch with my witch self.

"How about this?" I poked her tummy, making her giggle. "I promise we will stay here long enough that you can play with every single one of those toys."

"Again and again?" she whispered.

"Again and again. So, let's check out that tub."

She hopped off my lap. "Okay."

As was her routine, she *folded* baba into a bundle and set it on the foot of the bed. Then she scooped up her new jammies, which she declared were *perfect*, and wandered to the snug bathroom across from the second bedroom.

"This tub has holes in it."

I followed her in to see what she meant and laughed. "This tub makes its own bubbles."

"Really?"

"Not soap bubbles." How to explain? "You know how when you blow into a straw instead of sucking your milk through it?"

She nodded. "This tub will blow bubbles at me?"

"Yep. Want to try it?"

"Yes, I do!"

Once she was in the tub, playing with the toys that appeared while she got undressed, I grabbed my backpack to get the toothbrush and toothpaste the hotel desk clerk had given us. When I opened the door to my bedroom to put my pack inside, I stopped at the threshold. Where my granddaughter got her ballerina dream room, my bedroom contained a narrow camping cot shoved into the corner. A thin pillow and threadbare blanket lay at the foot. That was literally it. No chair, no curtains on the sliding doors to the balcony, no lamp. Just a single dim bulb hanging from the center of the ceiling.

"I assume you're mad at me too."

The bulb dimmed further, which hardly seemed possible.

"I'm really sorry. I thought I was protecting the family."

The bulb brightened slightly.

"I have to help Comfort at the diner tomorrow. Could I have something else to wear? These clothes smell like smoke."

The closet door popped open revealing a pair of ripped, ragged jeans and an old stretched out T-shirt with *AF* for Applewood Farm in a font that looked like apple tree branches.

"Ha! You think you're being funny, but this is exactly what I like to wear. And I'm proud to show off our logo."

The image changed to the words, "I support clear cutting" and a pile of cut down apple trees.

Looked like I had a lot more apologizing to do.

CRICKET CLUTCHED a purple stuffed elephant she'd found in the toy pile while I read to her. I don't think we'd made it five pages when she slumped heavily against my side, sound asleep. After settling her in the middle of her full-size bed, I tucked baba, the elephant, and the covers around her, then kissed her forehead.

I went out to the pink and green living room and sat on the pink sofa. While narrow, it was at least comfortable.

"Might just sleep here tonight," I told the apartment. "It's certainly better than the cot you gave me."

The house had given me a piece of paper with the start of a list so we could make a plan for gathering information to help Carly. I got it from where I'd set it on the kitchenette counter. So far all it said was *he was waiting for someone, did Carly speak with Beck,* and Beck's description. We talked more about me than helping her.

Instead of a plan, I wrote the facts as I knew them and questions that occurred to me. Ludo Beck remained at the breakfast counter to finish his coffee after Gwynne told him the diner was closed. Sounded like he was stalling. But why? Who could he have been waiting for? Considering we knew absolutely nothing about this man, it could have been anyone. Who could have killed him? Why? What had he done? Was the diner somehow important in this crime, or was it dumb luck that he ended up getting killed in our restaurant? Was this Beck's first time in town, or was he a regular?

That was a lot of questions. How was I supposed to get answers? Where should I start? Who should I ask? Maybe one of the other store owners saw him around. Or the townies. I could casually ask questions while helping at the diner tomorrow.

I sat back and stared at the list until it blurred. All of my questions were based on the probability that Beck had done something to get himself killed. What if he was an innocent victim in all of this? Like Carly.

The words from the note I'd found on my windshield came back to me.

HER MOTHER WAS FIRST. THEN HER FATHER.
IT WOULD BE A SHAME IF SHE LOST HER ENTIRE FAMILY.
THEN WHO WILL TAKE CARE OF HER?

What if whoever left that note for me followed me here? I pulled into town right around two, went straight to the farm, and then went to the diner. What if *her entire family* meant my family, too, not just Micah and Josie?

My cell phone rang, and my coworker Vic Lipinski's name flashed on the screen. Vic got hired to work in the finance department at my *former* company about a year ago. We'd been cordial, as coworkers are, and then one day during lunch about a month after he started, he sat at my table and began telling me that the guy he met at a club three weeks earlier had stopped replying to his texts.

"I can't believe I've been ghosted." He went on for fifteen minutes about how much he'd liked that guy and how he was sure they'd been heading for something meaningful. "Can't believe he was leading me on the whole time."

"Let me tell you a cautionary tale about picking up guys in bars." He sat riveted while I told him about Micah's father. Vic declared me the queen of relationships gone wrong, and we became fast friends.

With thumb hovering between the answer and hang-up buttons, I debated if I wanted to talk right now. I was tired and not in the mood for the lecture I knew was coming. I also couldn't handle anyone else being mad at me, so I owned up to my misdeed, which seemed to be the theme of the day for me, and clicked answer.

"Where are you?" he demanded before I'd finished saying hello. "Your house burned down? And you didn't call me? I've been frantic trying to find you. Didn't you get any of my twenty messages? They won't tell me anything at work other than you no longer work there. Did you quit? Tell me you're not stranded at the bottom of a ravine somewhere."

I smiled while accepting the scolding. "Considering I actually answered your call, I would have called for help."

He paused before saying, "Fair point. Seriously, though, what's going on?"

Might as well start with the easy stuff. "They fired me."

"They what?"

"I think Skylar wants my job."

"Who's . . . Oh. The strumpet who's always one jiggle away from popping out of her dress?"

"That's her. I'm only guessing she's the reason, so don't repeat that. She has gotten very close with Mr. Farnworth lately, however, if you know what I mean."

"Message received. I give it two weeks tops, and he'll be begging you to come back."

Vic could be very good for a bruised ego. "That happened yesterday morning, and then, yes, my house burned down last night."

"Did the strumpet do it?"

I couldn't help but laugh. "I doubt it."

"Where are you staying?"

"We went to a hotel last night, and then I decided to introduce Cricket to my family." He didn't know I was a witch. No one outside of Blackwood Grove did.

"You could stay with me, you know."

"In your tiny one-bedroom apartment?"

"You and Bug Girl can have my bed. I'll sleep in the recliner."

And he would, too. Vic had a big heart. While that option could have worked for one night, his building didn't offer the security we needed. And after reading the note left on my car, only the highest level would suffice. That meant staying here. For the time being, at least.

"Where are you exactly?" Vic asked.

"Blackwood Grove."

"Which state?"

"We're still in Wisconsin." I heard the sound of typing on his end of the call. "Are you looking it up?"

"I am. Deciding if I should come give you a hug."

Vic gave amazing hugs. "It would be a five-hour round trip."

"Ah, yes, I see. Southwest Wisconsin. A little far this time of night. Hang on. There's a witch's hat icon next to the name. You grew up in a safe town?"

Tread carefully, Dusty girl. "I did."

"What does that mean? Does everyone walk around with wands at the ready?"

"No."

And then he whispered the inevitable question, "Are you a witch?"

All these years of living in hiding. I must have felt really safe within the hedge because I whispered, "Yes."

That released a barrage of questions about what magic could I do, what could my family members do, was Cricket a witch, and so on. It was a potentially huge gamble, but I told him about my family, leaving out the Warren name. I also skipped over the part about the boat accident and the resulting threat because I just couldn't talk about that again. It was too draining. When I finished, I felt free. Saying the words to someone outside the town was liberating. And more than a little terrifying.

"Your story needs to be made into a movie."

Shizzle. "No. Do not start writing this."

Vic claimed to be a frustrated novelist. "I'll change the names to protect the innocent."

"Promise me, Vic."

He groaned something that sounded like an agreement. "Will you let me visit you at your enchanted farm?"

What had I done? "That's not entirely up to me, but I'll see what I can do."

"Cool. Now, explain safe towns to me. We all know they exist, but it's not like we study them in history class. How did they come to be?"

I knew that tone. He wasn't going to let this go, so I might as well give him something. "You're aware that witches have always been targets."

"Uh, yeah. Everyone knows that."

"My family was sort of . . . *feisty* is probably the best word. After generations and generations kept fighting for their rights, my family was given a parcel of land. They were the first family to receive one, but others started popping up all over the country soon afterward. On that parcel, they were free to live however they chose, including performing all the magic they wanted. As long as they were within their safe zone, they wouldn't be persecuted. Eventually, almost all of those safe zones became safe towns like Blackwood Grove and it's no longer illegal to be a witch."

"But it is illegal to perform magic. Talk about screwy. Have you really been living a double life all these years?"

"Not exactly. I stopped doing magic. I haven't cast a spell in more than thirty years."

"Nothing at all? No pinch of this, dash of that?"

"I've mixed cold remedies using specific plants, but that's medicine, not magic."

He hummed softly. A thought was forming. "Could you make a love spell and hook me up with my soulmate?"

"That would definitely fall under the magic category, so out of my wheelhouse." I explained my dreams and premonitions but not the gray witchcraft. "As a side note, you should know that there are always consequences to performing magic. Both for the witch and the Ordy, or Ordinary, which is what we call non-magical people."

"What kind of consequence could come from a love spell?"

"You could attract stalkers, serial killers, needy people who can't function without you at their side constantly . . . Any time you mess around with another person's timeline, there will be consequences." Images flashed in my mind. The boat coming to an almost instant stop. Kids getting hurt. Beau Balinski flying out of it, and his leg getting mangled from the impact with the submerged tree I'd tried to prevent them from hitting. The mystery person—Henry?—standing before me and issuing threats. "Sometimes consequences are major, other times they're minor. For example, you do a good deed by giving a driver's car a little magical push so they can make it to the gas pump two blocks away without running dry. Then your car runs out of gas two miles from the station or your car dies on the way to an important meeting. Things like that."

"I have so many questions."

"I'm sure you do." I looked around the living room for a clock. "What time is it?"

"Almost ten."

"Oh, man. I need to be up early. As in four-thirty early."

"Why? Cows to milk?"

"We don't have cows. We do have goats, however. Their milk makes amazing cheese and lotions. And no, I've been tasked with helping my aunt at the diner in the morning. Then I have to interview people about the dead man."

"Stop the bus, sister. What dead man?"

Dang it! I wasn't going to mention that either. I took a few more minutes and explained about Ludo Beck and how my cousin got mixed up in his murder.

"A murder minutes after you arrived," Vic summarized. "And you still feel your safe town really is safe?"

That was the million-dollar question, but what other choice did I have? "Remember I said Cricket was in danger?"

He sighed. "Poor little bug."

"Keeping her here is the very best option. Bad things might happen to some folks in the town, but nothing can happen to us inside our hedge. And as long as Cricket is with me or one of the aunts if we go outside the hedge, she will be fine."

"So you're staying."

"For now, yes. I believe Josie's disappearance, Micah's incarceration, and this threat against my girl are all related. Once I resolve all that, I'll reevaluate my life and figure out my next step. Other than this murder, of course, I'm glad I'm back. I missed my family and Blackwood Grove more than I realized."

"And being allowed to be yourself."

"That too." This shocked me. I thought I was just fine keeping to the shadows.

Vic let out a big sigh. "I'm sorry this has happened to you, but I'm so glad you're okay. I really do want to come and visit you on your farm. And squeeze Cricket's chubby cheeks."

"She hates that, you know."

It sounded like he'd slapped his hand against his recliner cushion. "Why didn't you tell me that? Now I feel bad."

"I swear, the rules change by the day with that girl."

"Can I call you again?"

"Of course."

"I'd say be safe, but it looks like you've got that covered."

After we hung up, I went to my bedroom, my awful jail cell of a bedroom, and changed into the T-shirt I bought at the hotel last night. I stared down at the cot and shook my head. Nope, not sleeping on that rickety thing. Grabbing the pillow and poor excuse for a blanket, I headed back out to the pink sofa. Despite my exhaustion, I couldn't fall asleep. I'd asked for decaf coffee with my pie. Pretty sure that wasn't what I got.

CHAPTER 7

*T*he apartment woke me early as expected. The bright lights and reveille bugle blast were over the top.

"Stop it!" I hissed. "You'll wake up Cricket."

The bugle kept playing, on a continuous loop, but much more softly.

"I apologized to everyone last night and meant it. How long are you going to punish me for leaving?" I tossed aside my whisper-thin blanket and pushed myself to a sitting position. Everything hurt. A combination of stress, sleeping on this sofa, and age. "Maybe the cot would have been better."

The bugle stopped. Was that a yes?

I checked the time. Twenty to five. Was I meeting Comfort at the diner or the house?

"Dusty?"

Speaking of my aunt, that sounded like her voice. Where was it coming from?

"Look by the refrigerator."

On the small apple-green counter between the pink-and-green range and pink refrigerator was a landline phone with an intercom. I pressed the button. "Dusty's still sleeping."

"I can see your lights are on," Comfort replied, unamused. "Are you ready?"

"Give me five minutes."

After washing my face and applying moisturizer, I brushed my teeth, pulled on the raggedy jeans and blasphemous T-shirt turned inside out. The property must have heard me mention how I'd wanted to get an environmental degree and was messing with me. No way would I ever support clear cutting.

Before leaving, I crept into Cricket's room. She'd had a bad dream last night. When she called out, the sound of chirping crickets filled the apartment. Or at least the living room. I went to check on her and was happy to find her still asleep. I stroked her forehead and whispered everything was okay. She hugged the stuffed purple elephant closer, and the scowl on her beautiful face smoothed. Now, she was sound asleep with the elephant next to her and her thumb in her mouth. She stopped sucking her thumb a year ago. Hopefully that would pass as she became more comfortable in her new home.

When I bent to kiss her forehead, I noticed a silver witch's knot pendant at her throat. It had a lavender crystal at the center where the loops came together. I gave the chain a gentle tug. It was stretchy. Good. If she snagged it on something, she wouldn't get hurt. My hand went to my throat as I closed the door. No witch's knot for me yet.

Ready to leave, I stood at the top of the steps and stared at Cricket's room.

"I'll be honest," I told the apartment, "even though Jett said she'd check on her, and the house is only twenty feet away, I don't like the idea of leaving her alone."

The chirping crickets sound returned.

"Not good enough. Maybe I should bring her over to the house. There's got to be someplace to put her over there."

But then she'd wake up in a different bed than she fell asleep in.

"Keep an eye on her for a minute," I instructed. "I'm going to send Jett over here."

Jail cell bars appeared in front of her room door. Still not good enough, not to mention disturbing considering where her father was, but at least she couldn't leave the room until Jett, or someone, got over here.

At the bottom of the stairs, I put on my hiking boots, then grabbed my backpack and found Jett standing on the other side of the door when I opened it.

"After you left last night, I realized how inappropriate it would be to leave a four-year-old alone. I said she could be with me today, so here I am to be with her."

My nerves settled immediately. "Thank you. I was on my way to get you for the same reason."

"Go on, Comfort's waiting for you outside The Apple Barn."

Comfort was dressed much as she was yesterday in dark wide-legged jeans, a loose pink Comfort's Food Diner T-shirt, and a red bandana holding her hair back. At eighty-two years old, there were wrinkles across her forehead that weren't there thirty years ago, naturally, and the skin around her neck was loose. Her shoulders rounded forward a bit, too, but she was still as spry as ever.

As I tried to fall asleep last night, Gwynne's comment replayed in my head. *Have you forgotten how much work there is to do around this place?* As kids, Brenda, Carly, her siblings Etta and Benny, and I were expected to do our part to support the family business by doing rotations through the diner, orchard, gardens, animal pens, or the house. After we'd done each position three times, we could pick the one that felt the most comfortable. For me, it was working in the orchard and gardens. It's not that I disliked working at the diner, but I hadn't especially liked it either.

"Finally ready?" Comfort snapped when I got close.

"Are you sure you want my help?"

She held my gaze but didn't reply.

"I recall only working in the diner the three required times," I said. "That was a long time ago. I also worked at a burger joint for about six months when I was pregnant with Micah twenty-nine years ago."

Comfort sighed. "What are you saying, Dusty?"

"That I have limited experience and will likely not be your best server ever."

She swatted her hand and grumbled, "You'll be fine. The diner will help, and our customers are *chill*, as the kids say, so if you make a mistake, they won't give you a hard time. The diner might, but the customers won't."

"I'm more concerned about the physical toll. It's not easy work, and for the last twenty-some years, I sat at a desk in an office. You're in better shape than I am. How are you still doing this work? Nine hours a day, five days a week. It's got to be exhausting."

She chuckled as the spot in the hedge that opened for Cricket and me yesterday opened now so we could pass. "Mindset is everything. If I sat on the back porch in a rocking chair all day, I'd seize up and die. The diner keeps me young. I love being around all those people. And watching while the first bite of my food makes their day better is like an elixir for me too."

For the first time since I got here, the scowl on Comfort's face smoothed. She meant what she said. She loved working at the diner.

She strolled along, head held high, mouth clamped shut. Not interested in more small talk. But there was something I had wanted to know for years. Comfort's magic wasn't gray, she didn't alter the course of people's lives, but I knew she suffered consequences for interfering. Even though it was to make them feel better.

"You've been taking on your customers' bad days and aches

and pains, both physical and emotional, for more than sixty years. It's got to be wearing on you."

"I've been working in the diner for sixty-some years but took over my mother's role as head cook and piemaker not long after you left."

"Okay, thirty years of taking in other people's negativity."

"Not everyone who comes in has a problem that needs comforting away. For those who do, my food provides the antidote. Then my consequence is I carry their woes around with me before I let them go."

"How do you do that?"

"The magic of pen and paper."

I laughed out loud as we approached the diner. "You journal about other people's problems?"

"Not exactly. Journaling implies I keep a record of it. After every shift, I write down the day's problems on a simple piece of paper, removing it from my brain, and then I burn the paper." She made explosion hands. "Poof. Problem gone."

"That's kind of brilliant."

"As Granny Sadie always said, better out than in."

So that's where I picked up the saying.

"Your pie soothed me last night, which means you took part of my pain. It also means you know how sorry I am."

She didn't reply.

"Comfort, how long are you going to be mad at me?"

She stopped walking abruptly and faced me. "Do you know how badly you hurt Carly?"

I nodded, ashamed. "I have a pretty good idea."

"Do you know how badly it hurts a mother to see her child in pain?"

More shame. "I do."

She jabbed her finger into my arm and demanded, "You need to make things right with my girl."

"I will, I promise. Whatever it takes."

She stared into my eyes for a long moment, then softened a little. "I'm going to hold you to that promise. I can't fully forgive you until you fulfill it."

Scouts' honor. Pinky promise. Swear on the *Bible* . . . or grimoire in our case. "I understand."

"Look at me, Dusty." I did. "I'm sorry for what you went through and what you're still going through. And I'm glad you're home."

Tears filled my eyes. "Can I hug you?"

She opened her arms and held me. Not for as long as I would have liked, but I'd take whatever she was willing to give.

"Thank you." I sniffled when she released me. "I will make this right. All of it."

We completed the half-block walk to the diner where she unlocked the back door. We were instantly engulfed by the aroma of freshly brewed coffee. How wonderful to have an enchanted kitchen.

Comfort dropped her purse in the office and then read a note left on the counter by the register. "Looks like peach is the pie of the day, and BLTs with a cup of chilled peach soup sprinkled with goat cheese is our special."

My mouth watered. I loved that soup and hadn't had it in decades. "You still let the diner decide those things?" I took my first sip of coffee. So good.

"I tried to do it once. The diner wasn't happy about it. The thing is, letting the diner decide means it also acts as a prep chef. This morning, I'll open the fridge and find cucumbers peeled and seeded, bell peppers chopped, and the peaches sliced. All I have to do is mix it all together, add my own touches, and whisper my intent."

Peaches, peppers, and cucumbers for the soup. Tomatoes and lettuce for the sandwiches. Specials of the day featuring produce fresh from our farm. I loved that.

"I assume your shirt is inside out because the property was

up to shenanigans." Comfort pointed to the retail section. "Grab a T-shirt and an apron. I'll leave your *laminated* opening instructions here on the counter. Carly keeps things very organized. Everything you need for the dining room including pie pans are under the counter. Dishes are in the kitchen. Glasses and coffee cups by the drink station."

"What about the register? How does that work?"

"It's all programmed with voice commands." She picked up a gadget that looked like an oxygen mask. "Put this to your face, tell it what the order is, and it will take care of the rest." She gave the diner in general a stern look. "No joking around today, got it? It's not Dusty's fault Carly isn't here."

A *cha-ching* sound filled the air. I assumed that meant okay.

Comfort turned toward me. "You'll be fine. If nothing else, we've got regular customers who know this place well enough they could fill their own orders if needed."

An hour later, someone knocked on the door. A woman with a head of soft gray curls that reminded me of a dandelion gone to seed stood on the other side of the door. A large willow basket hung from her elbow.

"Is that June Stanford?" I asked.

"Sure is." Comfort went to let her in. "Comes three times a week and sits here all day long doing her needlepoint or knitting. We must be getting a bonus day this week. She was just here yesterday." As the other woman crossed the threshold, Comfort explained that, "June sets up at that first table there next to the retail section so she can keep an eye on who's looking at her products."

"Market research," June agreed. "How am I supposed to know what the customer wants if I don't watch?"

"Except she talks their ear off with precise details about how she made each item," Comfort teasingly scolded. "I can't tell if people buy things because they like them or want to shut her up."

June chuckled then turned toward me. "Dusty Warren. I heard you were back."

"Dusty Hotte now." Since the day I got pretend-married to Micah's father, I never regretted my name change. Now, not using the Warren surname made me feel even more like an outsider.

June patted my arm as she passed by me. "Welcome home, honey. We've missed you." Then she turned serious. "I understand there was some trouble after I left yesterday."

I glanced at the spot on the floor where Beck's body had been. Comfort said the diner would clean things up, and there was no indication whatsoever that a man had died there. The two older women took a minute to discuss what had happened. Comfort's retelling was to the point with no over dramatizing, which was good. A man died. That wasn't fodder for gossips, although I'm sure we'd get plenty of that today.

While June set up, Comfort went over last-minute details with me. "Nina will be here soon. She'll float between helping me in the kitchen and assisting you if breakfast gets busy. She'll handle the booths and tables during lunch. You can run the counter and ring up takeout and retail orders. Avery will come in for the lunch rush to help me back there and deal with the dishes."

"Dishes? Isn't the diner self-cleaning like the house?"

"We tweaked that. Customers were either scared to death to see the tables reset on their own or so entranced by the magic they wouldn't leave. We take care of it while customers are here, and at the end of the day, the diner wipes down the counters and tables, scrubs the floors, and cleans the bathrooms. Oh, and to prevent confusion or embarrassment, Avery is non-binary and uses the pronouns they and them."

"Thanks for letting me know. And who is Nina?"

"Nina is my granddaughter." A smile warmed Comfort's

face. "She's twenty years old and plans to take over the diner when I step down."

"Carly has a daughter," I mused. "On top of missing out on the life Carly and I were going to have together, I missed out on things like her getting married and having a baby."

Comfort held up four fingers. "Carly has four kids. Nina, Alex, Emma, and Sebastian. Kyle, her husband, is a long-haul trucker and off on a trip right now. I talked to him last night about the mess his wife is in right now."

As the clock ticked closer to six and the opening bell, a young woman walked in. Everything blurred, and all I could see was what appeared to be my childhood best friend.

"Morning, Granny," she called out to Comfort and slowed her pace when she saw me staring. Her hands went to her face like she might have a smudge of something there. Then she checked her shirt for a stain. "Why are you looking at me like that?"

"Sorry." I held out my hand. "I'm Dusty, and you look exactly like your mother."

She took my hand but paused the shaking. "As in, Mom's cousin? Must be, because there's only one Dusty I've ever heard about."

It was seriously like stepping back in time. If the diner was still red, black, and white, I'd swear I was eighteen again.

Nina pulled her hand out of mine. "So you're back? As in permanently or just stopping in for a visit?"

The tone in Nina's voice made it clear Carly had told her all about what I'd done. "I'm back." I wasn't ready to commit to permanently unless that turned out to be best for Cricket and Micah. Whatever happened, I'd never lose touch with my family again.

Nina studied me while twisting the witch's knot ring around her right middle finger. "You need to make things right with my mom."

"I will."

She released the glare. "What's on the menu today, Granny?"

Comfort told her about the peachy dishes. "Think I'll give Avery a call and see if they can come in an hour early."

"Good idea. You know how folks love fresh peach anything."

"And drama," Comfort added. "Be ready for plenty of that today."

I checked the salt, pepper, sugar, and napkin dispensers on every table. All were full. Coffee was brewed. My apron was in place as was the nametag I found on the counter. I was ready.

"You'll be fine, dear," June said from her table. Enchanted needles off to the side were busy knitting while she embroidered something else. "Breakfast is easy. It'll be mostly Ordinaries, and they'll get their own coffee. All you have to do is relay their orders and bring them their food when ready."

"Thanks, June."

She was right, breakfast was pretty smooth, and fortunately my time as a server came back to me like I'd just done it yesterday. The rest of the mall didn't open until ten o'clock, so it was mostly townies early on. Some of them recognized me and wanted to know where I'd been. I wasn't about to tell my whole story to basic strangers, regardless of how well we'd known each other in the past, so simply said my job and son kept me away but, now that he was an adult, it was time for me to come home. None of it a lie. Most of it a shadow of the truth.

And Comfort was right about the gossip. Everyone was talking about Ludo Beck's murder and Carly's incarceration. Some seemed excited to have something to talk about. Most were in shock over this awful thing happening in their small town and had gathered here for consolation. I listened to their conversations when I could, trying to pick up information about Mr. Beck. A few times I came right out and asked if they knew him. Most hadn't, but a few confirmed what Comfort had said yesterday. That he had wanted to open a store in the mall.

"Any idea what kind of store?" I asked one woman.

"I own Tiny Togs, the kids clothing store." She pointed to the west. "We're two stores down. Mr. Beck had been targeting those of us in the center of the mall."

"What do you mean targeting?"

She shrugged as though it were obvious. "We're the prime spots. Smack in the middle of the action."

"Are you saying he wanted your building?"

"That's what I'm saying. There's one available at the end of the park right across from Silver Moon Apothecary. He said it was too far away from where he wanted to be, but it's a great location. Tons of people go past that shop to get to The Apple Barn, so I don't know what his problem was."

"Do you know what kind of store he wanted to open?"

"Yep. A grocery store that carried specialty meats and cheeses, oils and vinegars." She shrugged. "High-end stuff, I guess."

I didn't want to risk offending her, but I didn't see Blackwood Grove as a high-end-food-type town. Maybe it had changed more than I realized. After all, we didn't have a children's clothing boutique when I was growing up here.

What exactly had Beck been willing to do to get people to give up their prime locations? Bribery? Sabotage? Murder? Is that what happened yesterday? Had Beck perhaps pushed one of the store owners too far and they retaliated?

"Excuse me, ma'am."

I motioned to a woman waving her menu at me that I'd be right there. "I need to go take their order, but I'll be back with your credit card. And I'll bring my granddaughter into your store. She needs clothes in the worst way."

"Grow like little weeds on too much fertilizer." She laughed at the joke she probably made a dozen times a day. "I'm Miriam, by the way."

"Dusty." I tapped my nametag with my pen. "Nice to meet you."

Shortly after returning with Miriam's receipt and a promise to stop by her store later today or tomorrow with Cricket, someone wearing a Comfort's Food Diner T-shirt walked in. Either the shirts were trendy around here or this tall, striking person was Avery. They had long, gleaming black hair tied up in a bun and a strong jaw. Small pearl earrings dotted their ears, and a long-sleeve shirt was tied at their narrow hips over the T-shirt.

"Avery?" I guessed.

"Right. I know everyone who works here." Their voice was deep and warm. "Since I don't know you, you must be the missing niece."

"Is that how Comfort is introducing me?"

They nodded.

"My actual name is Dusty Hotte. Pleasure to meet you."

Chitchat time ended as fast as it started. Moments after Avery walked in, a flood of customers followed. Avery went back to the kitchen, and Nina came out front. She grabbed a stack of menus and instead of taking people to tables, she handed them the proper number of menus for their party and told them to pick one.

"Ready for lunch?" she asked me.

"I think so," I answered with confidence. "Breakfast wasn't that bad."

She laughed, deep in her throat, the same way her mother did. It basically meant *just wait* or *you'll see*.

Lunch flew by in a frantic blur that breakfast hadn't totally prepared me for. I remembered from my last stint as a server that lots of customers made for a fast shift so at least there was that. By one thirty, half an hour before closing time, my feet were aching. So were my arms from carrying trays of food. Fortunately, the diner helped me out with a beverage tray that wouldn't let the drinks spill no matter how far off balance I tipped it. I got better as the shift went on, so if I had to help out here again, I wouldn't need quite so much backup.

At one forty-five, Nina announced last call for drink refills and that the kitchen was now closed. "Slices of pie are available to go."

"What about ice cream?" a man called out.

"Happy to add a scoop," she told him, "but if it melts, that's on you. Hopefully not literally."

She had her mother's sassy attitude. Listening to her both warmed my heart and created a sad hole. I had missed Carly over the years but hadn't realized how much until now.

At five minutes to two, June was the last customer. As she put away her projects and supplies, she called me over to her. "I made something for you, dear."

"For me?"

"It's a sort of welcome home gift."

She handed me a round object made of two pieces of cross stitch fabric. The pieces were sewn together and filled with stuffing, so it was like a pillow the size of my palm. On one side, she'd stitched a witch's cross, my initials, and the date. On the other, she'd made a compass with little red apples standing in for N, S, E, and W. Instead of a compass rose at the center, she'd stitched a cross-section apple slice, one that showed the apple seed pentagram hidden at the heart of every apple. Curving across the top or north edge, she'd put *Applewood Farm*.

June winked. "Now you can always find your way home."

So creative and touching. "Thank you, June. This is very sweet."

As June left, a grim-looking Officer Beau Balinski entered the diner.

CHAPTER 8

*B*eau frowned at the empty pie case. "Dang. No more peach?"

Comfort appeared from the kitchen. "We always hold a pie in the back. In case of a pie emergency. I see my daughter isn't with you. Release her and you can have all the pie you want."

He cleared his throat and tried not to look like a scolded boy.

Nina matched her granny's temperament. "Something we can do for you, officer?"

"I stopped in to give you an update on Carly."

Comfort and Nina stood across from Beau on the other side of the breakfast counter, matching scowls on their faces. I grabbed a cup of coffee and sat two stools away from him, groaning with gratitude to finally be off my feet. I said, "I thought you were just taking her in for questioning. Why haven't you released her yet?"

"Because while we have no solid proof that she's guilty," he began, "we have enough circumstantial evidence to believe she might be."

"What does that mean?" Comfort asked and put an arm around her granddaughter's waist.

"Yesterday when I conducted my interviews here, you all indicated that Ms. Gwynne told the victim the diner was closing and a few minutes later Carly ordered him to leave. A short time after that, he was found stabbed, and it wasn't with a knife as we originally believed. When the weapon was removed during the autopsy, we found that it was one of those triangle-shaped spatulas with the serrated edges."

Comfort looked shocked by this. "A pie knife? We keep a couple of them beneath the serving window for slicing fresh pies."

"Pie knife," Beau repeated while writing on the small notepad he'd taken from his pocket. "We fingerprinted Carly when we booked her and then matched a thumbprint from the handle where it connects with the blade to hers."

Comfort looked at him like he was speaking gibberish. "It matched because she was serving pie yesterday. As she does every day. I cook, she takes care of the guests. How can that be evidence?"

"Hers were the only identifiable prints on the weapon," Beau explained.

Nina shrugged. "The killer wore gloves. That's pretty obvious. Talk about circumstantial evidence."

Beau remained respectful. "That's why I said we don't have solid proof. Other prints were smudged, but we can't know if that was from her repeatedly using the weapon or from possible glove fabric rubbing against the handle."

Or maybe because a telekinetic witch sent the pie knife flying at Beck. Gwynne didn't do it; she saw him before Carly did. But another witch could have. How many telekinetics did we have in town?

"Regardless," Beau continued, "the thumbprint was perfectly

clear. Based on the statements everyone gave yesterday, Carly was the last one to see him alive."

"Nope." Nina refused to back down. "The killer was the last one to see him alive. Mom didn't do it. No way."

"Were you here yesterday, Nina?" Beau asked.

"I had to leave early—"

"So you're offering an opinion, not a statement of fact."

She stepped back and leaned against the counter along the wall.

Beau closed his notebook. "Here's the deal, we're going to hold her for seventy-two hours. If we find proof that she's innocent, we'll let her go. If we don't, we'll have to charge her with murder. The clock started when we took her into custody yesterday."

Which meant we had about forty-eight hours to find the proof he needed. I thought of what Miriam had told me about Ludo Beck earlier.

"I might have a lead for you," I offered.

"Really?" Beau seemed pleased by this. He'd known Carly since we were little kids and surely didn't believe she was guilty any more than I did. He tapped his pen on the counter. "What have you got?"

When I told him about Ludo trying to convince people to give up their stores to him, Comfort agreed. "He had been in here before yesterday."

"Did he ask you to give up this building?" Beau asked.

"He did. This one is the best location in the mall. Compared to the others, we're backward. Their front doors face the park which used to be Crispin Street. This was the first building here, and my great-great-great-whatever grandmother wanted people to see the river while they ate."

We all glanced out the windows at the Mississippi River. From here, trees perfectly framed the site of the deep-blue water running slowly past and the lush green bluffs in the distance. It really was beautiful.

Beau faced her again. "What did you tell Mr. Beck regarding his offer?"

Comfort stood tall. "That he could stuff it."

Nina and I laughed.

Beau fought with a smile and reiterated, "You told him no. Did he ever talk to Carly?"

Oh shizzle. Gooseflesh covered my arms at the implications behind that question.

"I don't know for sure," Comfort said, "but I assume he did. He was very persistent."

"Carly is known to have a temper," Beau began.

Nina stepped up to the counter again. "No. I know what you're suggesting. Mom can be direct and always stands her ground, but I've never seen her lose her temper."

"Really?" Beau tilted his head as though confused. "Four kids and a husband who's gone more than he's here, and she never once blew her top at one of you?"

Nina paled but didn't respond.

"What's been going on at home lately?" he pressed. "Anything that might be stressing her? Other than Kyle being gone again."

"Mom is fully capable of existing without a man around, officer." Her words hit their mark if Beau's flinch was any indication. "Sure, it's great when Dad is home, but our lives don't shut down when he's gone. The five of us are a team. We take care of things just fine when he's gone."

After a short pause, Beau offhandedly asked, "What's Sebastian been up to lately?"

Sebastian . . . oh, yes. One of Carly's four kids.

Nina's jaw clenched. "Why ask? You already know."

"I mean *since* we held him at the station for vandalism."

"What?" Comfort demanded. "What did he do?"

"Do you want to tell her or should I?" Beau asked.

Nina crossed her arms in reply.

"Sebastian," Beau began, "wandered out to the Kramer farm, cut the fence, and herded a few cows out the opening. Caused a bit of a traffic problem."

Comfort crossed her arms, mimicking her granddaughter. "How do you know Sebastian did it?"

"Because Mason Kribs, who owns the farm on the other side of the road, saw him do it. Mason's been testing a solar powered irrigation system on part of his field this summer. Says it was working perfectly until someone disconnected the controller. Mason was out there making repairs when Sebastian showed up with a wire cutter."

Comfort propped her fists on her hips. "I suppose you think Sebastian vandalized the Kribs' property too?"

"Considering he confessed to it, yes, I do. When I asked what was going on with him, all he would say was that there were too many girls in his world."

"He's got Alex," Comfort protested. "They've always been good buddies. And he has friends from school."

"Most of his friends have been gone over the summer," Nina supplied. "Camps, vacations, visiting family, or helping on their farms. As for Alex, he's been hanging around . . . oh."

"What?" Beau asked. "Or should I say who?"

"Savannah."

For my benefit, Beau said, "Mason's daughter."

"Yeah." Nina sighed as though it all made sense. "Whenever he isn't doing chores on our farm, Alex is over there helping Mason with things on his."

"Sebastian vandalized the Kribs' farm," Beau concluded, "because, in his mind, they're the reason his big brother is away so much. Does your mom know all of this?"

"Probably," Nina admitted with less attitude. "She was on the phone the other night talking to someone about Bastian. She said she'd send him over to do chores."

Beau nodded. "Mason was out there waiting for Sebastian to show up that day. The boy made a stop across the road first. Vandalism can be addictive. He might just be looking for attention, though." He blew out a breath. "This circles us back to Carly and what might be stressing her. Working five days a week here, four kids to parent—"

"I'm twenty years old," Nina reminded him. "I don't need parenting anymore."

He fixed her with a *don't push me* look. "Three kids to parent, responsibilities at the family farm, her own house to maintain" —he glanced at me—"and the only one around to care for aging family members. When's the last time any of you saw Etta or Benny?"

Carly's sister and brother. I hadn't thought of them in years.

"It's been a while," Comfort confirmed, "but we 'aging family members' don't need a babysitter."

Dad seemed to think they did. Except he used the word *caretaker*.

"I recall," Beau replied gently, "having to pick Gwynne up at the saloon a few months ago and bring her home because she was causing a scene. Do you remember that?"

Comfort released a heavy sigh "I do. It was her and Filip's anniversary. The first since he passed and her first episode."

Uncle Filip died? I'd thought of him a couple times since getting here, but assumed he was just off somewhere. How awful. And what episodes? Did Gwynne have dementia? No wonder her magic was wonky.

"She told me about it after you dropped her off," Comfort continued. "She got to the saloon to have their regular dinner and a pint, and someone was at their table. Having to sit in a different spot was the first strike. The staff knew which day it was."

Comfort shook her head. "The blessing and curse of a small town. She was partway through her dinner when they turned on her and Filip's song, and that triggered . . . whatever it triggered in her."

"The server said she was looking for Filip," Beau said softly. "She started screaming his name and rushing around trying to find him. She even accused someone of kidnapping him."

"Gwynne remembered that she flipped a few tables." Comfort made hand gestures indicating Gwynne flipped them telekinetically. "Then she sent her beer flying at her server, who was just trying to calm her down. Finally, you walked in."

"Don't know exactly why I was able to calm her, but she relaxed and let me help her out to my squad car."

"Then I gave her pie," Comfort recalled, tears pooling in her eyes now. "Key lime, Filip's favorite, with an extra dose of comfort sprinkled on top."

Beau waited a respectable amount of time for us to collect our emotions. "Pepper also suffered an incident. She was looking for something at the grocery store—"

"And couldn't find it." Comfort knew about that episode too. "She magicked it to her cart but somehow took down three shelves of produce in the process. Telekinesis has always lingered in the background for her, more like a possibility than an ability, so it doesn't always work right."

Beau looked pained now. "No offense to you and the others who live at Applewood, Comfort, but it seems you do need a bit of care." She didn't object this time. He turned to Nina. "Your mom has been doing all those things we mentioned plus stressing over everyone at the farm by herself."

His comments weren't directed at me, but he couldn't make me feel more guilty if he tried.

"If pushed really hard," Nina admitted, "or if she's super stressed, she might yell, but she has never once been physical with any of us. Never a spank or even a slap to the back of the head."

He noted that on his pad. "She admitted that she raised her voice with the victim. As for her prints on the weapon, being the only one serving pie yesterday would explain that. I promise, I'm going to do my best over the next forty-eight hours to prove her innocent."

Comfort cleared her throat. "If we're done, I've got a few things to take care of before I can go. Dusty, you're free to leave."

She and Nina went back to the kitchen, and I remained on my stool. "At the risk of bringing up other negative memories, can we talk about the elephant in the room?"

"What elephant?" he asked.

"The accident."

It took him a minute, then he tapped his leg. "The one from a hundred years ago?"

I couldn't help but smile at his casual attitude. "Yes, that one."

"What do you want to talk about?"

Maybe he didn't know I was responsible. He didn't give so much as a hint that he blamed me. I'd enter this conversation through the backdoor, then.

"The last time I saw your parents, they were so upset about it."

"You know what, Dusty?" He tapped his temple. "I *know* what happened, but I don't remember much. I remember Nash asking some of us if we wanted to go for a boat ride after our graduation ceremony. Nine of us said yes, which was way too many people for that boat, and I remember Nash was going too fast. A couple of us told him to slow down. I think. The next thing I remember was waking up in the hospital with half my leg gone."

Some might say he suffered amnesia surrounding the event, but there was a glassy look in his eyes that could only mean one thing. He'd been spelled. Someone cast a memory spell on him. Or more specifically, a forgetting spell.

"Really?" I asked. "You don't remember any other details?"

He shook his head. "I think Nash remembers, but none of the others do either."

That glassy look was still there. What would a change in topic do? "Even though you don't remember, has it changed your life? Other than in the obvious way."

"*Knowing* what happened because of our stupidity that day, I've become a big advocate for boating safety." His eyes cleared. "When not investigating crimes, I patrol the town and surrounding rural area, but I spend as much time as possible patrolling the river. I give one warning and then a fine big enough to make people learn their lesson."

Warmth sparked in my chest. "Bet you've saved a life or two."

"More than two." He tilted his chin proudly. "I honestly couldn't guess how many. It never ceases to amaze me how foolish people can be."

"Something right came from something wrong."

"I guess that's one way to look at it. We never know the ripple effect our actions will have." He inhaled deeply. "I should get back to work."

"Thanks for talking with me, Beau. It eases my mind to know you're okay."

He held my gaze for a beat too long. "Are you okay, Dusty?"

Last night I wondered if the person or people who were threatening me had followed me here. Had they moved on from notes on windshields to attacks in diners? It was possible. It was also possible that Ludo Beck had done something to make someone angry enough to kill him. I should share my thoughts about who the killer might be with Beau. Being a cop, he should know who could be in his town.

Before I could say anything more, Jett and Cricket entered the diner. Cricket was literally bouncing with energy. Jett looked like she'd gone ten rounds with, well, a four-year-old.

"Lola! I had the bestest day ever."

I slid off the stool into a squat and braced myself for impact. As always when this excited, she launched herself into my arms. Fortunately, she didn't knock our foreheads together this time. She started talking about helping Jett with her chores.

"Did you know that chickens make eggs? And milk comes out of goats. I thought it only comed from cows and almonds."

I bit my lip to stop myself from laughing and glanced up at Jett. When Cricket stepped back, I found a few pieces of straw in her hair.

"I couldn't get her to go inside for a nap," Jett explained, "but she thought lying down by the chicken coop with one of the cats sounded like a good idea."

"I taked a catnap," Cricket declared. She looked up at Beau, frowned, and leaned against me.

It took me a moment to understand the problem. "It's your uniform. The last time she saw a police officer was the night our house burned down."

"I'm Officer Beau." He bent to look her in the eye. "Seeing your house burn must have been scary."

"Really scary. It looked like a dragon with fire shooting out of his mouth. But then the firefighters squirted it with water."

They talked more about dragons, and when he told her that baby dragons came out of eggs, her eyes lit up.

"Like chickens?"

"Sort of." He held his hands about a foot apart. "Dragon eggs are much bigger, and they're sparkly."

"Can I see one?"

"They're kind of hard to find," he told her after realizing his error. He mustn't talk to many preschoolers. "I'll look around, and if I find one, I'll show you next time we see each other." He leaned toward me and softly asked, "Is she likely to forget about this?"

"No time soon. You better start looking."

Beau left when the others came out of the kitchen.

"Nice to meet you, Dusty," Avery called out with a wave. "See you around."

Nina needed to get home to take care of things there. "And I want to stop by the jail and see Mom for a few minutes."

"That leaves us to talk with the other shop owners about Beck," Comfort said.

"Are you doing that with her?" Jett asked. "I've still got more chores at the farm."

"Cricket and I are in desperate need of clothes and supplies."

Before I could say more, Comfort dismissed us. "I'll check with the other shops. You three go do your thing. We'll meet back at the house. I told Nina to bring the others over for dinner tonight."

CHAPTER 9

*a*t Tiny Togs, I let Cricket choose seven outfits, one for each day. Along with shirts, shorts, and dresses, she insisted she needed a pair of jeans and boots if she wanted to ride the goat.

"Ride the goat?" I repeated.

She nodded and bounced excitedly.

I'd have to ask Jett what that meant.

Next, we headed to The Mercantile to stock up on necessities, like bathroom supplies, socks, underwear, and pajamas for both of us. *Safari* was the best word to describe my taste in clothes. Khaki pants, tank tops, loose button-up shirts, my hiking boots, and my favorite canvas jacket . . . which didn't survive the blaze. I found some T-shirts and jeans that fit well enough and grabbed a pair of light-weight sweatpants and a zippered sweatshirt, one for Cricket, too, in case the nights got chilly. Finally, I added a pair of kind of ugly but quite comfortable sneakers to my stash. I'd order more things from my favorite online store. Once I got a new laptop. The aunts must have one I could borrow.

After all that shopping, we were both ready to go home.

We cut through the park, making our way to the hedge, and had just passed the diner when Cricket spotted Comfort sitting on a bench beneath an oak tree near the little playground. Again, whoever designed this spot did it well. A playground surrounded by shade trees—the oaks, maples, birches, and dogwoods must put on quite a colorful show in the fall—and benches where parents could rest while their kids burned off energy either before or after browsing through the stores.

"Hi, Auntie Comfort," Cricket called and ran over to her.

Comfort was writing in a notebook. Or rather, her pen was writing for her. A few people stared, but in a town where buildings changed colors at will, a pen skittering across a page on its own was a fairly mild display. The pen dropped into the journal's crease, and Comfort held her arms out to wrap her great-grandniece in a hug. She noticed the bags hanging off my exhausted arms.

"Looks like your shopping was successful."

"For her, yes. I'll need to borrow a laptop to order some things for myself. Including a new laptop."

"Not a problem. Time to go home?"

"Can't I play first?" Cricket clasped her hands beneath her chin. "Please."

Comfort tweaked the child's nose. "For a few minutes. Everyone is coming over for dinner in an hour, so we need to get home and get ready."

The message was as much for me as it was Cricket.

My aunt gave me an apologetic look. "Probably should have cleared that with you first, hey?"

"Sitting for a minute sounds like a good idea." I groaned as I dropped next to her on the bench, set down all the bags, and shook out my arms.

Comfort chuckled. "You're too young to be making those kinds of noises."

"Even you must have had a few aches and pains at fifty. What did you learn over the last couple of hours?"

Her head tilted. "What did I learn?"

"When you talked to the shop owners. Did you learn anything about Ludo Beck?"

"Oh, that. I didn't talk to anyone. Like you, I needed to sit a spell."

Was this deviation from the plan purposeful or did she forget her assignment?

"I didn't forget."

I narrowed my eyes. "Are you reading my mind?"

"No need. The question is clear on your face. For the record, my body has its bad days, but my mind is still clear. Remember what I said about getting certain thoughts out?"

"I do."

"There were some doozies today on top of people being upset about the murder." She capped her pen and shut the notebook.

"Well, I found out a few more things about Mr. Beck."

"Do what you feel you must, Dusty, but don't worry about proving Carly innocent. She'll be fine."

She seemed certain of that. "How do you know?"

"Because she's not the killer."

"Comfort, jails and prisons are full of innocent people. Beau is searching for solid proof—"

"Which means he'll let her go. He said he'd let her go if he didn't find anything, and he won't because there isn't anything to be found."

"That's not exactly what he said. He said if they find proof that she's innocent, they'll let her go. If not, they'll charge her with murder."

"She'll be fine."

Maybe, but I wasn't content to sit back and wait for the truth to show itself. I needed to know that my kids and my family were safe. Plus proving Carly innocent would surely help prove my loyalty to the family and earn me a few points in the forgiveness column.

We let Cricket play for a couple more minutes, then it was time to go home and get ready for dinner. She pouted but didn't protest. Two minutes later, we arrived in the small courtyard formed by the main house, Apple Blossom Cottage, and the garage.

"We'll be right there to help," I told Comfort.

Inside the apartment, I distributed our packages between our bedrooms and the bathroom and then swapped my sweaty, food-stained diner T-shirt for a new one from The Mercantile. This, naturally, meant Cricket wanted to change clothes. While she decided, I ran my new hair brush through my short hair and swiped a bit of balm over my dry lips.

"Did you decide?" I called out.

Cricket appeared in the hallway and did a spin, showing off a sundress covered in big pink and blue flowers. "This one."

I stared at it. "I don't remember that one."

She pointed into her room. "It was in my closet."

I opened the bifold door to find her closet crammed full of clothes. Mostly dresses, her favorite, but plenty of shorts, leggings, jeans, and dozens of shirts.

Should have known. "Why did I bother buying those things from Miriam?"

"Because I love them." She pulled out a pair of purple rain boots with ballerinas all over them. "Look!"

"Guess I could take back the bunny boots."

"No! I love those too. I love *all* of my clothes."

Such a little fashionista. Where did this come from? Certainly not me, and her mother, Josie, was a jeans and blouses gal. Although she'd wear a dress if she and Micah were going out for a date night. I sure hoped she was okay.

I shook off the thoughts that arrived every time I thought of

Josie. The police and her family in the Philippines were searching for her. Not much I could do about a missing woman from more than eight thousand miles away. Of course, she might not have gone to the Philippines and was instead being held somewhere in Green Bay. Or somewhere else entirely. Or she wasn't kidnapped, and someone had—

No. The alternative was too horrible to think of.

Oh, Josie. Where are you, girl?

I handed Cricket her new brush and smiled while she waved it around her head, barely touching any strands of hair.

"You missed a spot." I took the blue brush with pink flowers and yellow bristles and finished the job. "Ready to go over to the house?"

"Yes!" She immediately started chattering about Jett and pointing out where all the animals were on the property. "We didn't have time to visit the bees. Jett says maybe tomorrow."

In the kitchen, we found Pepper at the range, Comfort arranging drinks on the island in some strange grouping I couldn't decipher, and Gwynne setting the table. Gwynne pointed at a cupboard, and a stack of plates floated over to her followed by flatware and napkins. Nothing exploded or dropped to the ground. Must have been her emotions interfering with her magic yesterday at the diner. And I hated knowing about the episode at the saloon. Now I was going to look at her for signs of dementia. Hopefully that was a one-and-done because it had been their anniversary.

"Hello, little love." Gwynne knelt down to get a hug from Cricket. "Want to help me set the table?"

"Okay. What should I do?"

She handed her the napkins. "Put one on the left side of each placemat. Do you know which one is the left side."

Cricket held out her left hand, thumb stuck out to form an *L*.

"You survived your first day at the diner," Pepper praised.

"I did all right. And what do you mean first day? How many days will there be?"

"Depends on where your interests lie." Comfort was now sorting the beverages seemingly by color.

She meant which area of the farm I wanted to claim as my territory. I'd always loved working in the gardens and orchard best. But what if I wanted to find an office job in town . . . Who was I kidding? I hated office work. I only did it because it was my best means of supporting Micah and me.

"We'll be fine tomorrow," Comfort stated. "There are a few kids from the high school who work on the weekends. They probably could have helped today but . . ."

She let the rest of that sentence hang. I presumed it would have been something like *Dusty had dues to pay*. This provided a decent enough segue, so I asked, "Can we talk about Carly's situation for a moment?"

"Only until her kids get here," Gwynne insisted, "which should be soon. They could use a fun night with family where they're not worrying about her."

That was fair. "Okay, I'll be quick. Miriam at Tiny Togs told me Ludo Beck wanted to open a specialty grocery store."

"Grocery store?" Pepper perked up at this announcement.

"That's right." Comfort turned away from her drink station. The house instantly rearranged her display by beverage type. "I did hear that. I stopped listening to him when he asked to buy our building."

"Which building?" Jett asked, joining us.

"The diner," Comfort clarified.

"Who wants to do what with it?" Jett smiled apologetically. "Sorry for being late to the party."

I lowered my voice so Cricket wouldn't hear. "Ludo Beck, the man who died at the diner, wanted to open a specialty grocery store. He was trying to convince shop owners in the prime locations at the center of the mall to give their buildings to him."

"Got'cha. Sounds a little desperate. Or slimy. Or both. What are specialty groceries?"

"Items you generally don't find at a regular store." Pepper turned away from the range, letting the kitchen continue stirring whatever was in the pot. She seemed excited by this grocery store prospect. Looked like Beck would have had one customer for sure. "I get most of my salts, peppers, and other seasonings from specialty stores. Since there's nothing like that nearby, I order from a trusted online source. In person would be better so I can taste them."

"So, a spice store?" Jett asked. Cricket had skipped over and latched onto her leg.

I smiled at her. "Specialty meats and cheeses too. Oils and vinegars. That's what Miriam told me."

"Oh," Pepper sighed. "That would have been lovely. Remember that sampler box I ordered for Mabon last year?"

"Oh, yes," Gwynne replied. "It was delicious."

This led them to recall a night of playing sheepshead, a card game I never took the time to understand, late into the night while eating everything in the sampler box. Then they each mentioned their favorite item. Was this how discussions would always go with this group? Weren't we talking about Ludo Beck?

"One of the questions I have," I raised my voice a bit to bring them back to my topic, "is what exactly was Mr. Beck willing to do to get the owners to give up their buildings? You spoke with him, Comfort. Did he try to bribe you?"

"Like I told you, I spoke to him once. He tried to convince me to sell, I told him I wasn't interested, never would be, and told him to go away." She scowled at the memory then told me, "You should talk to Carly."

"You should," Pepper agreed.

"You should absolutely go talk to Carly," Gwynne added.

I was pretty sure they didn't mean just about the murder and that they wanted me to go now. I had every intention of talking to my cousin, but it was dinner time, I was hungry, and it would be time to put the little bug to bed soon. Besides, I couldn't imagine visitation hours at the jail went all day.

"Oh, so sorry to interrupt," came a new voice from the top of the basement stairs, located between the kitchen and family room. "Looks like you're getting ready for dinner."

I turned to find a Black woman standing there. She was dressed in a white tank dress, had frizzy silver hair streaked with black strands, and wore jewelry that looked to be crocheted—a purple necklace, matching earrings, and multi-colored bracelets.

"Winnie." Comfort held out a beckoning arm. "Come in and meet Dusty."

She gave the woman a quick rundown on who I was and then explained to me that Winnie Monroe was a visiting witch from a safe town in southern Illinois. She was staying at the farm for a couple days.

I recalled Dad telling me that, along with the aunts, witches from other safe towns stayed at the house now and then. Witches were always welcome to stay with others in the collective, as we called the safe towns as a whole. Every house kept a room ready for a witch or witches in need. No questions asked.

Winnie inclined her head in greeting. "Pleasure. I'm on my way to northern Minnesota. I like to drive, but my nerves can only handle three or four hours at a time, then I need to rest for a while."

"So what would be a two-day drive for some will take you five?" I guessed.

"Including rest time, two weeks." She chuckled. "I'm not in a hurry. I look at it as a vacation."

"Winnie helped me in The Apple Barn today," Gwynne explained. "As you can see, she has a great talent with jewelry and set up a display of adorable crocheted apple earrings and necklaces for us to sell."

"Whatever Gwynne takes in for the sales," Winnie added, "can go toward my room and board."

"How long will you be here?" I asked.

"Another day or two. I got here late Wednesday night. How long will you be here?"

Before I could answer, Gwynne said, "For as long as she wants to, up to and including forever."

I met her gaze and put my hand over my heart.

"Very nice." Winnie nodded her approval. "I just came up here for a cup of tea and a snack."

"We're having fajitas for dinner." Pepper indicated the huge pan of sautéed vegetables and the other of chicken on the stove.

"We've also got plenty of pie." Comfort pointed to the dessert collection at the far end of the kitchen island.

"I've had many slices of your pie." Winnie patted her backside. "Each one more amazing than the last. I had a late lunch so don't need a whole dinner."

A potato the length of my hand appeared on the kitchen island.

"I know you think you're funny," Winnie told the house, "but that's actually perfect. Will you bake it please?"

The potato disappeared, and seconds later, the microwave beeped. Winnie removed the steaming potato on a plate, then found cheddar cheese and sour cream in the refrigerator.

"Don't forget a twist of pepper and a sprinkle of salt," Pepper reminded her as though they'd just discussed it.

Pepper pointed at the huge cabinet that took up almost the entire wall to the right of the sink. The shelves on the top half were crammed full of labeled apothecary jars. The bottom half had doors that hid spellcasting supplies like candles, cauldrons, incense, crystals, essential oils . . .

I'd been obsessed with mixing herbs and plants since I was a child and often found myself in the kitchen gazing at all the glorious bottles and jars. The cabinet seemed bigger now, and it took a minute for me to realize that was because there was now an entire shelf of different types of salts, another of peppers, and a third of salts or peppers mixed with other ingredients. This had to be Pepper's doing since the kitchen appeared to be her domain.

"Which do you suggest?" Winnie strode to the cabinet and pulled out a clear acrylic pepper mill filled with black peppercorns.

"Pure black pepper is for prosperity," Pepper informed.

"Can always use more of that." Winnie tucked the mill under her arm and investigated the salt collection.

"Sea salt for protection," Pepper told her. "Himalayan pink will open your third eye. Both are useful when traveling. The pink is stronger, so use less of it if that's your choice."

Winnie added a twist of the pepper and a sprinkle of sea salt to her potato, grabbed an iced tea, and headed back to the stairs to the lower level. "I'll leave you all to your dinner. Nice to meet you, Dusty."

A minute later, Maks and Freddie entered the kitchen followed by Carly's kids. Looked like we were done discussing murder for tonight.

"I could have handled dinner," Nina reminded us as her siblings hugged aunts and chose beverages.

"Yes, but Granny Sadie insists," Jett interpreted for our ghostly matriarch, "that we should be together at a time like this. Meaning the trouble your mom is in. And she says the others needed to meet Dusty and Cricket."

Emma, Carly's fifteen-year-old daughter, and Cricket connected immediately.

"I love little kids," Emma told me while Cricket clung to her back like a backpack. "If you ever need a babysitter—"

"Yes," I replied immediately. "I don't have a daily schedule yet but should soon. When does school start?"

"In like two weeks." She exhaled like the thought exhausted her. "I'll be off at three every day and can come straight here."

"I'll be in touch," I told her as though we'd just negotiated, and I found her demands to be acceptable. It's not that I didn't trust the aunts to watch her if I couldn't for some reason, but Jett was the youngest at 70. I had a hard time keeping up with the preschooler all day and was twenty years her junior. Besides, the aunts had things that needed their attention.

"Is there a preschool in Blackwood Grove?" I asked the group in general.

"Autumn Trainor," they said in unison.

"She runs a preschool at her organic flower farm." Alex smiled in a way that made me think Autumn must be pretty.

"The school is exclusively for witch kids," Emma explained, "and she teaches them by doing things like putting them to work sorting flowers. Like she'll tell them to work in teams of two or three and put four purple pansies and two pink pansies in the big yellow bin. Stuff like that."

"The kids love it," Maks agreed, "and don't even know she's teaching them."

Learning while having fun. What a concept. "I'll get in touch with her ASAP."

"Dinner is ready," Pepper announced. "Kids, will you take these to the table, please?"

They each took loaded serving dishes and made short work of the job. While we ate and talked about our days, I watched Carly's kids. Nina was the oldest at twenty. Seventeen-year-old Alex was a handsome boy with a teenager's appetite. He ate two plates of fajitas and side dishes before I'd finished half of my dinner. I saw a bit of Carly in him—around his mouth mostly—

but his eyes and the cleft in his chin had to be from her husband. The girls also had her smile and wavy hair, although Emma's had an auburn hue where Nina's was medium brown like their mother's. Thirteen-year-old curly-haired Sebastian was gloomy. He didn't say a word other than "hi" to me, nothing to anyone else even when Alex tried his best to get a rise out of him, and barely looked up from his plate. Despite being a little on the scrawny side, he ate as much as his big brother.

"Everyone knows she didn't do it." Nina opened the Ludo Beck topic out of the blue, surprising us all. "A lot of people at the diner told me as much today. Something's going on in this town. There's a mood."

I felt it the moment I entered the mall yesterday.

"Yeah, we're witches." Alex said and, as though proving it, held a hand up over his head. The flatware drawer from across the kitchen opened, and a fork floated over to him. "If Mom was going to kill someone, she wouldn't do something as mundane as stabbing. She'd get creative with herbs and stuff."

Maks chuckled at him and then adopted a serious expression when Comfort shot him a scolding look.

My attention went to Cricket. I didn't want her to hear about things like someone getting stabbed, but she was distracted by the floating fork and the familiars wandering around.

"Let's keep this G-rated for little ears," I began and saw Sebastian sit tall as though about to protest. He settled back again when I indicated my granddaughter. "Do any of you have thoughts on who could have done this? We were talking about Mr. Beck trying to intimidate shop owners earlier."

Neither Alex, Emma, nor Sebastian had any ideas. It seemed that other than their mother getting blamed, some old guy getting killed didn't affect them so wasn't on their radar.

"You know who might be able to help?" Nina locked eyes on me. "Mom."

Message received. "I'll go to the jail tomorrow. Comfort doesn't need me at the diner. Do either of you need help?" I asked Jett and Gwynne.

"I get to do the eggs," Cricket reminded from where she sat on the rug near the fireplace with Emma and the familiars. Collecting eggs was now her job. Period.

"You can help Jett if she needs you," I said.

"I did say she could be the head egg collector," Jett agreed, "but after that, I've got to patrol the orchard."

And I knew full well how easy it was for little ones to get lost in there. Carly and I zigzagged around it for hours one time before Maks finally found us.

"I'll need some help in the shop," Gwynne said. "Tomorrow's Saturday. Our busiest day. We're open until six, but you can take off and talk with Carly whenever you're ready."

"What do I get to do?" Cricket leapt to her feet and jumped up and down, excited about this concept of chores. I expected that would change before too long.

"You can hang out with me." Emma picked her up and spun her around. "We'll find all sorts of things to do."

I smiled at the girl and touched my chest over my heart in thanks. She replied with a nod.

"Um, Granny." Alex meant Comfort, not Granny Sadie who stayed in the kitchen with us the whole time. He pointed at the dish in front of him. "What is this?"

He was the first to dive in when the dinner dishes disappeared and the desserts arrived.

"Peach galette. It's like a peach pie but without the pie dish."

For a galette, the filling was placed in the center of the dough then the dough got folded over the filling about an inch or so to keep it in place.

He made a face. "I don't think it's right."

All eyes turned on him. He was criticizing Comfort's dessert? That wasn't done.

"What's wrong with it?" I asked. He struck me as a joker.

He pushed the plate with the galette toward me. "Take a taste."

I did. He was right.

"What?" Comfort pointed at both the galette and the key lime pie and flicked her fingers for the kitchen to slide them to her. She took a bite of each and spit out both. "The galette recipe called for a quarter cup of sugar in the filling. I added salt by mistake. The key lime pie uses sweetened condensed milk. Seems I grabbed unsweetened coconut milk by mistake. I'm so sorry."

"No, Granny," Alex began, "it's okay."

"It's not." She looked so embarrassed my heart hurt for her. Since Carly was taken away, Comfort had done her best to make everyone believe everything was fine. That she wasn't affected by the murder and her daughter's incarceration. I didn't understand how she *couldn't* be affected. And for her to not be able to comfort her grandchildren with pie?

She could act like the big, tough witch if she needed to, but I understood what this meant. And it gave me more motivation to be the caretaker and figure out what exactly was going on.

Thankfully, the sound of a clock's chimes rang throughout the house and broke the tension.

"Seven o'clock," I told Cricket. "Bath time."

"Can Emma give me my bath?" she asked.

"And just that fast," Jett griped while winking at me, "I've been replaced."

"You'll see Emma tomorrow," I told Cricket.

"Yeah," Emma agreed, "I have to go home and take my own bath."

"Please do." Alex waved his hand beneath his nose, which earned him a small snort of laughter from Sebastian.

Cricket, the kids, and I said goodnight to the aunts and left. Fortunately, the house could take care of cleanup.

"Where exactly do you live?" I asked Carly's kids as they headed toward The Apple Barn.

Nina pointed. "There's a path on the other side of the store. Follow it along the hedge for about five minutes and there you are."

They lived among the apple trees. That was funny because after she and I got lost that time, Carly had been scared of the orchard. She insisted there were creatures living in it, "And I don't mean deer, coyotes, and raccoons."

"Glad to know you're close. See you all later." I turned away then turned back. "Can you see? It's pretty dark tonight. Do you need a flashlight?"

I'd barely finished asking when Sebastian cupped his hands together, and as he pulled his right hand away, a bright ball of light hovered above his left hand. "We're good."

So the boy could say more than hi.

$\mathcal{W}$hile I helped Cricket with her bath, we talked about her going to preschool.

"Like a big girl?" she asked, eyes glittering with excitement.

"Yes. Remember how your—" I almost said *mommy*. Thank heavens I caught myself. She'd had such a nice night with Emma and the familiars. Reminding her of her missing mother would ruin it. I was going to ask if she remembered Josie bringing her to daycare. She had loved it. Instead, I pretended to cough, and she patted me on the back. With a very wet hand.

"Are you okay, Lola?"

"I'm fine, sweetie." I cleared my throat. "Yes, you can go to school like a big girl with other witch kids. And then—"

Her mouth dropped open, and she gasped. "Am I a witch?" She held her hand up in the air like Alex had earlier when he magicked the fork. She pouted when whatever she had been trying to summon didn't come to her.

Was she a witch? I hadn't noticed any abilities. Magic skipped generations sometimes, and some family members simply never developed powers. If Cricket had them, she would have gotten them from me because Micah never revealed any either.

Or had he?

There was one time . . . He was a little younger than Cricket and had asked for his toy helicopter when I tucked him in one night. I kept it on a high shelf at night because it had hard edges, and I didn't want him to sneak out of bed to get it and then roll over on it in his sleep. When I went to check on him before going to bed, the helicopter was next to him and his stuffed animals. He either climbed the shelf to get the toy or he summoned it, and I could find no evidence that he'd climbed. It never happened again, so I dismissed it as one of those weird things.

If he did have powers, I could have helped him develop them, but using powers outside of a safe town, even within one's own home, was dangerous. I couldn't take the chance he'd get caught.

Another event came to me. Micah, Josie, and Cricket were staying overnight at my house. They'd come for dinner, but a sudden storm made driving home treacherous. While I was in the hallway getting an extra blanket and pillow from the linen closet, I saw Josie in the bathroom. She held out her hand, and manifested a toothbrush, much like my father and his pencils.

This meant Cricket could have gotten powers from her mother's bloodline too. I wasn't sure how I felt about that. If she wasn't a witch, she wouldn't be able to go to Autumn Trainor's school. And she was already excited about it. Although, there must be a preschool for Ordinary kids too.

My sad little bug looked about to cry, so I asked, "Are you trying to do what Alex did?" She nodded. "Being a witch takes lots of practice. What Alex did tonight, he had to try many times before it worked."

"Will you show me?" She reached out her hand again. "I'm trying to get my hairbrush."

I wasn't at all prepared for this conversation. It seemed she had decided I was a witch, too, even though she hadn't seen me do anything, and wasn't likely to let the topic go. No sense trying to hide or deny what she'd seen with her own eyes.

"Every witch knows different kinds of magic. I can't teach you to summon because that's not the kind of magic I know. If you are a witch, you might do something different than Alex."

She dropped her hand into the water, splashing herself and me. "Will you show me what you know how to do?"

Nothing very interesting about watching someone have a dream or premonition. And I prayed that my gray witch ability didn't pass on to her.

"Another time," I answered. "Ready to get out?"

She showed me her water-wrinkled fingers. "Prunes!"

That meant yes. I helped her dry off, then told her she could play in her room for a few minutes. "I'll be right there to read stories."

I stepped into my bedroom and pulled off my wet T-shirt. When I flicked on the dim bulb hanging from the middle of the ceiling, I saw the cot was still there, but there was something new too. A thicker blanket, better pillow, and a laptop computer lay on it.

Afraid to touch anything lest it was an illusion, I asked, "Are these for me?"

The bulb brightened a few watts. And stayed that way.

"Thank you. I'm extremely grateful, but why? What did I do?"

The laptop made a *ping* sound, like a message had just come in. I opened it to find a message on the screen:

> *You helped today.*
> *The family forgives you.*

"I'm so glad. I hope you can too."

The property became enchanted when the witches who lived here two hundred years ago began to pass on to Summerland. I had long believed that homes, other buildings, and even outdoor places took on a bit of the moods and personalities of the people who had occupied them. That was true of the Warren house. And because their bodies were buried here, even more of them was absorbed by the land. All those temperaments. That was why we never knew what we'd get from the property. Sometimes it was loving and provided warmth and security. Sometimes it was a little wicked, like when it turned on the air conditioning during a blizzard or lit all the fireplaces on humid summer days. Other times, like giving me this cot and not much more, it wanted to teach a lesson. I hadn't done anything to purposely hurt, scare, or worry my family, but I wouldn't push my luck and try to defend myself anymore. I'd simply continue to do all I could to prove that I cared, get Carly out of jail, and catch the real killer.

After reading Cricket two bedtime stories and tucking her in with baba and the purple elephant, I decided to order some clothes. It was a beautiful mid-August night, so I took my new laptop and a mug of herbal tea outside to sit on the small balcony off my bedroom. And I literally sat on the balcony, because the apartment wouldn't give me a chair. After repeated requests, it relented and produced a rather comfy floor cushion.

Once I submitted an order to replace my favorite pieces plus a few new ones, I sat in the quiet, sipping my tea and appreciating the night. To my left, I watched a barge float down the river. The tugboat, that pushed the load along at about four miles per hour, shined its spotlight back and forth across the width, searching for any obstacles in its path. Beau would be pleased with their attention to safety.

The light from the waxing moon gave off enough light that I could see the white barn/workshop where we kept all the farm equipment to the right of the balcony. The chicken coop and goat pen were over there as well.

Straight ahead was the garden. Herbs and edible flowers were closest to the kitchen. Vegetables, tomatoes, and berries were next. I wasn't even sure what all was in there anymore but recalled the one-acre spread had always produced more than enough to support the family for an entire year. We preserved items by canning or freezing them. On especially bountiful years, anything we knew we wouldn't consume got sold during the annual Samhain Harvest Celebration in October. Folks came from all around to pick apples in our orchard and buy our produce and remedies.

As I gazed around, something in the distance caught my eye.

Past the house, barn, garden, and animal pens at the end of the driveway was the entrance to the orchard. We installed a gate there years ago when some inebriated driver thought our driveway was a road. He sped down it late one dark night and smacked into three of our apple trees.

A light. Like a flashlight. I immediately thought of the killer. Were the people threatening me and my kids out there? No, it wasn't possible. The property wouldn't let anyone through the hedge. Not without permission.

Could it be Sebastian and his magic orb of light?

Blink, blink, blink, blink. They turned the flashlight on, off, on, off. A few seconds later, they did it again. *Blink, blink, blink, blink.*

What was going on?

This blinking continued until the backdoor light on the main house flashed off and immediately back on again. Then one of the witches exited that door and used a small flashlight to illuminate their way. I kept mute and watched.

The thin beam of light led them all the way to the gate and stopped. Straining my ears, I listened for any conversation, but either they didn't speak or they spoke in whispers. Or it wasn't a person who had made the flashing light. There were plenty of rumors of beings and creatures in the orchard, the ones Carly claimed weren't deer, coyotes, or raccoons. Generations of town kids were sure unicorns lived among our apple trees.

The witch was only at the gate for about thirty seconds before turning and making their way back to the house. I couldn't see their face, but as they got closer, the light from the back door allowed me to see their shape. Long hair and loose-fitting clothes. Gwynne. Although, Pepper favored tunic-style dresses, and while she had on a headwrap every time I'd seen her, a few longer strands poked out the bottom, so it could have been her. Comfort had short hair. Jett, too, with that floppy mohawk down the middle. Maks wore baggy clothes but hardly had any hair. Winnie had shoulder-length kind of frizzy corkscrews. Could it be her?

Why was either Pepper, Gwynne, or Winnie wandering out to the orchard late at night? And who or what did they meet over there?

The back door light went out, and when nothing more happened after five minutes, I decided to call it a night. I lay down on the cot. Might as well give it a try since the apartment gave me gifts. The pillow was comfortable and the blanket warm enough for a summer night. The cot was far more comfortable than the pink couch.

I fell asleep fairly quickly . . . and had a dream.

Eighteen-year-old Beau is lying in a hospital bed. Scratches and bruises cover his face and body. His left wrist is in a cast. His right leg has been amputated above the knee. He looks absolutely miserable. Of course. His entire life has changed.

I walk over to the bed. "How are you doing, Beau?"

He doesn't react. Just blinks and stares at the spot where his leg used to be.

"Everything will be all right. This is a mere detour in your life."

Still no reaction.

I hold up my left hand, palm cupped, and add three drops of essential oil to the well. "Cedar for courage. Apple blossom for happiness. Sandalwood for healing." I dip my finger into the oil and touch his right leg. I dip again, touch the center of his forehead, and chant, "Take his pain and the memory of its cause. Grant him a wondrous life after this dreadful pause. As I plead, so mote it be."

He looks up. His eyes have taken on a glassy sheen.

I jerked awake. My lungs heaved for breath. A thin veil of sweat covered my body. After sitting on the edge of my cot for a moment, waiting for the room to stop spinning, I pushed myself up to stand. I stumbled into the kitchen, filled a glass with water, and then sank to the floor to drink it.

"A dream shows what actually happened," I reminded myself as my brain tried to process what it had seen. "Beau *is* charmed. Someone *did* put a memory spell on him."

As the sweat on my body started to dry, I shivered with cold and . . . dread? Concern? Fear?

In the dream, I saw the events happen through the eyes of the witch who spelled him. That wasn't my voice. Those hands . . . The pinkie of the right hand was bent badly at the first knuckle, slightly at the second. That was what I saw, wasn't it? It could have been a shadow or simply the way she was holding it, but it looked bent. Which meant they were my mother's hands. She broke the pinkie on her right hand when she was young, and it never fully straightened again.

My mother went to Beau's hospital room to clean up after me. I destroyed his life that day, and she went in and made things better for him. How many times had she cast a spell to restore justice or right a wrong and make someone's life better?

Where was she when things were going wrong for me? When my "husband" conned me and re-ruined my life?

She's not ready. She's far too unpredictable.

I was never the witch she wanted me to be. No wonder she never contacted me after I left home.

But why would I want to be like her? Abandon my child and let his life fall apart while restoring justice for strangers? I was better off on my own all those years.

I set the water glass on the floor, unsure if I wanted to cry or scream.

After another few minutes of sitting there in a confused, angry daze, I pushed myself up off the floor and went back to my bedroom. I tried to fall asleep again, but my racing thoughts wouldn't let me. They took me from a wounded teen to a scared young adult to a fed-up and exhausted middle-aged woman. Anger at my mother surged. For passing this gray curse on to me. For never showing me how to handle it. For cleaning up after me rather than teaching me about the magic.

Then I started doubting myself. Maybe those weren't her hands. But Mom and I were the only gray witches in Blackwood Grove, and I hadn't cast that spell on Beau. But, could I have blocked that memory? Would I have dared to try and correct my mistake on my own? No, never.

Mom cleaned up after me. It was the only answer.

CHAPTER 11

I tossed, turned, and finally dozed lightly until Cricket came in and told me she wanted, "Chocolate chip pancakes!"

Of course. She'd had way too many sweets since the house burned down. That had been fine for a day or two, but it was time to wean her off sugar. "How about something like—"

"Chocolate chip pancakes," she insisted.

The pout in her voice told me reasoning or negotiating wasn't going to work. And I wasn't in the mood for a fight. I'd go at the weaning a different way then. Once we were dressed, we crossed the courtyard and entered the main house kitchen.

"Good morning," Pepper greeted from her standard place between the kitchen island and the range.

"Every time I come in here, that's where you are," I teased.

"I spend much of my day right here. When I'm not cooking or baking, I'm preparing various things to sell in The Apple Barn. My salts, peppers, and apple pie spice blend are the most popular. I also make mixes in jars."

"Where's everyone else?" I helped myself to a cup of coffee. "Comfort must be at the diner."

"She is. Jett is tending the animals." Before Cricket could protest, she added, "She's waiting for you to come collect the eggs. Gwynne is in The Apple Barn. Maks is in the workshop tinkering with the tractor." She looked down at Cricket, who was bouncing impatiently from foot to foot. "You, little miss, look like you want something."

"Chocolate chip pancakes!" she announced.

"Isn't that what you wanted yesterday morning?"

"Yes, because I love them."

Pepper chuckled. "All right, but you'll have to help me today."

"Go easy on the chips," I whispered and sat across the island to watch Pepper help Cricket tie on a well-used child size apron. Then Cricket climbed up on a short stool and helped measure, pour, and mix. Only a little of the ingredients ended up on the counter instead of in the bowl. I was impressed.

"Tell me more about yourself, Pepper," I requested. "I know you've lived here for twenty-five years. Where did you come from? Do you have a family?"

She set a cast-iron skillet on the stove and adjusted the heat beneath it. "This will get very hot, little one. Don't touch it."

"Okay," Cricket whispered. She was so calm. Was that because she was eager to learn or the influence Pepper seemed to have on people? "To answer your questions, Dusty, I came here from New Orleans. I met Gwynne there when she was on vacation with Filip. She came into our shop and started asking question after question about the things we sold."

"What kind of shop?"

Pepper flicked some water drops on the skillet. "Oh, see how they dance around?"

"They look happy," Cricket decided.

"Or they have hot feet," Pepper suggested.

Cricket giggled and hopped from foot to foot. "Hot feet."

"That means the skillet is ready. You get to watch this part. When you're bigger, I'll watch you do it." Pepper carefully ladled batter onto the skillet and distributed six miniature chocolate chips in a smiley face formation—one for each eye and four for the mouth. Perfect. Then she told me, "When you have time, go into Silver Moon Apothecary. I opened it about a year after I moved here and called it Pepper's Place. It's a replica of our store in New Orleans." She paused as though wondering what she'd been doing. "What else did you ask?"

"Do you have kids?"

"Oh, yes. I have a daughter, Fleur. She took over the store there and is married to Marshall Bergeron." She chuckled. "My independent daughter. She always insisted she would never marry. They have two sons, Remy and Claude. Remy is married to Annette, and they have a little boy named Milton." She expertly flipped the pancakes, switched off the heat beneath the pan, and then tapped her fingertip to Cricket's nose. "You and Milton would be good friends."

"How old is he?" she asked.

"Milton is six."

Cricket counted her fingers out loud. "He's two more than me."

"Very good, little one. All right, your breakfast is ready."

While Pepper filled the plate with cakes and orange slices, I got Cricket settled in *her* seat at the table by the fireplace, then topped off my coffee and returned to the island. "I had a dream last night."

It took mere seconds for Pepper to understand. "What did you see?"

I gave her all the details from finding Beau in the hospital bed to the memory spell at the end.

"Why do you feel a gray witch enchanted Beauregard?" Pepper asked.

"This was a definite wrong thing for the right reason spell. The witch who cast it interfered with the course of his life."

As I had. More precisely, I interfered with ten that day. How had the lives of the others who were on the boat turned out? Had she . . . Mom enchanted all of them?

Pepper climbed onto the stool next to me and sighed like she was relieved to sit for a moment. Then, as though reading my mind, she said, "You paid your dues, child."

That's what Dad said at the park Thursday morning. The words meant more coming from Pepper.

"You've seen that Beau is okay," she continued. "You can find out about the others if you want to, but it might be best to let things be. Nothing can change at this point. All the magic in the world can't turn back time." She stretched out her arm, coffee cup in hand, and it refilled. "Perhaps the dream wasn't as complicated as you think. You felt Beau was spelled. The dream showed you that's what happened, so maybe it was meant to let you know that you can trust your instincts."

I hadn't thought of that. "Maybe."

"But you think there's more to it."

I held out my hands, fingers spread wide. "In the dream, I saw the witch lay her hands on Beau as she cast the spell. They weren't my hands."

She stared at me as though looking into my thoughts. "A wrong thing/right reason spell cast by someone who is not you. I know of only one other gray witch in Blackwood Grove. You think your mother did this."

There was my opening. Time to confess my thoughts. "In the dream, the witch's right hand had a bent right pinkie."

"Ah. You do think it was your mother. Why does that bother you? Don't *think* about it. What is the first thing that enters your head?"

I'd already thought about that last night. "She had to clean up after me and restore happiness to Beau's life."

"That isn't a bad thing."

"Restoring happiness, no. But cleaning up after me and then surely suffering a consequence for casting the spell?"

"According to your dream, it was her choice to cast that spell. She went to the hospital with the specific intention of doing so. Yes, she was making things okay for Beau. He no longer remembers any of the details. I understand that none of the other passengers do either. Yes, she likely paid a price, but that was not new to her." Pepper paused. "There are two reasons people repeat actions. They either can't stop or they gain something from doing it. Consider that by making things better for others, your mother gains satisfaction. In this case, she made things better for Beau while also protecting you. That's what mothers do, after all."

I scowled. "Everything is after the fact. I made a mistake that day because she never taught me anything about being a gray witch. She and Dad knew what I was capable of. I heard them talking about it many times. But instead of guiding me, she let me flounder and cause an accident that cost a boy his leg."

"But saved ten lives. Tell me, are you sure you saw what you think you did?"

"Meaning did I misinterpret something?"

"Mm-hmm," she hummed while drinking coffee.

"What?"

"Think about it. What could you have misinterpreted?"

I sighed and let the dream replay in my head. "It's possible the pinkie in question wasn't bent, so they might not have been Mom's hands."

"That's true." When I didn't say more, she nudged, "Is it possible this was a regular dream and not a prophetic one? You've wondered about Beau all these years. Now you're back and see that he's okay, so your brain now has the missing piece to the puzzle."

If not for the way I jolted awake, I might agree with her. Beau's eyes turned glassy at the diner when we talked about the accident and cleared again when we changed subjects. My brain could have borrowed that for the dream. But what about the bent pinkie?

"Those were the bestest pancakes ever." Cricket stood between us, empty plate in hand.

"There's no syrup on the plate." I gave her a side-eyed glance. "Did you lick it clean?"

"Wasn't me." She pointed across the kitchen at Gumbo happily licking his chops.

I DROPPED Cricket off with Jett who promised to bring her to The Apple Barn once they were done tending the animals. Then I went to join Gwynne and check out this store that wasn't here when I left thirty-two years ago.

It was an exact replica of the white barn, which meant it wasn't fancy inside, but it didn't really need to be. The stone floors were charming, as was the high peaked roof. The walls had been insulated, covered with sheetrock, and painted crisp white, but they added tons of character by leaving the wood trusses exposed. A simple checkout counter stood immediately to the right of the front door.

Past the counter was all retail space. One side had products made from primarily apple tree wood, but surely other trees contributed too. Wooden spoons and bowls, walking sticks, picture frames, smoking chips to toss on the grill, bags of runes, and wands for casting spells. Then there were the bee products including honey, of course, and candles made from beeswax. The list went on and on.

The other side of the barn was for food—pies, apple butter, chutneys and jellies, fresh and frozen fruits, fruit juices, applesauce . . . In the fall there would surely be cider, caramel apples, baked apples, apple crisp and cobbler. There were also eggs, goat milk, goat cheese, and Pepper's seasonings.

Between the food and the retail goods were Gwynne's remedies. She used to sell a small amount at The Mercantile. From the size of the display, people had taken nicely to her natural treatments and goat milk lotions and soaps. This was what I always dreamed of doing.

At the back of the barn were shirts, pants, and shorts with The Apple Barn and Applewood Farm logos. Even towels, blankets, and pillows.

"When did we become a corporation?" I murmured to myself.

"Impressive, isn't it?" Gwynne appeared from the back room. "A few years ago, a woman asked if we had T-shirts. I said no and smiled, thinking who would want a shirt with our name on it? A couple in line behind her said they'd buy two if we had them. That night over dinner, I discussed it with the others. They loved the idea, so we had logos designed. That one question turned into this. And yes, we sell all of these things."

"Tell me you don't do all of this yourself."

"Oh, heavens no. I mix my remedies, take care of the store layout, and manage the business end. Pepper and Jett contribute a lot, and we hire witches from town for the rest. We try to stay local. There's a team that helps Jett with the orchard, animals, and gardens. I've got people who work part-time here, and plenty of folks provide products we can sell."

I pointed out some dishtowels with apples embroidered on them. "Did June Stanford make those?"

"She did." Gwynne pointed at a stack of towels. The towels reorganized into a neat row. "The woman always has a needle of some kind in her hand. She rotates her stock between here and the diner to keep things fresh. How was your night? Are you getting by okay in the cottage?"

"Would be nice if I had more than a cot to sleep on, but a laptop showed up last night, which I appreciate. I've got new clothes on the way." I made a mental note to check on the insurance for my house. And file for unemployment.

Gwynne frowned. "Sounds like the property's coming around. Sorry it's been giving you a hard time."

"Can I ask you something?"

"You just did." She chuckled at her little joke. "Of course. You can ask anything."

"I was sitting on my balcony last night and saw a light flashing at the gate at the end of the driveway. After a few minutes, someone came out of the house, walked down the drive, and then went back to the house. I could only make out a shadowy shape, but it looked like someone in loose clothes with long hair."

She waited for me to say more. "Is there a question?"

"Was it you?"

"Wasn't me. I went up to my room right after dinner. I took a bath, watched a little television, and then fell asleep reading."

"Does Pepper have long hair under that head wrap?"

She thought about that. "Last I saw it out of the wrap, it was shoulder length."

Not sure that answered my question. "Any idea what that was about?"

"Yes. There are a number of Ordinaries around here who point fingers at us during the day and then come begging for our help under the cloak of darkness."

My jaw dropped. "You perform magic for them?"

"No," she insisted immediately. "We give them the bits, bobs, and instructions they need to cast their own spells." At my shocked expression, she explained, "Ordies aren't magical, and there's nothing I could do to give them, say, telekinetic powers." She pointed at a messy stack of sweatshirts. The stack burst apart, flew into the air, and landed in a heap on the ground.

I bit back a laugh and teased, "Not sure why they would want to be able to do that."

She blushed, pointed again, and the sweatshirts reformed into a neat stack like the dishtowels had earlier. "Arthritis in my fingers. My aim is a bit off. We enchant everything they'll need for their spell—herbs, oils, crystals, amulets, candles, etc.—so it will provide the requested results when the instructions are followed. The rest is up to the caster."

"What kinds of spells do the Ordies ask for?"

"Nothing of the murderous variety. As far as I know. At least no one's ever asked me for anything like that. Sure hope none of the others would fill such a request. Mostly people want love, money, or beauty. Lots of people ask if we can make them younger but—"

"You can't turn back time," I concluded, echoing Pepper's words from earlier. "Have spells ever gone wrong?"

"Let's see," she adjusted her glasses, "one time a woman was desperately in love with someone who didn't return her feelings. She cast the spell and then ended up in the hospital when the guy's girlfriend attacked her. Another time, a woman wanted a little more *attention* from her husband. She came back a week later begging for a sleeping spell for him so she could get some sleep."

Oh my. "And they pay you for this, I assume."

"Handsomely. We always price high enough that people have to really, truly want the thing they ask for. And we have a waiting period. They make their request, and we make them wait a week. We also explain what could go wrong, especially if they don't follow our instructions exactly. That way, we're not responsible. We don't mix or even pre-portion anything because as you're aware, a spell is fifty percent intention. Many times, even after the waiting period and handing over the money, they don't follow through with it. No harm done. Nothing will come from enchanted items if the spell is not cast."

This didn't quite sit right with me. I think it was the *we're not responsible* comment. It felt like they were justifying their actions or trying to trick karma.

"Is this practice okay? I mean, it doesn't go against a creed of some kind, does it?"

She twirled her finger at a shelf of candles, making all the labels face forward, then pressed her palms together, straightening the rows. "Witches' abilities are completely natural. We didn't ask for them, and we didn't do anything to bring them about. We were born with the magic inside us as surely as a singer was born with the gift of a beautiful voice. Why shouldn't we also be able to use and share the gifts we're given?"

She was right. One hundred percent. Yet we still got accused of being freaks and abominations. Anger flared in the center of my chest.

"I never thought of it that way before, Auntie. If they want to make a law that says we can't use magic on the streets of non-magical towns, fine. But why not within the walls of our own homes? Artists, actors, athletes . . . anyone with any other sort of natural ability doesn't have to hide who they are. I spent the last three decades tamping down what's natural inside me for fear of getting caught. My son may have powers, but I never allowed him to try for the same reason. No wonder my blood pressure is up, I can't sleep, and my brain gets fuzzy. I'm blocked."

"More fiber helps," Gwynne stated. "And prune juice."

I stared at her. "Not that kind of blocked."

"It could also be menopause."

"It could be that." I laughed at her, but my newfound fury returned a heartbeat later. "Think I'll be angry at society for a minute."

She took a step back. "By all means, my dear. Express your rage."

The confidence in her shined like starlight.

Two Ordies, a mother and her teenage daughter, came to

help with customers and stocking. In lieu of a paycheck, Gwynne gave them the equivalent in merchandise. Gotta love the barter system. The store opened at ten o'clock, and I was shocked to find a small crowd waiting when Gwynne gave me the go ahead to open the doors. I mostly hung in the background and learned about the business. Jett brought Cricket to the store a little after ten, and fortunately three cats followed them in. Not only did the customers love seeing them lounging about, the familiars kept Cricket busy until lunchtime. That's when Emma showed up to babysit.

"Let's go get lunch." She propped Cricket on her hip and looked at me. "And then?"

"She should lay down for an hour or so." We stopped calling her afternoon rest time *naps* because according to my wise for her age granddaughter, only babies took naps. When I said I liked taking naps sometimes, she restated, "Only babies and old grandmas."

After taking my own short lunch break, I planned to start organizing the storeroom at the back of the barn. The place was . . . chaos. I couldn't figure out any sort of system whatsoever so asked Gwynne if sorting by area within the store made sense to her.

"Oh, sure. That would be a lot better than alphabetically."

I stared at the shelves but still didn't see it. "Alphabetically using what language?"

She made a face at me. "You can work on that next time. For now, you need to get going."

"It's only twelve thirty. I can keep working. It's not like I'm on the clock."

She propped her fists on her hips. "There's something else you were going to do today."

It took me a minute. In my defense, I was already thinking about the inventory. Then I remembered. I said I'd go visit Carly today.

CHAPTER 12

*B*efore going to see Carly, I stopped at the apartment to brush my hair and teeth. I was nervous to talk to my cousin. We'd been inseparable as kids. Living in the same house meant we walked to and from school together and did our homework together every night. We shared a bedroom, except for those rare times when we were fighting, and even shared clothes. As I dabbed a wet washcloth on the teensy drip of syrup Cricket got on my Applewood Farm T-shirt, I laughed, remembering Carly digging one of my shirts out of the laundry hamper because that's what she wanted to wear to school that day. Didn't matter if it was wrinkled or a little grimy as long as it didn't smell.

Of course, we weren't girls anymore. We were middle-aged former best friends about to reconnect, I hoped, after missing out on each other's life for three decades. Three important, glorious, and at times painful decades when we could have used a best friend. At least I could have. Maybe I'd been replaced. All of it was completely my fault.

After successfully removing the syrup drip, I added a little more deodorant for good measure. Then I laced up my boots, hopped into my car, and psyched myself up to make the biggest apology of my life.

As I waited for a pickup to pass so I could turn left onto River Road, I watched the sun sparkle off the Mississippi. Being one of the last weekends of the summer, the river was crammed with fishing boats, runabouts, pontoons, and jet skis. Farther down the street, the boat dock across from the diner was filled to capacity with people floating down the river and stopping at the mall to get something to eat or do a little shopping.

"Be safe," I whispered at them and envisioned everyone making it home happy and well.

Two miles and five minutes later, I entered the station and found Officer Leezza Chapman sitting behind the tall desk in the lobby. As she had been when I first met her at the diner, she was very smiley.

"Hey," she greeted like she'd been expecting me. "You're from the diner, right? Bet you're here to talk to Carly."

"Yes and yes. Are there specific hours for visitations? Do I need an appointment?"

"Only when we have a full house, which isn't often." She had me sign in and then motioned for me to follow her.

She led me down a hallway painted the same soothing shade of medium blue as the entrance. A glass wall on one side of that hallway revealed a large room with eight or ten desks. Four officers were in there at the moment. Beau wasn't one of them.

Officer Chapman stopped at a room with four table-and-chair sets. The tabletop and four chairs of each set were bolted to a heavy metal frame. The frame was bolted to the floor.

"This is our visitation room. Go ahead and have a seat and I'll get Carly. Sorry, what's your name?"

"Dusty Hotte."

"Be right back."

I chose a chair facing the door and had been waiting so long for Officer Chapman to return, or so it felt, I started to think

Carly didn't want to see me. Finally, Carly appeared in the doorway. And she didn't look happy.

There were handcuffs around her wrists, and the officer attached them to a metal loop on the edge of the table. "I'll give you a little privacy but will be watching you." She pointed to a camera mounted to the ceiling. "You have fifteen minutes."

Now that Carly was in front of me, I didn't know what to say. We sat in awkward silence for a few seconds, then Carly asked, "What are you doing here?"

Here at the jail or in town? Did it matter? Should I take care of business or beg for forgiveness first? The cold glare in her eyes led me to believe business was best.

"I'm trying to find the proof Beau needs to let you go."

She made a move like she wanted to cross her arms, but the cuffs wouldn't let her. Instead, she let out a frustrated sigh and sat back. "You don't think I'm the killer?"

"Of course I don't. We talked to Beau yesterday, and he told us the only things they've got on you are that you were alone in the dining room with the victim shortly before he was found dead, and they found your thumbprint on the weapon."

"That's what Nina told me yesterday. Supposedly, I stabbed him with a pie knife. Didn't know those things were sharp enough to do that kind of damage."

"I could see it." I made an upward stabbing motion, beneath the ribs and into the heart. "With enough force behind it."

She didn't react.

"Your prints on the weapon muddies the water a bit, but there is a valid reason for why they were there." I paused before asking my next question. "Please don't take this the wrong way, but is there any legitimate reason Beau would suspect you? I talked with Miriam from Tiny Togs, and she told me the victim, Ludo Beck, wanted to open a store in the mall. Comfort said he tried to convince her to sell the diner to him. Beau wonders if he came at you, too, and maybe that's why you—"

"I didn't stab him."

"I know that. He made you angry, though."

"Not angry enough to stab him."

I counted to ten, letting her deflate a bit, then cautiously said, "That's what Beau sees, though. You were mad and now the man is dead. What did he do that made you angry?"

She adjusted the cuffs around her wrists. "The first time Beck asked if we'd sell him our building, I told him no way. We were the first ones there and would be the last ones standing. Then he started pressuring me. Every day for the last week, he'd either come to the diner or stop me out in the park and ask again. Multiple times some days." She pursed her lips, growing angrier. "No matter how many times I told him it wasn't for sale or just flat out no, he kept pushing. I told him to put in an application for the building across from Silver Moon." She gave me a pained look and hissed, "That should be our place."

Memories of late nights, papers spread out all over the floor in our bedroom, while we planned the store we wanted to open together after college flashed in my mind. I shoved them away. We could talk about that later. I needed to get her out of jail first.

Officer Chapman appeared in the doorway. "You've got seven minutes."

I glanced at one of the four clocks, one at the center of each wall. "You said Beck should put in an application. What application?"

Carly blew out a breath. "That will take more than seven minutes to explain. Talk to the aunts about Marilyn Kramer's process."

Marilyn? What did Nash Kramer's mother have to do with this?

"Beck offered a ridiculous sum." Carly shook her head in a disbelieving way. "Regular grocery stores are always busy, but a specialty grocer? I can't imagine him ever earning back the amount he offered for the diner."

"Maybe he planned to carry something other than groceries."

One of her eyebrows arched, and she paused to consider that. "That would help explain how desperate he was, but why was he so set on our place? Location for a business is super important, and we've got the best spot, but the mall is only three blocks long. If a store has great products, they'll do well. Why wasn't the empty one good enough?"

"Because the location isn't right," I suggested, thinking of the boat dock. "What if he wanted the diner for a different reason?"

"What do you mean?"

"Miriam said Beck had been targeting the stores in the center of the mall because they're the prime spots in the middle of the action."

"Right," she said. "We're running out of time. Say what you're thinking."

"The river. If he was going to sell something illegal, there's that flight of stairs directly across the street from the diner that goes down to the boat dock when it's out in the summer. Hop in, speed off, disappear into the river traffic. Since they pull in the dock in the winter, they could use snowmobiles or four wheelers."

"Airboats," she corrected. "The main channel freezes inconsistently due to the undercurrents. It could be two feet thick in some areas and two inches in others so driving anything heavy is risky."

"Okay, they could pull an airboat up near the stairway and set out a board to walk on to get to shore."

We sat quietly for a moment, mulling over this possibility.

I looked at the clock again. "Our time's almost up. I'll come back, but trust me, I'm doing everything I can to prove you didn't do this."

"Trust you?" She shot an incredulous look at me. "Where have you been for the last *thirty-two years*, Dusty?"

"Time's up, ladies." Officer Chapman came in and unhooked the chain through the loop on the table. Then she took Carly's arm while she stood from the chair.

The last thing Carly said to me before leaving the doorway was, "Hope you know you've got a lot of making up to do. Since you're not actually dead."

$\mathcal{I}$ left the jail and drove directly home, my mind spinning. I tried to come up with a plan of attack for getting Carly out of there but kept getting distracted by the residual fury she directed at me. The best way for me to get back in control when it got like this was to be outside. The urge to dig in the dirt, breathe in fresh air, and soak in some sun became almost overwhelming the closer I got to Applewood Farm. If Jett didn't need help in the garden, which was unlikely, I'd go for a hike.

A pickup truck I didn't recognize caught my attention the moment I entered the driveway. It was parked in front of the workshop barn, so I tucked my car into the garage slot beneath the apartment and walked over. Long drawers pulled out of the back and were about half the length of the six-foot bed. They were loaded with what looked like medical supplies. Metal boxes in the front half of the bed opened to the side for access to more supplies. What was going on? Why was there a doctor here? Then I read the words on the side of the truck. *Kramer Veterinary Services*. Kramer?

I looked up to find the bald man I'd seen the other day

coming out of the workshop. Being closer to him, my eyes immediately went to the tattoos on his head. They were contained to within his hairline, and if he let his hair grow, I wouldn't know they were there. Those on his temples, neck, arms, and hands covered almost every inch of skin. Then I looked at his face and gasped. Nash Kramer.

"Lady," he called. "Come here."

I thought he was talking to me and was about to yell at him for being rude when his pit bull trotted out of the workshop. Cricket came running out a second later and headed straight for the dog. Unsure if the dog was dangerous or not, I was about to holler at Cricket to stop, but as she got close, the pittie with the bright-pink collar dropped to the ground and rolled to her back so Cricket could give her a two-handed belly rub.

Emma appeared from the workshop next and gave me a wave.

Shocked, both at my granddaughter climbing all over this dog and Emma's carefree attitude . . . and seeing Nash Kramer in our driveway, I stepped closer to find out what was going on.

He looked at me, his expression neutral. "You were staring at me the other day. Thought you looked familiar."

"Same, that's why I was staring. You look a little different now." I pointed at the dog. "I assume she's the lady you were calling."

He nodded his tattooed head. "That's her name and her temperament." He pointed at Cricket. "She's yours?"

"My granddaughter, yes." I watched as he went to his truck, put some items back into the drawers, and then pulled other things out. "What are you doing here?"

He pointed at his business' name on the truck. "Taking care of the animals. I come every few months to check on the goats, chickens, and familiars."

"Dr. Nash is a animal doctor. I didn't know animals had to

get shots too." Cricket winced and put her hand to her arm as though she'd received a vaccination along with the goats.

"I understand the nickname," Nash said. "She asked approximately two hundred questions."

"That all? You got off easy."

His eyes remained cold, but his mouth twitched with a hint of amusement. Carrying what looked to be a tackle box, he headed for the chicken coop, Lady at his side. When Cricket started to follow, Emma scooped her up.

"Let's let Dr. Nash do his job now." Emma spun Cricket up onto her shoulders and looked at me. "We were going to the playground before Dr. Nash arrived but decided to learn what vets do. Okay if we go now?"

I hesitated. There was a killer on the loose who could possibly be the person who threatened my granddaughter. But they'd be in a public location with plenty of people around. "Okay. I was going to see if Jett could use help in the garden. I assume I don't have to say it but—"

"Don't take my eyes off her." She appeared to understand my fear. Or at least the *killer on the loose* fear. "Don't worry, I'll keep her safe."

My throat tightened as I hugged Cricket goodbye, so I was immensely grateful when Jett put me to work weeding the flower beds around the house and then harvesting raspberries and a few herbs. I couldn't say how long I was on my hands and knees reaching, pulling, and tugging, but it was long enough for my mind to forget about my life and Carly's troubles for a while and focus on the plants. With each one I came to, I tried to remember what it was for. Raspberry leaves, I recalled, helped with the pain of childbirth. Dried, powdered yarrow staunched bleeding cuts. A tincture of mugwort and honey made an effective cough syrup. It was also great for cleansing and charging divination tools.

The physical work was tiring yet satisfying. I knew I'd be

achy tomorrow, but I also felt motivated to re-learn these things I'd let myself forget while outside Blackwood Grove.

This was the life Carly and I had talked about. I had great respect for nature, and I'd wanted to become an herbalist. I'd wanted to grow my own herbs and flowers for various remedies. The parts of plants I didn't use for tinctures, poultices, or for other medicinal or magical reasons would have been used for crafting. The raspberry brambles that I cut to the ground in the fall or spring could be tied into bunches with twine and hung over windows for protection. Grapevines were perfect for wreaths. Like the aunts did, I'd planned to raise bees and use the wax and honey in handmade cosmetics. I'd had notebooks filled with ideas for garden layouts and all the items I would make and sell in our shop. Where were those notebooks? Did the aunts or Carly get rid of them when they decided I'd died?

Carly had also loved plants and herbs, but her skill lay more with food. With Comfort for a mother, that wasn't a surprise. She'd wanted to learn about food as medicine and study ancient recipes that could help with ailments. She'd also wanted to become an acupuncturist, so we'd added a space for her to do that on our shop layout.

We had such big dreams. And I ruined them.

"Lola," a little singsong voice called. "Where are you?"

"Over here," I singsonged back and smiled at our little ritual. The first time she disappeared on me, we were in the backyard. She had chased a little frog into a viburnum bush and sat among the tall snowball-like flowers to play with it. I looked everywhere and was starting to panic. Calling out angrily would have only scared her, so I sang out, "Cricket, where are you?" It became the way we found each other.

"You're all dirty," she accused and made a disapproving face.

"I know. That happens when you work in a garden."

"Aren't you mad?"

"Not at all, this is a good way to get dirty. I love working with the plants."

"Auntie Jett says we can get the night eggs now."

Already? Time flew when working in the garden. I stood, brushing dirt from my jeans and hands. "Okay. Let's go collect those eggs and then get ready for dinner."

After I had showered and put on the jeans I bought at The Mercantile, Cricket and I went to join the others.

"It would be so much easier if we lived in the main house. If the property could move a whole barn and create a new one, it could surely add on two new bedrooms for us."

"I like my room." Cricket's big brown eyes filled with tears. "I don't want another new room."

I didn't realize she was listening. Sweeping her into my arms, I promised, "You don't have to get another new room. We're fine right where we are. I just thought it would be easier when we want something to eat."

She swiped a lone tear trailing down her cheek. "We don't have a very big kitchen, so we hafta go there to eat."

"If we had a bigger kitchen," I said more to the apartment than her, "I could make our dinner. And lunch. And breakfast."

She giggled when I gently poked her tummy at the mention of each meal. "But Auntie Pepper makes good food, and we get to see everybody."

Guess I needed to leave well enough alone.

"There they are." Jett opened her arms wide. "I want a bug hug."

Cricket ran over and launched herself into Jett's arms.

"Did you visit Carly?" Comfort's semi-threatening tone meant I was in trouble if I hadn't.

"I did." I told them about our theory that Beck wanted the diner location because of its easy access to the river.

"That could be," Comfort agreed. "Especially since our main entrance faces the river while all the others face the park."

"This guy's name is Ludo Beck, right?" Maks asked.

"Correct." I smiled as Cricket climbed onto her chair, carefully fanned out her dress around her legs, and then folded her hands properly in her lap. "Did you learn something about him?"

"Possibly. I had to run over to the hardware store today. Ran out of screws. Never in my life have I run out of screws." He thumped his forehead with a knuckle. "Must be losing it."

"You're not losing it," Comfort assured.

"Maybe the property hid them," Gwynne suggested. "What did you learn?"

Maks glared at the property in general, presumably over the misplaced screws. "Naturally, the buzz around town is about the murder. Folks are upset and scared that there's a kil—" He looked at Cricket. "That there's a criminal wandering around. As for this Beck fellow, they were saying he hung out at the saloon every night and seemed kind of sketchy."

Making drug deals? Trying to find folks who would buy from him? Or maybe it wasn't drugs. He could be trafficking anything small enough to carry down those stairs without drawing a lot of attention. Jewelry. Car parts. People.

"Dusty?"

I blinked and found them all looking at me. "What?"

Maks repeated what he'd said. "We should go to the saloon. We can eat dinner there and ask around about Beck. Might result in nothing, or it might lead to something."

Pepper stood at the island and indicated the spread of bowls filled with taco add-ons laid out there. "But I made tacos."

"We can have those for lunch tomorrow," Gwynne soothed.

Pepper sighed. "Put it away, please."

The house copied her sigh, and the bowls disappeared.

"All right," I agreed. "Are all of us going?"

"Not really a place for little ones," Jett advised. She looked from Cricket to Freddie who was waving his arms about to get her attention. He vanished a moment later. "He went over there to scout around. Whatever that means."

"Let me call Emma." Two minutes later, I asked Cricket, "Do you want to go spend time with Nina, Emma, Alex, and Sebastian? I promise to be back in time to tuck you in and read your stories."

"What about my dinner?" she whined and rubbed her tired eyes. All of these new people and places in only two days. It was a lot for a four-year-old. It was a lot for a fifty-year-old. "What would you like?"

"Chicken nuggets, applesauce, and sweet potato french fries."

All of that appeared on the table in big serving dishes a second later.

"Weren't you listening?" Jett scolded. "We're going to the saloon. The lass is going over to Carly's house."

The platters disappeared as fast as they'd appeared. The sound of footsteps stomping up the stairs echoed throughout the house followed by a door slamming.

"That's a bit dramatic, don't you think?" Comfort scolded the house.

"It doesn't like it when we eat out," Pepper explained in a cautionary tone.

"Where did all that food go?" I wondered.

Pepper grumbled something I couldn't hear. She seemed out of sorts. I understood. She'd been ready to feed us and now had to pivot. Some folks, myself included at times, needed a minute to readjust to a sudden change in plans.

The seven of us—Comfort, Maks, Gwynne, Pepper, Jett, Cricket, and me—all piled into a full-size van with the Applewood Farms logo on the sides. I drove while they all shouted directions at me before I'd even made it out of the driveway.

"Go down to Braeburn Lane and take a left."

"Why all the way to Braeburn? She can turn on McIntosh and get there faster."

"There aren't any stop signs on Braeburn. We have to stop every other block on McIntosh."

I turned left out of the driveway onto River Road, the only one in town *not* named after an apple variety, and came to McIntosh Street first so turned left there. Then they said to take a left on Honey Crisp Road and a right on Fuji Court.

Carly's house was a classic barn-red saltbox farmhouse with a covered front deck. It wasn't there when I lived here, so unless the property had magicked it here from elsewhere, it was built to look old.

"You all stay," I told them. "I'll just run Cricket inside and be right back."

She wrapped her arms and legs around me tight the moment I pulled her out of her booster seat.

"Are you okay, bug?" She nodded, her face pressed into my shoulder, but didn't say anything. I stopped walking and waited for her to look up at me. "What's the matter?"

I knew what was coming.

"I miss mommy and daddy."

There it was. It was what she said whenever she got tired. And it broke off a little more of my heart every time.

"Oh, honey, I know you do. I do too. Daddy will call you on Monday."

She sniffed. "When is that?"

"Hold up your fingers." She held up her little hand with fingers splayed. "Today is Saturday. Tomorrow is Sunday. The next day is Monday." I gently folded two fingers. "How many is that?"

"One, two, three." She touched each *up* finger with her other pointer finger. "Three more days."

"But this day is almost over."

She put one down. "Two days."

"Not so long, right?"

"Right." But she didn't sound soothed by this and rested her forehead against my chest.

"Do you want me to take you back to the apartment? The aunties and Uncle Maks can do this by themselves. You and I can eat dinner together then snuggle on the couch and watch a movie."

The front door opened, and Emma stepped out. She immediately knew that there was a problem and turned down her normally bubbly personality. "Someone must want chicken nuggets. A big plate of them showed up on our table a few minutes ago."

Cricket turned her head a little. "Is there applesauce?"

"And sweet potato fries," Emma said like this was an amazing choice. "My favorite."

"Mine too." Cricket lifted her head all the way up.

Three cats, one wearing a tutu, trailed after Emma.

Cricket perked up when she saw them. "You have kitties?"

"We do. A hamster and a chameleon too." Emma reached to pet the cat in the tutu. "This is Bary. He's Nina's cat, and she named him after the famous ballet dancer Mikhail Baryshnikov because Bary bounces around when he gets excited, and it looks like he's dancing."

Cricket squirmed in my arms, so I asked, "Are you okay to go with Emma?"

"I'm okay, Lola."

"Good girl." I kissed both cheeks and tilted her head back to put one beneath her chin too. "I won't be long. Promise." To Emma, I said, "Bring her back to the house at seven. If we're not there yet, we will be soon."

"Sounds like a plan." She held her arms out and waited for Cricket to reach out for her.

I returned to the van to find a much more subdued group of seniors.

"Everything okay?" Gwynne asked.

"She's tired but will be fine. Let's be quick about this, though."

Maks agreed. "Eat, gather information, then go back to the house to discuss."

And eat pie. Discussions always required pie. After seeing my little bug so upset, I needed some of Comfort's comfort.

CHAPTER 14

The Paddle Wheel was one part Old West saloon, one part restaurant, one part nightclub, and very welcoming. What first caught my eye was the ornate bar area. The wall behind it was covered by a huge mirror and glass shelves filled with bottles of liquor. A long bar made of hand carved, polished wood—similar to the breakfast counter at the diner—provided space for customers to pull up a stool and eat or place their orders and sit elsewhere. Bronze-colored decorative tin tiles covered the ceiling. Deep-forest-green walls made for an atmosphere that was both moody and soothing. The wood floor used to have a pattern stained onto it but was so scratched from wear now I couldn't tell what it used to be. A stage and dance floor took up the far end of the building.

Along with the seating at the bar, several four-top rectangular dining tables lined the wall opposite the bar, built-in bench seating on one side and mismatched wood chairs on the other. Round high-top tables were also scattered throughout the space.

"Have a seat anywhere," a server wearing jeans and a Paddle Wheel T-shirt told us. "We'll find you."

"I say we split up," Maks decided.

Comfort nodded. "Divide and conquer."

"I agree," Pepper said. "I'll go with Gwynne."

Pepper watched her lifelong friend make her way across the dining room and stop at an empty table. Gwynne's mouth turned with a small smile.

Comfort's smile, however, was sad. "That was their table."

Hers and Filip's.

I asked, "Is it good or bad for her to be here?"

"As long as someone familiar is with her," Pepper offered, "she should be fine."

Pepper scurried off to join Gwynne while Comfort and Maks went in search of a table, leaving me with Jett. I turned to ask her where she wanted to sit and found she'd already taken a seat at one end of the bar. Freddie hovered behind the counter across from her and the middle-aged men in motorcycle chaps who sat on either side of her. Guess I was on my own.

I took a stool at the other end and ordered a local lager and a veggie burger, which the bartender assured me was "pretty good for not being meat." I had the impression *meat* made up the majority of his meals, so that seemed like a safe recommendation. Happy to see sweet potato fries on the menu, Cricket's request had sounded good to me, I added those instead of regular fries.

With beer in hand, I turned on the stool to face the tables and scanned the room for any familiar faces. After almost thirty years, it was hard to know for sure, but some of them looked like people I went to high school with. From the way they looked at me, whispered to their tablemates, who then also looked at me, my guess seemed like a safe one.

The homeless man I'd seen in the park yesterday, the man Nash had been talking to, was meandering around the dining room. When patrons left, he swooped in and ate items they had left on their plates. He took a half-full glass of beer from one table, took a long drink, and then stopped at a table of younger men who had pitchers of beer in front of them. Somehow, he convinced them to refill his glass. All of this appeared perfectly natural to him. In fact, after he ate what he wanted, he cleared the dishes from the tables and took them to a tub near the swinging door to the kitchen. He even wiped down the tables using a towel and a spray bottle of cleaning solution. A server gave him a pat on the back, presumably for helping, so I assumed this was his regular method for getting a meal.

"His name is Wayne."

I looked left to find Beau standing next to me. "Wayne?"

"That's all he'll tell me. Quite a character."

"Isn't he panhandling or stealing?"

"He's not begging for anything so not panhandling. Taking the uneaten food is considered theft. Yes, it's garbage, but it belongs to the restaurant. If they make a complaint, I'll do something about it. That's why he cleans the tables. He does a service for them, so they don't care if he eats the food. Hygienically not a good idea, but no one's upset about it."

"Why don't they hire him?"

Beau blinked his blue eyes at me. "Why pay someone who's willing to work for literal table scraps? And Wayne says he doesn't want a job because he's only passing through and won't be here that long."

"How long has he been here?" I drank some of my quite tasty lager.

"About a week?" Beau estimated. "He pitches a tent in the mall's park every night. I told him there's a state park with camping sites available on the other side of your orchard. Says he doesn't have money to pay for a site. Since he's not bothering anyone, I told him he can sleep in the park as long as he doesn't damage anything and has everything cleaned up before shoppers arrive."

I couldn't decide if Beau was a good person or a sucker.

"Veggie burger and sweet potato fries," the server announced and set a plate on the bar behind me. "Enjoy."

"Those burgers are really good." Beau took the empty stool next to me but positioned himself so he could see the dining room.

He was still in uniform. "Are you here for dinner or . . ."

"I'm off shift soon and thought I'd do a walkthrough before heading home. It's good for the public to see police presence in random places at random times. Although, that veggie burger looks really good. Might need to get one."

A thought struck me. "Does Wayne come here every night? Help yourself to some fries. I'll never eat all these."

He took two. "Yep, he's here every night. Someone inevitably gets him something for breakfast from Comfort's Food or the teahouse across the park, but he seems to get most of his food for the day from here. If he stays much longer, I'll put a stop to the food stealing. It's kind of gross."

Kind of? Yuck. But I was less concerned with the man's eating habits and wondered more about how much time he spent here.

"The reason I asked is because Maks overheard a conversation at the hardware store about Ludo Beck. They commented that he had also been hanging out here. If Wayne is primarily here or in the park, the two places Beck also spent time in—"

"You're wondering if Wayne could give any information on Beck. Yeah, I questioned him about that. He insisted he never saw Beck here. Too focused on customers getting ready to leave their tables, I guess. Says he saw him going around to the front of the diner many times. During the time the stabbing occurred, Wayne remembers seeing a few people leaving Comfort's shortly before they closed at two o'clock but didn't see anyone going to it at that time."

I chewed and swallowed a bite of the indeed decent veggie burger. "Which means Carly is still your only suspect."

Beau appeared genuinely saddened. "If no one entered or left the diner during the time Beck was stabbed, the killer had to be someone inside the diner."

I needed a big swig of lager to wash down the lump of burger suddenly stuck in my throat. "Carly couldn't have done this, Beau."

"I don't think she did either, but right now the evidence says otherwise. I need proof."

He did. I knew and understood that. I thought back, again, to what I had seen when I entered the diner that day. "Gwynne told me June Stanford was there right up to closing time."

"I talked to her too." He shook his head. "She was really shaken up by the stabbing. She says Beck was alive when she left and doesn't remember anything helpful." He sat for a few seconds, then tilted his head side to side as though making a decision. "Look, don't misinterpret what I'm about to say as being encouragement for you to get involved with this investigation, because you shouldn't. It could be dangerous. If you hear anything from the other store owners let me know. They're being shut-mouthed with me."

While Beau chatted with a woman who came over to tell him about some possible vandalism on her farm, I finished my dinner and wondered why the store owners would be shut-mouthed about something that could affect them directly.

"I'll have Officer Danville stop by your place in the morning," Beau promised the woman, then apologized for the interruption.

"Don't apologize. You're doing your job. It gave me time to think. I stopped by the jail and talked to Carly this afternoon."

He nodded. "Saw your name on the visitors' log."

"Beck harassed Carly daily about selling the diner."

"I know. She made a formal complaint the day before he was stabbed. I told him to leave her alone."

"You should have added that he shouldn't even go inside the building."

He shook his head. "The diner is a public place. Unless she filed a restraining order or he was causing a disturbance, there's not much more I could do. Everyone I spoke to agreed he sat at the counter and drank coffee the day he died. He didn't harass anyone."

Guess I saw his point. "When I stopped to visit her today, Carly and I talked about why Beck wanted that building so badly. We have a theory."

He gave a small eye roll, then flipped his notepad open. "Let me hear it."

"We think he might have been involved with something illegal. Or was planning to be. The diner is the only building with a front entrance that faces the river. Directly across the street is that stairway."

"That leads to the boat dock." He concluded and seemed interested in the possibilities this presented. "Locations near highway on-ramps are often targeted by thieves. They grab what they came for, get on the highway, and speed away before the police can get there."

"And rivers are like highways. No one would set up a store to be stolen from, but what if Beck's grocery store was going to be a sort of distribution point?"

"Instead of steal and run, it would come get your stuff and run. Interesting thoughts, Dusty. I'll dig further into Beck's past business dealings." He stood from the stool. "I should go mingle with the public."

"See you around, Beau."

A different bartender, Stella, a woman big and strong enough that she could surely fill in as a bouncer, asked if I'd like another beer.

"Like one, yes, but I'll have an iced tea now, please."

I continued to face the dining room. Jett was still at the other end of the bar with Freddie hovering nearby. She held up her drink in acknowledgement when she saw me looking at her. Comfort and Maks had drawn a small crowd around their table. Not surprising. The two of them were cute individually. Together they were absolutely adorable, and people had always been drawn to them. Pepper and Gwynne were still at their table, glasses of wine before them. Gwynne seemed to be okay. Seemed Pepper was right and having someone familiar with her helped. Or maybe the episode happened that night because it had been her first anniversary without Filip and she was overloaded with emotion.

Were any of them asking about Ludo Beck, or had they simply conned me into bringing them here for dinner? I checked the time on my watch. Only six o'clock. We could stay for another half hour, forty-five minutes tops, and then I wanted to get home to Cricket.

I was about to go ask if any of them had learned anything when Nash Kramer took a seat near the center of the bar. Lady sat on the floor by his side. Within seconds, Stella placed a tall glass of something in front of him just as a server arrived with a dinner plate. He hadn't even ordered. Maybe he called ahead. Or was a regular here.

An older man with white flyaway hair, a horseshoe mustache, and a huge black short-haired dog sat next to Nash. The dogs sniffed noses and then ignored each other. The man finished off his current pint and asked for another. Partway through that one, he started complaining, loudly, about *that dead guy*. There was no empathy in his voice. In fact, he seemed annoyed that Beck had dared to *bring his sorry self into our town. Deserved what he got.* The man went on for long enough that Nash finally said something while taking the still mostly full beer glass away from him.

The man sat and pouted when the bartender gave him a glass of water instead. Then he devoured a plate of deep-fried cheese curds and didn't say anything more about the dead guy.

I turned away from them and found someone standing in front of me. A little too close for my comfort. It took me a moment to recognize Henry Kramer. His hair and beard were mostly gray beneath his cowboy hat; his face, lined and weathered from the sun.

He glared at me, jaw clenched and nostrils flared. "I heard you were back in town."

I flashed back to the person standing before me by the river all those years ago. My mouth went dry, but I screwed up my courage. We were in a public place, and Beau was somewhere nearby. Henry wouldn't do anything to me here. "Did you all get together and vote on that being the way you'd greet me?"

His bushy brows knit together in confusion.

"Something I can help you with, Henry?"

"Yeah, you can leave."

"The saloon is a public place—"

"Not the saloon. You were warned to stay away."

My memory of that day intensified. Maybe it was being back in town. Maybe it was having Nash and his angry father in the same room with me, but this time, I remembered something different.

The aunts and uncles had planned a graduation celebration for Carly and me. Before the festivities began, I wanted a couple minutes to myself. I went down by the river and was happy to find no one else there on the shore. I sat, looked out at the water, and thought about what was coming next for us.

Then Nash sped past with his boat full of kids. Did any of them see me? No one acknowledged me. They were probably all too busy holding on for dear life. That's when I had the premonition and saw the boat hit the tree. It flipped, and all ten of them went flying. I blinked out of the vision, saw the tree, and looked around for help. Not sure what I thought anyone else could do from the shore or even right there on the water with them. Stopping what was about to happen seemed impossible.

My hand instinctively shot out. The boat flipped. Someone screamed.

But the scream didn't come from the river. It came from above me on the road.

Marilyn Kramer was standing there, probably watching her son having fun with his friends. Then she turned and saw me with my hand out.

I gasped and blinked. Henry's face came back into focus. "It was Marilyn. *She* threatened me."

Why had I forgotten that? Had she cast a spell on me? No, not possible. Marilyn was an Ordy, and that kind of magic required more than *bits and bobs* as Gwynne called the ingredients they sold at the orchard gate.

The scowl on Henry's deeply lined face intensified. "She told you what would happen if you ever came back."

"Nothing but words, Henry. Words from an angry mother looking for someone to blame for her son's foolishness."

"Don't you speak about my son. You don't think she meant what she said? People know what you are."

My pulse pounded in my ears, but I tilted my chin up and maintained my composure. "And what am I exactly?"

I expected him to call me a witch. At worst, a gray witch.

His hand shook as he pointed a wrinkled, gnarled finger at me. "You're just like your mother, is what you are." He meant to wound me with my biggest fear, and he hit his mark.

My breath caught in my lungs for an instant, and I leaned my back against the bar. I remembered being afraid of this man when I was eighteen. He was a big and strong farmer, a tough guy with a temper who hated my family. Why, we didn't know. He stayed in the area because he owned his family's successful farm outright, but he could have sold it and bought land somewhere that didn't border our farm.

My eyes focused on that finger still pointed at me, still shaking. Was it age or something else causing the tremor? Anger and fear mimic each other. Was he afraid of *me*? He knew what I was capable of.

The longer he stood there trying to intimidate me, the more my fear of him faded and annoyance set in. I didn't come back to Blackwood Grove to make enemies, and the last thing I wanted to do was cause more problems for my family.

"Henry, we have nothing against you or your family. We never have."

"How would you know?" He stepped close enough that I could smell his alcohol and tobacco-tinged breath. "You were a stupid kid when you left. What did you know about anything then? Nothing, that's what. And if you think you know everything about your family now, you've grown into a stupid woman."

Henry might be older, but he was still strong, and his hands were now fisted. I looked around hoping Beau was nearby. Out of the corner of my eye, I saw Nash get to his feet.

"That's enough, Henry," Stella said from behind the bar, her raised voice stern. "You should walk away now."

He glared at me, then shrank back and stormed off. I exhaled and sank back onto my stool. Maybe I was still a little afraid of him.

I looked down the bar at Nash—not sure what, if anything, I expected him to do—and as he met my gaze, a scuffle broke out between two men at one of the pool tables set off to the side. Nash went over to them, said something that ended the argument, then returned to his stool.

He slammed back whatever was in his glass, then signaled Stella for a refill. When the scuffle started up again seconds later, he called out, "Either knock it off or one of you has to leave."

"Those Kramers." Stella topped off my tea and took my empty dinner plate. "Never quite sure what you'll get with any of them. You okay?"

"Yeah, Henry was just puffing his chest at me." I jutted my chin at Nash. "What's going on with him?"

"He's here every night. Sort of a hero around town."

That got my attention. "Nash is?"

"It's not a secret, he tells everyone, but he's a recovering alcoholic."

A man stepped up and rudely demanded a soda refill because he hadn't seen their *girl* in an hour. Stella told him to quit being rude, pointed at the server standing by his table, and told him to ask her for a refill. Nicely.

She sighed. "We get all kinds here."

"Not to be nosey, but if Nash is in recovery, why does he hang out here?"

"Again, he tells everyone, so I'm not spreading gossip. Says it's part of his process. He comes here and breaks up fights or drives people home when they've had too much. In payment, Curt and Annie give him dinner. And all the glasses of seltzer water he can drink."

Wayne cleared tables. Nash acted as a bouncer. Gwynne paid townies with merchandise. There was a lot of bartering going on in this town. I liked that, and I liked knowing that Nash's life seemed to be okay. He spent five years in prison after the accident and had clearly had some bad times, but it looked like he'd found his path, and that was the best any of us could hope for. What was the rest of his story?

I thanked Stella and then went to gather up my aunts and Maks. Time to go home and find out if any of them had learned anything helpful tonight.

CHAPTER 15

The moment the aunties, Maks, and I stepped into the kitchen, Comfort called out, "Pie, please."

Happy to be able to feed us, the house filled the table with three kinds of pie—graham cracker and a do over on the peach galette and key lime from last night—vanilla ice cream, a carafe labeled *decaf coffee*, the creamer and sugar tray, and six plates and forks. I went straight for the graham cracker pie—vanilla custard in a graham cracker crust topped with meringue.

"What did we learn?" I asked once they all had food in their mouths so had stopped chattering.

"Apparently," Comfort began, "Mr. Beck was quite a talented cook. He had worked in restaurants his entire life and was ready for something different."

"You were right, Dusty," Maks added. "He wanted to open a small specialty grocery store that sold only the highest quality meats, cheeses, wines, oils, and select ingredients. Cookware and bakeware as well."

"I only repeated what Miriam told me." I gave credit where it was due and then waited for someone else to add to the knowledge base. "Did we learn anything else?"

Jett shook her head. "I got caught up in discussions about Freddie with some of the patrons who used to ride motorcycles with him. Turns out they miss the big oaf."

Nearby, Freddie took a bow.

"Pepper? Gwynne? Did you learn anything?"

Gwynne looked expectantly at me. "About what, dear?"

A feeling of dread formed in my chest. I worried whether going to the saloon was a good idea.

Then she asked, "Oh, about Mr. Beck?" She shot a grin at Pepper, the kind girlfriends gave each other after a fun night out. What did they do when I wasn't looking? "We started talking about old times and suddenly there you were telling us it was time to leave."

Did I want to know what their *old times* involved?

Basically, the only thing they learned tonight was what we already knew. They were too busy having fun. I couldn't be mad at them for that, but the clock was ticking down on Carly's 72 hours.

"Oh, pie," Cricket squealed. "Ice cream! Can I have some?"

I cringed. We'd usually done the bath and were settling in for stories by this time. "You may have a taste of one or the other. Which would you like?"

She decided on the ice cream, and since quantity rarely mattered, I placed a tiny scoop in an equally tiny bowl. All Cricket knew was that she got some . . . in a "so cute" little bowl that fit in the palm of her hand.

"We have something fun to tell you," Emma announced after Cricket had a taste.

All eyes were on the teen.

"Should we tell them what you can do," she asked my granddaughter, "or do you want to show them?"

Cricket pondered this. "Both."

That's my girl. Why have one thing when you can have it all?

Emma cleared her throat importantly. "Cricket has powers."

My jaw dropped. "She what?"

"She was playing with Bary," Emma explained, "and he batted a Ping-Pong ball across the room. It rolled right for the TV stand and was about to go underneath when Cricket reached her hand out, and it stopped. Then it rolled back to her."

Telekinesis? That's a fairly strong power. Then I got a flash of the boat flipping after I'd reached my hand out.

Dear goddess, please not gray magic.

"Okay, witch girl," Emma prompted. "Show them."

Cricket's eyes took in the room and landed on the food spread out before us. She reached for a napkin that was about eight inches out of her reach. A second later, it fluttered, lifted, and flew to her hand.

Telekinesis. Thank heavens. Then the same disappointed feeling I got when Micah called to tell me she was walking settled in my chest. I'd missed her first summoning.

For a family of witches, powers turning on was reason to celebrate. Everyone around the table—Freddie and Granny Sadie included—cheered. The house released a gentle trumpet fanfare, and confetti rained down around us.

Everything was wonderful until I announced it was bedtime.

"But I'm not sleepy," she insisted when I tried to pick her up. "I don't want to go to bed."

Tantrums from her were rare, but more common when she was tired, which she'd already been when I dropped her off with Emma. I'd pushed it too far today.

"Goodness, what's going on up here?" Winnie appeared from the basement, smiled at the confetti, and then frowned at Cricket's upset state.

"We were celebrating that her powers have turned on," I explained, "and now someone doesn't want to go to bed."

Cricket crossed her arms tightly and pouted.

Winnie went to the pantry cabinet, studied the labeled

containers, then pulled out two quart-size jars. Holding them out for the gang's approval, she said, "Lavender and mint?"

Of course. I was so out of practice.

"Oh, yes," Gwynne approved, then told the house, "we'll need a sachet bag and a container for an infusion." A moment later, a small cheesecloth sack and glass jar big enough to hold a cup of dried herbs appeared on the table in front of her.

Winnie brought the bottles to Gwynne, who placed a healthy pinch of each herb into the bag and tied it shut while Winnie added herbs to the jar.

I was to hang the sachet beneath the tap as the bathtub filled and give her a small cup of the infusion before we started reading stories.

Winnie winked at me. "She'll be asleep in no time."

Pouting now and on the verge of tears, Cricket refused to say goodnight to anyone, not even Emma, who assured me it was all good.

I carried her across the courtyard and gently traced a fingertip over one eyebrow and then the other. The soothing technique always worked on Micah when he was overstimulated. I was happy to see it had a similar effect on his daughter.

Bath time was only long enough for cleaning off the day's grime tonight. The lavender and mint scent relaxed both of us nicely. And Cricket loved drinking out of the child-size teacup with ballerina slippers all over it that we found waiting for us in the kitchenette.

"When will Daddy and Mommy come home?" she asked as I set the empty cup aside.

That was a question I couldn't answer, but I could deflect. "We talked about Daddy earlier. He's going to call in two days. Remember?"

She shook her head and mumbled through a yawn, "I don't 'member. When will Mommy call?"

Anger, not at her but at the unfairness of it all, flared in me. I deflected that question by opening one of her favorite bedtime stories about a ballerina mouse. She was asleep by the fourth page.

"Is the alarm activated?" I asked the apartment.

It replied with the sound of chirping crickets.

"I'll be outside. Alert me there if she wakes, please."

Chirping again.

While we were eating pie, Maks, tonight's social director, had mentioned it was a beautiful night to sit outside. I agreed and found most of them gathered around the firepit.

"How is the lass?" Jett asked when I dropped into an empty Adirondack chair.

"The sachet and infusion worked perfectly." Feeling relaxed and ready for bed myself, I leaned my head back and looked up at the house. I swear I saw someone looking at us from one of the top windows. "Is someone in the attic?"

They all looked.

"Maybe Freddie or Granny Sadie," Comfort suggested.

Looked more like Gwynne to me. "Pepper, how did Gwynne really do at the saloon?"

"Okay overall." There was a bit of hesitation in her voice. "She does perfectly with her regular day-to-day routine. It's new situations when she gets a little unsettled."

"That can happen to anyone," Comfort defended, "at any age."

"By the time our food arrived," Pepper concluded, "she had forgotten our mission."

I took them all in with a pointed look. "I think that was true for all of you."

Honestly, I had gotten more accomplished with Carly in fifteen minutes than two days with this lot. But I did get to bounce some ideas off of Beau, which wouldn't have happened if we hadn't gone to the saloon, and the aunts got a night out.

Conversation drifted to more mundane things. Jett reported one of the goats had an infection in her eye, so Nash gave Jett an ointment to use on her. All the other animals "passed their inspections." Comfort hoped something chocolate would be on the menu tomorrow. Maks could finish his project now that he had screws. Pepper wondered how long it would take to ride a raft on the river down to her kids in New Orleans. They all took guesses.

"You look content, Dusty," Maks noted.

"I was thinking what a nice way this is to end the day." I gestured at the sky. "And I wish I had a camera that could capture all those stars."

"Camera," Comfort repeated as though that had reminded her of something.

We sat there for a little while longer, then I decided I was done for the day. The others agreed, so Jett reached to switch off the gas fire.

"Wait!" Comfort tapped her forehead with her fingers.

For a moment, I worried she was having a medical episode. "What's wrong? Are you okay?"

She swatted away my concern then blurted with relief, "The security system!"

"What security system?" Jett pulled her hand away from the off switch.

"At the diner," Comfort replied. "By the window between the kitchen and counter is that old ticket wheel hanging from the ceiling. We don't use the wheel anymore because orders come in on a computer screen, but we left the wheel as decoration. There are small cameras hidden in the ticket clips circling the wheel."

"When did that go in?" Maks asked.

Comfort blushed. "A couple years ago. Remember when there was that break-in at one of the mall stores?"

He agreed he did.

"I panicked," Comfort admitted, "and put in a system. Since it was a rush job, and the cameras are tiny, it cost a lot. Carly would've been furious at the price, so I never told her. Turned out we didn't even need it because there was never another break-in. After the first month, I stopped checking the recordings. I forgot it was even there."

"You have a security system," I concluded. "Which means there should be a video of who killed Ludo Beck."

MAKS HEADED OFF TO BED, and Jett said she'd sit with Cricket while Comfort and I went to the diner to watch the video from Thursday afternoon.

I followed her into her office, a closet-size room off the kitchen that contained an eight-foot-long counter with two three-drawer filing cabinets beneath it. The counter was covered in stacks of paper and supplies. The office manager in me cringed at the sight, and it took all my willpower to keep my itchy fingers from digging in and organizing the mess.

It was nearing midnight as Comfort excavated her laptop out from beneath the mess, figured out which icon was the right one, and brought up the recording from Thursday. I was running on fumes but perked up when an image of the dining room filled the screen.

"Let me see," she mumbled. "Mr. Beck was stabbed just after closing." She clicked ahead to the 1:50 mark.

"There he is." I pointed to where he sat on the first stool at the breakfast counter.

We watched while Gwynne came out and spoke to Beck. June was still working on her dishcloths, and the six customers Gwynne had mentioned were still at their tables but left a couple of minutes later. At two o'clock on the dot, Carly came out of the kitchen, said something to Beck, took an aggressive stance, pointed angrily at the door, and then went back into the kitchen. June loaded her needlework supplies into her big basket, then stepped into the retail area to straighten her inventory.

As Beck drank the last of his coffee, tipping his head back to get the last drop, someone wearing a baggy flannel shirt, dark gloves, and a Milwaukee Brewers baseball cap pulled low on his forehead entered the picture. We couldn't see his face because of how he wore that hat. He stood face to face with June and appeared to say something to her. She immediately snatched up her basket and raced out of the building. Then the man charged past Beck and appeared to be heading for the kitchen. First, he went behind the counter, rummaged around, and when he turned back he had the pie knife clutched in his hand. Beck went up to him—to stop him?—and the man stabbed him in the stomach, then left the building.

My thoughts shifted between *I knew she didn't do it* and *was he really going to enter the kitchen?*

Comfort let out a sigh of relief and dabbed her eyes with the hem of her shirt.

"Why didn't June say anything?" I asked. "Beau talked to her."

"I did too. She says she doesn't remember anything other than being here."

"Did someone cast a memory spell on her?"

"That's possible. June isn't one to lie. Maybe it was the trauma of seeing this man come into the diner that way. I wonder what he said to her."

"Is it that, or is she too scared to say what she saw?"

Comfort considered this. "Despite her mild appearance, June doesn't back down from conflict. If she says she doesn't remember, I believe her."

I blew out a hard breath. "Okay, even though June may not remember anything, we can now prove Carly didn't stab Beck.

We need to make a copy of this video for Beau. Do you know how to do that?"

"I think so." She clicked a few buttons, and the screen went blank. "That wasn't me. What happened?"

When she tried to bring up Thursday's video again, I pointed out there were only two files—Friday's and today's. "Did you delete it?"

"No." Her eyes narrowed as she thought. "Oh. What time is it?" She uncovered a clock buried at the back of her desk. "It's after midnight."

When she didn't say more, I pressed, "Is that important?"

"I had the installer set the system to keep videos for two full days. That meant the one from Thursday would be available for Friday and Saturday."

"And now it's after midnight, so it's Sunday." I let my head drop back. "And you don't save them anywhere else?"

She shook her head. "The system already cost so much I didn't opt for cloud storage. On the bright side, we have proof she's innocent."

"We *had* proof. Beau isn't going to just take our word for it."

CHAPTER 16

*B*ack at the apartment, I found a small wobbly bedside table and a dim lamp next to my cot. A little reward for trying to prove Carly's innocence? Except I wasn't really any closer to doing that than I had been this morning.

"The clock is ticking," I murmured to myself. "The seventy-two hours are up tomorrow at two thirty. How am I going to make Beau believe the truth?"

Across the room, my new laptop binged. I opened it to find a message from . . . the computer? The property?

Spell him was written in the middle of the black screen.

"Spell him? As in cast another spell on Beau?"

Those two words disappeared, and *Yes* took their place.

I immediately felt uncomfortable with that option. Never mind the fact I was having a conversation with a laptop. "Not a good idea. His memories have been messed around with enough."

Although, in this case I wouldn't be altering anything, simply allowing him to know the truth. While we didn't see the killer's face on the video, Comfort and I saw that Carly did not stab Ludo Beck. She was one hundred percent innocent. Spelling

Beau to understand that . . . was implanting a memory and therefore playing with gray magic. I couldn't do it. There had to be another way.

The compass rose June Stanford cross stitched for me fell off the little table next to my cot, as though an invisible cat had pushed it overboard. I picked it up and put it back on the table. It was after one in the morning, and my granddaughter was an early riser. I needed to get some sleep, so I closed the laptop, turned off the light, and willed my brain to be quiet for a few hours.

I was almost asleep when a premonition hit me.

"Guilty!" A man in black judge's robes hammered his gavel on his desk.

Carly, wearing inmate orange with her hands cuffed behind her back, looked stunned and despondent.

A few feet away, her kids huddled together, sobbing. Sebastian reached for her as Alex held him back and the bailiff took her away.

My eyes flew open, and I sat up on the cot. Carly would go to prison for a murder she didn't commit if I didn't do something. I knew the truth and could come up with only one solution. I had to cast another spell on Beau.

I'd only get one shot at this, so I had to do it right. That meant going to the attic and looking in the Warren family grimoire for the right spell.

"I'm sorry, Beau," I whispered as I switched on the lamp. The compass rose was on the floor again. I put it back on the table. The compass immediately fell to the floor again. What was going on with this thing? And how did it even get here? Could have sworn I put it on a shelf in the closet.

I held the gift from June . . . who had been there. She'd looked the killer right in the face. The target of my spellcasting changed.

Grabbing my cell phone, figuring I'd need the flashlight app,

I asked the apartment to, "Activate the alarm, please. I'll be in the house."

It replied with chirping crickets.

I entered the house through the back door and turned on the flashlight. Lordy that was bright in the middle of the night. The house had changed the floor plan many times over the years. One of the iterations removed the staircase off the kitchen that went to the second floor. There only the one to the basement now. The stairs to the upper levels were by the front door.

I crept through the kitchen and family room to the front entry, jumping when I saw a shadowy shape move. Sure hoped it was a familiar. The second floor appeared to be the same. The room Carly and I shared was above the kitchen. I smiled as memories started to wiggle around my brain, but I pushed them away. Now wasn't the time for a trip to the past. I needed to do this quickly before either the aunts or Cricket woke up.

The door to the attic used to be across from this stairway. Saying a little prayer that I wouldn't find a bedroom and a sleeping aunt on the other side, I slowly opened the door. Another stairway. Thank heavens. It went straight up toward the back of the house, came to a landing, and then made a full turn back the other direction.

The attic was wide open, unfinished, and stuffed full. Old furniture, steamer trunks, dozens of cardboard boxes, holiday decorations . . . all the standard things Ordinaries would keep in their attics. Ours also included a huge grimoire and an altar.

From overhead, the house resembled a giant witch's knot, each arm of the knot squarely facing a cardinal direction. My family had always had a special connection to the earth. Not that air, water, and fire weren't also important, but it was the earth, this parcel of land, that allowed us to be our true selves and kept us safe. Without it, we'd be exposed to countless dangers. Therefore, earth being the element of the north, our altar table sat beneath the window facing north. Our grimoire sat on a lectern a few feet away from the table. Despite its penchant for redecorating, the house would never move those two things. Now, to find north. Between the twisting staircase and the darkness, I'd gotten all turned around.

A shuffling sound came from somewhere nearby. Was someone up here? Freddie? Granny Sadie?

"Who's up here?" I whispered. "Gwynne?" I still thought it was her I saw in the window when I was out at the firepit earlier.

Straining my ears to hear the sound again, I nearly jumped out of my skin when something scurried across the floor in front of me. I shined my phone's light toward the thing and found a black squirrel sitting a couple feet away. She startled me at first, but she didn't seem at all scared of me. In fact, her innocent-as-can-be expression and calm demeanor settled my nerves. What a beautiful creature.

"How did you get in here?" Not that it mattered. In here she was.

She turned away from me, took a few steps, looked back, and repeated the process. Message received: *follow me.* As reliable as my GPS, she led me straight to the grimoire.

The aunts and other family members must have added more pages over the years. The sizable book was thicker than I remembered but just as beautiful. A witch's knot was carved into the leather cover and crystals had been affixed. I remembered Comfort explaining their purpose to Carly and me when we were old enough to view the grimoire.

"Black tourmaline and amethyst for protection. Hematite to absorb negative energy. Labradorite to enhance intuition. Moonstone for focus."

My favorite crystal adorned the center of the knot. The rainbow-colored *super seven* contained seven different types of quartz and helped open a connection with the divine.

"Now, how do I find a memory restoring spell?" It's not like the grimoire had a table of contents or index.

The squirrel chirped, and I swear it sounded like she said, *ask it*.

Okay. I laid my hand on the cover and felt a gentle vibration. It was reading me, making sure I was a Warren and therefore worthy. I held my breath, unsure of the *worthy* part, and exhaled when it allowed me to open the heavy cover and flip to somewhere near the middle.

"Please show me a spell to return a lost memory." Remembering Gwynne's words, *as you're aware, a spell is fifty percent intention*, I added, "I want to help June Stanford recover the memory of who killed Ludo Beck in order to prove Carly's innocence."

Seconds later, I took a step back when the pages began to flip so rapidly I worried they'd tear. It settled on a page conveniently titled "How to Restore Lost Memories." I tried to take a picture of the page, but the image came out black. Instead, I typed the ingredients and instructions into a note-taking app, vowing to delete the note when I was done casting. It had been many years since I'd purposely cast a spell, and knowing the importance of following the steps precisely, I triple checked what I'd typed.

According to the grimoire, I needed a white votive candle, rosemary and thyme herbs and essential oils, a sheet of paper, something to write with, a fireproof bowl, matches, and an item connected to the object of the spell. I had shoved June's compass into my pajama shorts pocket.

"Thank you," I whispered. "I promise my intentions are pure."

A nearby cabinet held candles and matches. I'd need to get everything else, plus a jar of plain white table salt, from the kitchen. As quietly as possible, I tiptoed back downstairs, collected the items, and went out onto the patio. Since I didn't have an altar table out here, I cast a circle around me using the salt and spread the tools across half of the circle. I knelt in the other half, pressed my open palms to the patio stones, and took a few deep, grounding breaths. Then I began.

After adding two drops each of the rosemary and thyme oils to the center of my palm, I anointed the votive and set it directly in front of me on the ground. Next I added one drop of each oil followed by a pinch of dried rosemary and thyme to the well surrounding the candle's wick. Then I lit the candle, asking Goddess Hecate—the goddess of magic, witchcraft, and the night—to illuminate my words and intent.

On the paper, I wrote my intent.

I cast this spell in order for Carly to be proven innocent of the murder of Ludo Beck and released from jail. I know that June Stanford saw the killer, but she cannot remember who the person is. The purpose of this spell is to allow June to recall the necessary details to set Carly free and give those details to Officer Beau Balinski.

Sure hoped I said it right and hadn't forgotten anything.

Holding the compass June gave me in my left hand, I read my intent out loud three times. Then, with June's face clear in my mind, I held the paper to the candle's flame and chanted, "Pen and paper, thyme and rosemary, may your memories return to thee."

I held the burning paper over the bowl until the heat nearly burned me, then I let it go. Instead of dropping into the bowl, the paper burst into embers no bigger than the grains of salt surrounding me. They rose into the air and floated off into the night. Hopefully directly to June.

"So mote it be." I winced, feeling a piercing pain in the center of my chest. My consequence for interfering with the path of June's life. Regardless of the purity of my intentions and the fact

I was truly restoring, not planting a memory, I'd interfered. Less than seventy-two hours after returning to Blackwood Grove, I'd performed a gray spell. The one thing I had vowed long ago to never do again. Please, Goddess, let it work.

The little black squirrel had followed me outside and chattered something that sounded like *good work*. She reached out a front paw and ran it through the salt, breaking the circle and closing my spell. It seemed, like the other witches did, I now had a familiar.

"Thank you for your help." I held my hand out to her and smiled when she placed her paw on it, slapping me a tiny high five. "You need a name." She sat back and waited while I went through a list of things that meant black. "Too obvious. Oh, I know. How about Pearl? As in Black Pearl."

I really loved those pirate movies.

She tilted her head one way, then the other, then place her paw on my hand again. We had a winner.

After cleaning up my tools, I returned the oils, herbs, and bowl to the kitchen. I would let the candle burn in a safe place in the apartment until it extinguished on its own. As I stepped outside again to go back to the apartment, I found Winnie Monroe waiting for me on the patio.

CHAPTER 17

From the disapproving look on her face, the witch obviously had words for me.

"Something I can help you with, Winnie?"

"You performed a gray spell."

What business was that of hers? And why was she awake at three in the morning? "Were you standing there watching me the whole time? Because if you were, you heard my intent."

She backed down a little. "I did hear you."

"Then you should know that we're out of options. In less than twelve hours, Carly will be accused of a murder she didn't commit. I found the necessary proof to clear her, but Comfort had the security videos set to delete after only two days." I shook my head in frustration. I scolded her over that, and she immediately changed the setting from two days to one week. "June was there, she saw the killer. Looked him right in the face. I'm not asking that she lie. I simply restored her memory."

Why was I justifying my actions to this woman?

"You haven't performed a gray spell in thirty-two years. This could go horribly—"

"Hang on." I held out my hands, silencing her. "How do you know that?"

She pulled what looked to be a thin wallet from the pocket of her crocheted bathrobe. From it, she took what looked like a credit card or driver's license. It was an ID card. "I'm a Council member."

My spine stiffened with shock. "You're here to spy on me?"

"Basically, yes." She shrugged as if this were no big deal.

"Did my father send you?"

"Only in that he is also a Council member. We need to know if we can trust you to honor the contract you signed. You and Cricket are, of course, welcome to stay here, but if caring for the witches and the town isn't something—"

"You don't think I can? Is that what this is about?"

She returned the card and wallet to her pocket. "You agreed to be your aunts' caretaker, but you've spent an awful lot of time away from the house."

"Because we . . . *I* need to prove Carly innocent of something she did not do because no one else seems capable of doing so." I ran my hands through my hair. "Look, what I know is that this family is stronger when we're all together. I don't know how Carly did all this on her own, but I see why I'm needed. *Can* one person handle the job? Sure, but it won't be done well. On top of everything else, I'm also trying to figure out where I belong in this equation." I flung a hand at the house. "Apparently not inside the home with my family, which is where I should be if I'm supposed to be aware of what they're up to." My voice broke, so I blew out a breath and blinked to staunch my threatening tears of frustration. "I love my family, Winnie. So much I left to keep them safe. I returned for the same reason, to keep Cricket safe. Do you see the pattern here? My family means everything to me. There's nothing I won't do for them."

Apparently including performing gray magic.

She waited until I was done speaking, then said, "I

understand your situation was a bit . . . murky when you left all those years ago, but you understand if you had returned your family wouldn't have been in any danger. Right?"

"Yes. I see that now."

"And if you would have talked to us instead of just leaving, we would have explained that."

I spoke through a clenched jaw. "The Council knew I was leaving and gave me two loans in three years. They never asked why. But my father, a Council member as you pointed out, knew why I left. *He* could have explained things to me."

That shut her down.

"Winnie, I don't commit lightly and deserve more than three days to prove I'm capable of doing what I said I would do."

"Yes, but technically you didn't see the fine print until after you'd signed the contract."

"Which is part of the reason I've wondered if I made the right decision." Why did I suddenly feel like I might have been conned? I glared at her. "What's your conclusion? Are you going to go before The Council tomorrow and report that someone else needs to take my place?"

After a pause, she admitted, "No. We . . . *I* believe you are the best person for this."

I couldn't decide if that comforted me or added more stress. "What's really going on here? I heard what you said a minute ago, about me caring for the witches *and* the town. There was nothing about the town in that contract. Or was there more fine print I didn't see?"

She stepped closer to me and spoke softly. "I think you've already sensed it, and your instincts are correct. There is something going on in this town, but we're not sure what yet."

"I have noticed things but dismissed a lot of it as the town having changed over the years. You're saying this *something* has to do with the witches?"

After a very long pause, she gave a single nod. "As the saying goes, everything old is new again. Even backward thinking and hateful beliefs."

Tingly gooseflesh covered my body as her meaning sank in. "You think someone wants to harm the witches here."

"And elsewhere. Maybe. Like I said, we're not sure what they're up to yet. There are only quiet rumors at the moment. There could be a group of folks getting ready to act, or simply one unhappy someone with hurt feelings. We're hoping it's the latter. Either way, Blackwood Grove was the first safe town. If it falls—"

Oh, dear goddess. "The others will go down like dominoes."

She locked eyes with me. "*That* is what we're afraid of. The fallout would be catastrophic for witches everywhere."

Banishment. Dunking. Burning at the stake. All those horrors we thought were long gone.

Everything old is new again.

I looked at the main house, across the courtyard to Apple Blossom Cottage, at the shadowy shapes that made up the rest of Applewood Farm, and then out toward my town. Maybe it was because I was a kid the last time I lived here, and kids don't usually pay attention to much going on outside their personal spheres, but something *was* different now. Something dark had moved in. We tended to not notice changes when they happened slowly. Did the witches and Ordinaries who lived here see it too?

"I can do this, Winnie. I can care for my aunts if that's what they need. I can't tell for sure, but at times, I feel like they're on their best behavior the moment I walk in the door."

"That may be," the Council witch suggested, "because they're afraid you'll leave again if you see the problems. They love you, Dusty."

My hand went to my heart. "I understand that leaving wasn't necessary, but I learned things. Like how to fight for myself and my family even when my family was just me and my son. That *can* extend to fighting for the town, too, but one thing at a time. The aunties come first. In order to do what you've asked me to do, I need the right tools. That means my cousin out of jail and a place inside that house. Not sure who you need to talk to about that last part."

Winnie clapped her hands softly. "Brava, Dusty. I hope you understand why we had to do it this way. I could tell from the start that you're capable, but I had to know that you're fully invested. If I had told you what I was really doing here, you would have been on *your* best behavior. Surely you can see that this is too important for anything less than absolute certainty."

"I do." My anger and irritation cooled. "You'll keep me in the loop. That's a demand, not a question."

"A fair one. I can't promise anything, but I will do what I can." She turned to go back inside. "For the record, there's no need to worry that other visiting witches are on a secret mission for The Council. As far as I know, anyone else will just be visiting."

As far as she knew. "Good. I'm already paranoid with the property watching every move I make."

After Winnie went inside, I picked up the still burning votive candle and turned to go back to the apartment. I jumped to find Granny Sadie standing there. "Did you hear all of that?"

She smiled sadly while nodding her head, then placed her fingers to her lips, blew me a kiss, and vanished.

I must have said the right things to Winnie because when I got back to my bedroom, an actual bed was waiting for me with the covers folded back, beckoning me to climb in. It was only a twin-size but a vast improvement over the cot.

CHAPTER 18

I honestly couldn't say when the last time was that I slept well. Between worrying about Micah as a teenager, which flowed into perimenopausal night sweats, and now worrying about Cricket's safety *and* being scared for Micah and Josie, if I got a couple of sound hours every night, I considered that a win. There was also Carly and the aunts to add to my worry list now. The night sweats were still a thing too. Even though I can't say that I slept more soundly, I was grateful for the new bed. At least I was comfortable while tossing and turning.

Cricket was awake and wanting pancakes at six o'clock. Three hours would have to do. I convinced her to play in her room while I took a shower, and the apartment agreed to keep her in there. At least I didn't have to worry about her wandering away while I had shampoo in my hair.

"Good morning, you two," Gwynne greeted when we entered the kitchen.

"I bet I know what you want, little one." Pepper presented Cricket with a plate of pancakes hot off the griddle.

"Yummy!" Cricket darted over to her favorite spot at the

table and waited patiently while Pepper cut the cakes into bite-size pieces. She didn't even notice there weren't chocolate chips today.

I got her a glass of milk and half a banana, then settled in with a bowl of yogurt and berries with a drizzle of honey.

"You look tired, Dusty," Jett noted.

"Did Comfort fill you all in on the security video situation?" She hadn't, so I did. When Jett, reminding me of a Scottish mob enforcer, said we needed to go over to June's house and do whatever was necessary to get her to remember who the killer was, I almost told them about the spell I cast.

Fortunately, Winnie came upstairs with her packed bags and distracted them. Today she wore a long crocheted necklace that resembled tiny red berries on a green vine and tiny matching red berry clusters at her ears. She definitely had her own style. "Good morning, everyone."

"Time to head out?" Gwynne asked.

"It's time." Her gaze paused on me for a moment. "I'm ready to continue on my way."

"Where's your next stop?" I asked.

"The next safe town is this side of St. Cloud, Minnesota. I should be able to make it that far today. That's partly why I decided to get up and out early."

"Would you like breakfast before you go?" Pepper asked.

"I'd love to take something with me," Winnie said. "A big coffee and something like a breakfast burrito?"

Minutes later, Winnie had both in hand and was thanking the aunts for their hospitality. "You have a beautiful home in a very pretty little town. Maybe I'll stop by again in a few weeks on my way back home."

"We'd be happy to have you," Gwynne assured and then went off to get The Apple Barn ready to open. Jett took Cricket to gather morning eggs. I wandered around the house, willing Beau to call and let us know Carly was free to leave.

"You're pacing," Pepper noted while washing dishes even though the house could do it and there was a dishwasher.

"I did something last night." I confessed my middle of the night spellcasting.

"Rosemary and thyme." She nodded her approval. "You had an item that connected you to June?"

I pulled the compass out of my jeans pocket. "Did I do something wrong? Why haven't we heard from Beau yet?" I sounded like a teenager waiting for the boy she liked to call. "Should I have burned the compass along with the note? The grimoire only said to hold it."

Pepper caught and held my eye, settling me. "I can only speak to regular spells but assume the same is true for the gray ones. You should follow the instructions exactly. If it says hold it, hold it. If it wanted you to burn it, you would have been instructed to do so. Any deviation will create an entirely different result."

"Okay, good." I sighed with relief. "While I'm waiting for Beau, can I help you with anything?"

The kitchen was absolutely spotless. Not a utensil out of place nor a crumb on the counter or floor. Honestly, it was like she hadn't even cooked.

She shook her head. "Why don't you go work in the garden? It's a beautiful morning. Get outside and enjoy this weather. It's nearly Labor Day, and then Mabon will be here with the autumn chill before we know it." She paused as though needing to gather her thoughts. "Jett will need your help in the orchard by then. Next will be Samhain and the Harvest Fest."

What did Pepper do all day? She mentioned blending spices for the shop, but she couldn't do that all day every day. I usually ate and ran off like the others. The rest of us were surrounded by people all day. Even Jett had the farmhands around her. Pepper was alone in this big house until Jett came in for lunch and the others got home at dinnertime. Then we all scattered again for the night.

"Think I'll have another cup of coffee first." I went to the coffee and tea station at the end of the counter closest to the stairs. "I was up late, and Cricket was up early. Care to join me?"

She seemed to like that idea.

We chatted about her plans for the day—more recipes in a jar to make for The Apple Barn, and she'd tidy the guestroom now that Winnie had left. I was about to ask her to tell me about Silver Moon Apothecary when the phone rang.

She pointed. "I bet that's your officer."

The caller ID read Blackwood Grove PD.

"Is this Dusty?" the voice sounded like him.

"Beau?" My heart was in my throat waiting to hear if my spell worked.

"We've had a development in the case." He explained how June Stanford had showed up at the station early that morning. She'd insisted on talking only to Beau and waited patiently for nearly an hour for him to get there. "Anyway, all of that to let you know June identified the killer. Or rather, she assured me it was a man and absolutely not Carly. She offered to hand over her craft basket as proof of her honesty."

"Can't get proof more solid than that. Carly can leave, then?"

"She's free to go and would like you to come get her."

Uh-oh. "She specified me?"

"Yep."

"Am I in trouble?"

"Maybe. Be prepared, I guess."

"I'll be right there."

Pepper agreed, happily, to watch Cricket once she'd collected the eggs. She even insisted I take my time coming home. Was that so Carly and I could have a bit of time together, or was she bored and wanted to have Cricket around? Either way, I headed to the jail and found Beau had waited until I got there to formally release Carly.

"All charges are dropped," he said, handing her a bag with her personal items and paperwork of some variety, "but please stay in town until the case is concluded."

Carly fixed an unamused stare on him. "And here I was planning to skip off to Fiji tonight." She walked past me with her bag of possessions in hand. "Come on."

I followed her out to the parking lot, where she paused and sighed. "Which car is yours?"

"The teal-blue hatchback." We got in, and I pulled to the parking lot exit. "Anywhere you want me to go?"

She pointed left, away from the house. "There's a pull-off next to the river up ahead. Go there."

The spot she meant was a half mile away and offered a nice view of the Mississippi. I turned off the engine and waited.

"Catch me up," she ordered, cold anger radiating from her. "Beau filled me in at the end of every day with what he'd learned, which hasn't been much. As of lights-out last night, he didn't have a clue how to clear me. I assumed I was doomed. Then this morning, June Stanford shows up with a clear memory. June's memory hasn't been clear in years. The only thing I could figure was that a witch did something. What do you know?"

While she stared daggers at me, I explained what Comfort and I saw on the security video. "And then it deleted at midnight."

Carly threw her hands in the air, nearly catching me in the jaw with her left. "I told her we didn't need a security system. I can only imagine how much she spent if she was afraid to tell me."

I blinked at her then said, "Good thing she got one, though, hey?"

She grunted something that might have been an agreement. "You said the video showed June and the killer?"

"They literally stared each other in the face."

"Did you somehow retrieve the deleted file?"

"No, but we both saw the same thing. Then I had a premonition."

She turned in her seat to face me but said nothing.

"I saw your sentencing. You were found guilty, and your kids were devastated. Especially Sebastian."

With a little less bite in her voice, she asked, "And then what happened? Did you tell Beau what you saw? Was that good enough? How does June coming in this morning play into this?"

I looked her in the eye, wanting her to understand what I'd done *for her.* "I cast a spell."

Carly listened slack jawed as I gave her the details. "You swore you'd never cast another gray spell."

I snorted softly. "I haven't cast *any* spells since that one."

"I don't know what to say." Her face had softened, and more of her anger faded.

"If it makes you feel better, it was partly selfish. I had to get you out." I told her about the contract I signed with The Council. "It'll probably get easier, but I don't think I can do this by myself."

"Unbelievable." Her anger was back. She shook her head as though disgusted. With me?

"I can only guess at what you've had to do," I began, but she cut me off.

"Bring me home now. I need to see my kids and call my husband. And take a shower."

With that, we were done talking. She was still mad at me and likely would be for a while. But whatever I needed to do to make up for hurting her so badly, I'd do it.

CHAPTER 19

*a*fter dropping Carly at her house, I went back to the farm, made sure Pepper was still okay watching Cricket—she was—and decided to burn off energy by pulling weeds. Getting Carly out of jail was just the first step. There was still the matter of catching the killer. This was personal. A man had been murdered in our town. Inside *our* diner. The residents were understandably scared because Beau didn't have any answers for them. The aunts were acting tough, but they had to be scared as well. I was.

Other than offering proof Carly hadn't stabbed Beck, there was one thing from that video I couldn't get out of my mind. It was right after June left. The man had charged past Beck and went behind the counter to get the pie knife. To me, it looked for a moment like he was going into the kitchen. Was this man in the Brewers hat and flannel shirt really there for Beck, or had one of the aunts been his target? Were they truly safe?

At five o'clock, I took a long hot shower to remove the dirt that had gotten everywhere, and then Cricket and I went over to join the aunts for dinner. The moment we entered the kitchen, they pounced.

"How did you get her out?" Comfort wanted to know, wrapping me in a grateful hug.

"I'm starving," I told her. "Let's start eating, and I'll tell you everything once I have a few bites in my stomach. What's on the menu tonight, Pepper?"

"Her famous jambalaya," Maks reported, rubbing his hands together greedily. "We're celebrating."

Again, if they were scared, they were hiding it well.

Pepper went to the stove to retrieve a big pan filled with chicken, shrimp, andouille sausage, vegetables, rice, and a savory sauce. I took a small spoonful from the pan. As I feared, the jambalaya was too spicy for Cricket. I wasn't going to let her taste it, but when I said, "I don't think you'll like this," she insisted on a bite.

She swallowed one tiny mouthful, then wiped her tongue with her napkin. "It's too hot."

"I told you. Drink some milk." Once she'd downed almost half a glass, I asked, "What would you like instead?"

"Scrambled eggs," she announced. "With monster cheese, toast, and applesauce."

Monster? "Do you mean muenster cheese? How do you know about that?"

"Alex gave me some when I was at their house."

A plate of steaming, perfectly prepared eggs with a slice of toast and a small cup of applesauce appeared before her.

"Grape jelly on the toast, please," she added, and it appeared a second later. "Thank you."

For a child who had never seen a lick of magic until three days ago, she had adapted remarkably well.

While we ate, I told the aunts and Maks everything I knew. They all praised Comfort for remembering the security system and me for noticing the killer had looked June in the face. No one asked how exactly June got her memory back, but I was pretty sure they knew. Since none of us had any more details about either Beck's murder or his somewhat sketchy plan to open a grocery store, we talked about their days instead.

Comfort reported there were some looky-loos coming in to see where the murder had happened. "One woman claimed to be a psychic but stood at the opposite end of the counter and insisted that was where the body was found even after I said I'd been there at the time. The residents are getting a bit annoyed with this. Saying people are treating Blackwood Grove like a roadside attraction."

"It'll settle down," I promised, although I couldn't know that. We needed to find the killer. Once he was locked up, things would return to normal. I hoped.

Jett was pleased to see that this year's apple crop looked to be coming along nicely. Gwynne said that was good news because she was starting to run low on all of her apple products, especially apple butter and the frozen pre-sliced pre-seasoned apple pie filling.

Pepper and Cricket told us about their day together. Pepper taught her how to assemble recipes in a jar, read to her, took her for a walk along the river, and let her help make dinner.

"Best day I've had in a while, but that little one wore me out," Pepper said, then her smile faded.

The others worked outside the house. We needed to find something to give more purpose to Pepper's days. Maybe one of the businesses needed help in the form of a volunteer.

After dinner, Cricket and I convinced Pepper to play Hi Ho Cherry O and Candy Land with us at the kitchen table. Then it was Cricket's bath and story time. She insisted she wasn't tired, but she was once again overtired. The lavender-mint infusion and a story put her right to sleep.

I activated the cricket alarm and sat downstairs on the carriage house's patio to take in the night. I'd been there for about ten minutes when someone plunked a bottle of wine and two glasses on the small table next to me.

"We need to talk," Carly announced. She looked much better than she had a few hours ago. Resting, reconnecting with her kids, and washing off the jail grime appeared to have a positive effect on her. "But first, Emma tells me there's a little person upstairs."

My heart clenched with happiness. Finally, I got to show her my little bug. I'd thought dozens of times about calling her over the years, especially after Micah and then Cricket were born, but I was terrified to bring a curse down on her.

I led her upstairs, quietly opened the door to her bedroom, and whispered, "Her name is Alice, but we call her Cricket because she's always chirping about something. She's four years old, loves ballerinas, and anything purple."

Carly smiled. "She's beautiful."

We stood there for another few seconds, watching the little sleeping bug, and then backed out.

"Do you have anything to eat that will go with Riesling?" Carly asked.

"Not sure, let me check." I opened the small refrigerator and found a peach cobbler inside. Perfect. Back down on the patio, she poured while I dished up the cobbler.

"All right," she began after a bite and sip, "tell me where you've been and what your life has been like. Don't leave out any details or worry about the time. If we're here until dawn, so be it. The diner is closed on Mondays, so I don't have to work tomorrow. For the record, I'm still mad at you, but I'm hoping that hearing your story will help."

She didn't say a word, just let me talk. I told her about the mysterious someone who threatened to make life miserable for the family if I didn't leave when I was eighteen. And that after the altercation with Henry at The Paddle Wheel last night, I now believed that person was Marilyn. I explained how The Council gave me a loan for college, about my bigamist fake husband, and the joy and terror of learning I was pregnant with

Micah. The second Council loan. My success at being an office manager. The horror of learning Josie was missing and watching my son get led away for either her murder or kidnapping.

"And then minutes after I get here, you're hauled away for murder. Honestly, I was sure it was because I had returned and brought a curse with me."

"Why *did* you return? Pretty sure it wasn't to become a co-caretaker." There was no anger in the question this time.

"Oh yeah, I didn't tell you that part. I lost my job Wednesday morning, my house burned to the ground Wednesday night, and I found a note on the windshield of my car that said *Her mother was first. Then her father. It would be a shame if she lost her entire family. Then who would take care of her?*"

Her mouth dropped open. "Someone threatened Cricket?"

I took a long, fortifying sip of my Riesling. "Don't know which other *her* or *she* they could mean. I wasn't about to take a chance, so we holed up in a hotel Wednesday night, and when I couldn't come up with a single solid idea for how to keep her safe, I contacted Dad."

"And instead of simply helping you, they made you sign a contract?" Her anger returned but was directed at The Council this time. "You know you could have come home."

My face heated with a blush, or maybe it was the wine. "I understand that now, but all this time I truly didn't think I could. Marilyn, or whoever, made me believe something terrible would happen to the family."

"Something terrible did happen." Her voice shook slightly. "We thought you were dead. Why didn't Jasper tell us where you were?"

"I have no idea."

"Did Griselle know?"

"I assume so, but I never heard from Mom. Not once. Where

is she anyway? I've been here for three days and haven't seen so much as her shoes by the door."

"She comes and goes. No idea where." Carly tilted her head, pondering. "I stop by here every day, and it's been a while since I've seen her."

I added another scoop of cobbler to my bowl. "Guess I shouldn't be surprised. Mom straddled the parenting line my entire life. Dad too. I practically raised myself."

"Not true. I know it felt that way, especially after Brenda left, but you had a houseful of people, along with the house itself, happy to tell you what to do."

I gave her a grateful smile. "I can't tell you how good it feels to talk with someone again who knows my backstory."

We sat quietly for a minute, then Carly said, "A couple of years ago, when the aunts' magic started going kerflooey, they asked me to sign a contract too. In exchange for being their caretaker, the kids' post-high school education would be covered. We do okay, but putting four of them through college or vocational school or whatever they choose will be a lot. So I agreed. But four kids, our house, the diner, and the farm on top of the aunts? Trust me when I say, I fully understand 'don't think I can do this by myself' because I've lived it for years. I finally pitched a fit and threatened to let the aunts run wild if they didn't get me some help."

She was right. She'd watched over this place while also running the rest of her life, and here I was whining after a couple of days. "What, in your experience, does their magic going 'kerflooey' mean?"

She ticked things off on her fingers. "Pepper set the kitchen on fire when she flambéed bananas foster one night without a torch." She wiggled her fingers, which told me all I needed to know about how she started the fire. "Jett attempted to fix the goat pen with a sticking spell rather than a hammer and nails, which was less her magic being off and more that her body is wearing down from the physical labor of farming. Still, the goats got loose and treated the flower beds in the mall park like a salad bar. Gwynne tried to magic the sign onto the side of The Apple Barn. Every farmer in a ten-mile radius ended up with our logo painted on their barns."

I told her about how with a point of her finger Gwynne messed up the retail area in the diner and the stack of shirts in the shop. "She blamed it on arthritis. That's all I've seen so far. Of course, the property is making me stay in the cottage, so I don't really know what's going on with them." I suddenly felt like I might cry. "I'm sorry, Carly. For leaving that way and never getting in touch. It was torturous for me being alone and away from you all, but I honestly thought I was doing the right thing."

How many times had I said that since I arrived? Did anyone believe me yet?

As though offering a verbal olive branch, Carly said, "We all know that gray spells come with consequences, so I understand why the power scares you. Your mother has paid dearly. The evidence of every gray spell she's ever cast is written all over her." She paused then said, "Maybe everything that happened to you after the accident was your consequence for casting a gray spell."

Ten lives altered, ten consequences? "I'd rather take on a few wrinkles or another ache. Those are coming no matter what I do." We both gave irritated chuckles at that. "Has Gwynne interfered with people's lives? She told me about selling spells to the Ordies, and I was sure I saw her go out to the gate the other night. A spell doesn't have to be a gray one to qualify for interference. Are these episodes she's been having consequences for her?"

Carly paused before saying, "Hadn't considered that. She also *really* misses Filip, so it could simply be grief. Not that grief is ever simple."

I felt an odd combination of gratitude and envy that I would never miss a partner that much.

"Enough talking about me," I declared. "Tell me about you."

"Not a whole lot to tell. After you left, I went to college as planned but couldn't do it. There was no way I could move forward with our plans without you."

I winced and whispered, "Sorry."

She shrugged, but I saw her disappointment. Still there all these years later. "Granny Sadie was slowing down then, so Mom needed help at the diner. I dropped out, moved back home, and planned to go back to school, because the diner was never my thing. A few years later, Marilyn Kramer decided to turn 'The Blackwood Grove Mall' into something big, which meant business was picking up. So I stayed.

"I met Kyle, my husband, at The Paddle Wheel one Friday night. He was there again on Saturday, so I told him I'd dance with him if he bought me a beer. He was in town for the summer, helping one of the farmers, so we hung out a lot. When not on the farm, he worked on getting his commercial driver's license." She smiled. The only moment of warmth thus far in her business-like recitation. "He said life on the road sounded like a good one to him. He left after Labor Day, and around the beginning of October I realized I was pregnant."

"The two of you must have stayed in touch. Obviously. You're married."

"He promised to stop by and see me whenever he was in the area. It was February, and I was huge when he finally did. He asked me to marry him, and I told him he didn't need to be chivalrous. The baby and I would be fine on our own. The aunts and Granny were thrilled to have a little one around and started making babysitting schedules as soon as I told them."

Micah missed out on so much. I should have returned sooner. "They're really good with Cricket. You taught them well."

Carly inclined her head in a bow of thanks.

"How'd you two finally end up together?"

"Kyle stopped by again in late June to meet Nina. He called regularly during that stretch and said even though his job kept him on the road, he wanted to be involved with his kid. He saved up, bought his own rig, and took jobs that kept him as close to Wisconsin as possible, which meant he could stop by more often. Nina was about a year old when he asked me to marry him again. He was honest and said he wouldn't stop driving so I'd be home alone a lot. I said that suited me fine, and it does. It hasn't always been easy, but I've always had help. I talked to him after you dropped me off at home earlier. He'll be home soon, so you can meet him." She fanned herself with her hand.

"You seem excited about that," I teased.

She fanned herself harder. "Just a little."

"You really like this lifestyle."

She shrugged. "I do. The kids miss him when he's gone, but they're used to it. And right about the time he starts getting on my nerves, it's time for him to hit the road again. Retirement will be a challenge." After another pause in the conversation, "I said we could talk until dawn, but I think I'm ready to call it. Sleeping in my own bed tonight will be a blessing."

"I agree." Sad as that made me. She was just starting to warm up.

She scooted to the edge of her chair. "I overheard some of the officers talking about investigating Beck's death. Sounds like they're searching hard but aren't finding anything."

"It doesn't make sense." I flung a hand toward the mall. "Those three blocks were loaded with shoppers and people hanging out in the park when I got here on Thursday. Beau says the shop owners are being shut-mouthed and no one has come forward even anonymously with information."

"They're either afraid or are purposely covering something up."

"That's what I think too."

Carly leaned back in her chair again. "What if the killer is still wandering around Blackwood Grove? What if he's one of us?"

"If folks are afraid and won't talk to Beau or the other officers, they might talk to us. Could be worth a try."

She blew out a breath. "I can walk around with you tomorrow since the diner is closed. I think Emma is free, so she can take Cricket for the day. I need to be at the diner on Tuesday, though. Mom is pretty tough, but sometimes it's an act. She can't handle running the kitchen by herself anymore."

"I understand exactly."

She pushed herself up to standing then. "Okay, we'll see you in the morning."

Warmth spread through my chest. "The Warren girls, at it again." It's what people always said when they saw us together around town.

Carly paused. "Your last name is now Hotte?"

I nodded. "Has been for twenty-five years. I thought about changing it when I found out my *husband* was a bigamist but didn't feel like doing the paperwork."

A tiny smile turned her mouth, and she jerked her thumb at herself. "Flasch."

"What?"

"I've been Carly Flasch for nineteen years."

"So together we're a Hotte Flasch?"

We laughed loudly enough that one of the goats across the yard bleated in response. Which made us laugh louder. But the smile on Carly's face didn't quite reach her eyes. She was trying to forgive me, and I'd give her all the time she needed. Maybe if . . . no. Maybe *when* I caught the killer, she finally would.

CHAPTER 20

*C*arly and Emma met us as planned in the main house kitchen for breakfast. Comfort and Maks had gone to Carly's house yesterday afternoon, but the others hadn't seen her yet. Gwynne, Pepper, Jett, and the ghosts were so thrilled to see Carly, it was like she'd been released after serving a ten-year sentence rather than not quite seventy-two hours. I understood, though. There was a fear factor that they might not see her outside of prison again as well as the anger factor over her being accused of something she hadn't done.

We all chatted over a buffet breakfast of scrambled eggs, muffins, fruit, yogurt, and plenty of coffee. Cricket was thrilled to see Emma first thing in the morning and listed all the things they would do that day.

"First we have to get the eggs," she began like a pint-size event planner. "Then we're gonna color lots of pictures and go to the park and play games . . ."

Emma nodded enthusiastically, her bright eyes never leaving Cricket's excited face.

"Has she always been this good with little ones?" I asked Carly.

"She was always the most popular one on the playground," Carly recalled. "This side of her emerged a year or so ago. Before that, she was very much like Sebastian, quiet and moody. Not sure what happened, but one day she decided she liked little kids better than kids her age."

"There are days I feel the same way," I admitted.

After breakfast, Jett went off to tend the animals and gardens. Emma and Cricket followed, egg basket in hand. Gwynne went off to do something in The Apple Barn, and Comfort was going to take care of paperwork at the diner.

"Okay," Carly began, "should we go talk to people?"

Pepper wandered over to where we sat at the kitchen table. "What's going on, girls?"

I explained how the shop owners weren't talking to Beau. "We're not sure if they're afraid for some reason or covering up something, but we're hoping they'll talk to us. Want to help us make a plan?"

Pepper's eyes lit up. "Sure. Let me get some tea."

At Carly's questioning look, I said, "I think she's a little bored and a lot lonely. Plus, she might have some ideas for us."

"What do you already know?" Pepper asked, taking the chair next to Carly.

Carly deferred to me. "Dusty knows more than I do."

"We know that Beck wanted to open a specialty grocery store in the mall. Even though the building across from Silver Moon Apothecary is empty and available, Beck had been pressuring other shop owners to sell their buildings to him."

Pepper shook her head. "Not sell. It would be that he wanted them to move out so he could move in. Marilyn Kramer has been buying up those buildings for years."

"Right," Carly agreed. "Good point, Pepper."

"She owns all of the buildings?" I asked.

"Except for the diner and the apothecary," Pepper clarified.

"Marilyn tried to buy the diner from us," Carly recalled.

"That was a few years ago. She wants to expand the mall, but to fully realize her vision, she needs all the houses on the next block to the north."

"It's all or nothing," Pepper said, "and few of those people are interested in moving."

I pictured the town's layout. "She can't go south because of the river. The Mercantile is to the east, and they'll never sell. Applewood Farm is to the west, and we'll never sell. She's landlocked."

"And greedy," Pepper said. "She has enough and needs to stop now."

I brought us back to the murder. "Beck was mostly interested in the buildings on the Mississippi side of the mall. The diner in particular. Carly and I think it's because of the easy access to the river."

We explained our theory to Pepper, and she was simultaneously repulsed and oddly excited by the idea of illegal activity in our little town.

Carly smiled, amused by the elder witch. "Our goal today is to find out who was angry enough to stab Ludo Beck."

"The shops are closed today," Pepper mused, "but many of the owners catch up on office work on Mondays. Like Comfort does."

"Want to come do some investigating with us?" I asked her.

She thought about it and decided, "I don't think I'll go everywhere with you, but I have been meaning to stop in at the apothecary and chat with Silver and Moon."

Carly patted Pepper's hand. "You know the apothecary is literally on the other side of the hedge."

"I do. I can see it from my bedroom window."

"You also know," Carly continued, "that Silver and Moon adore you. They wouldn't mind if you stopped in every day."

The light in Pepper's eyes dimmed a bit. "I don't want to be a bother."

I hated she thought that way. "Oh, please. No one would ever think you were a bother."

We waited while she went to put on better shoes and grab her purse.

"It takes her forever to go up those stairs," Carly whispered. "I was thinking about putting in one of those chairs that will give them a ride."

"Have you ever seen one of those things in operation? They move so slow it'll take her even longer. Maybe the house can put in an elevator."

Carly approved of this idea and pointed toward the front of the house. "There's room in the formal dining room, which we never use. If we put one there, it would open right into the second-floor hallway." She told the house to, "Consider that, please."

The lights dimmed in reply.

"Okay, I'm ready." Pepper had added earrings to her ensemble.

"Are those voodoo dolls?" I stepped closer, squinted, then pulled my glasses off the top of my head to get a better look.

"My granddaughter-in-law sent them to me. I told you they live in New Orleans, didn't I? Aren't they cute?"

They had tiny pins sticking out of their heads and chests, and their little mouths appeared to be stitched shut. "You did and they are."

The closer we got to the apothecary, the more excited Pepper became. She talked about the new line of skincare products they'd recently started selling. "The girls learned how to make them from a witch up north. Morgan in someplace called Whispering Pines. I want to try some of their lotion. My hands get so dry."

As we approached the small shop that was both charming and a little eerie, Carly grew quiet. She'd told me this should have been our place. I was eager to see it.

Inside, I couldn't decide where to look first. The wall to the right of the front door was covered with various sizes of triangular shelves that held a rainbow of crystals and stones. The wall to the left was lined with freestanding wooden bookshelves which displayed bottles of dried herbs and flowers. Then there were the walls themselves. They were a shimmery silver color, and enchanted so it looked like fog or mist swirled beneath the surface.

Scattered randomly through the center of the shop, tables of different shapes and sizes were piled high with merchandise. In the back left corner, a table with two chairs was set up for tarot readings. In the right corner, a sign hanging above a curtained door announced acupuncture services. A stairway in the middle of the store directly across from the front entrance led to a narrow second-floor loft. The loft was lined with bookshelves, and ornate wingback chairs at either end beckoned customers to come up and read.

As I took in the loft, I couldn't help but be mesmerized by the ceiling. It was a deep purple-blue hue painted to look like the night sky. Then I realized it was moving. They hadn't merely painted stars, but whole constellations, and like the walls, they'd enchanted it. As the stars slid across the sky, the moon slowly shifted through its phases from new to waxing crescent to full to waning crescent.

Finally, near the checkout counter, which stood in front of the acupuncture door, was a glass case loaded with skulls, voodoo dolls, small skeletons with painted faces, chicken feet, beads, feathers . . .

"They say that's an homage to Pepper's voodoo side," Carly explained and pointed to the two young women who owned the store. Silver, who currently had Pepper locked in a hug, had dark skin and dreadlocks that hung nearly to her waist. Moon had ivory skin and dozens of braids pulled up into a high ponytail.

Both were in their twenties and dressed in flowy, colorful, bohemian-hippie clothes. Silver wore a long dress and about a dozen necklaces in various lengths. Moon wore palazzo pants, a tank top, and a single scarf that encircled her throat like a turtleneck. Both were barefoot.

"Look at them," I said with a sigh. "We were never close to that cool."

"True," Carly agreed, "but this could still have been our place."

"Is it too late?" I asked.

Before Carly could reply, Silver came over and introduced herself to me.

"I'm Dusty—"

Silver gasped and glanced at Carly. "Another Warren Witch. Oh my gosh, it's so awesome to meet you." She reached out and clasped my hand between both of hers. I couldn't help but notice the rings on every finger and badly chipped deep-blue nail polish. Somehow the less than perfect manicure worked for her.

"I'm Moon," the other young woman greeted. To Carly she said, "We heard you were free. Glad that got sorted."

"Me too," Carly replied with a laugh.

"That's kind of why we're here," I said. "Carly, obviously, isn't responsible for that man's death."

"And you want to know," Moon supplied, "if we know anything about it. I don't have a clue."

"Me neither," Silver agreed. "He wasn't super friendly, but I don't know why anyone would want to kill him."

"You interacted with him, then?" Carly asked.

"Once." Silver straightened her rings. "He wanted to buy the building."

Another shop on the river side of the mall.

"He didn't hound us or anything." Silver looked at Carly. "We heard he gave you a hard time."

"He did. I could definitely see him making someone mad enough to take a swing at him."

"What we can't figure out," I added, "is why they attacked him in the diner."

They shook their heads in unison. Silver looked genuinely sad. "Wish we could help you."

"Don't worry," Carly soothed. "We'll figure it out."

"Are you two on your way, then?" Pepper asked like we were pesky kids she wanted to be rid of.

"In a minute," I answered. "I'd like to look around."

With a big smile on her face, Moon asked, "Pepper, are you going to hang out with us for a while?"

"If I won't be in the way," she answered.

"In the way?" Silver's mouth hung open. "Never."

"We were actually talking about you the other day," Moon told her. "What would you think about working the tarot table now and then? Weekends, special occasions, major moon phases . . ."

"She gives amazing readings," Silver added.

I glanced over at the table. Three decks of tarot cards lay in the middle, waiting to do their jobs.

"Pick a card," Silver encouraged. "No charge."

I wanted to stay and explore everything, but we needed to move along. I could take time for one card, though. One deck was classic with drawings that made me think of King Arthur and his court. The second had modern renditions of the same drawings. The images on the third deck were done in soft watercolors. I chose the third deck.

"Keep it face down and give it a shuffle," Silver instructed. "Then fan the cards out across the table and pick one."

"Remember that the cards aren't magic." An almost mystical quality had come over Pepper. "They don't predict the future but are instead a tool for introspection. They offer help arriving at answers or making decisions about your life."

I could certainly use help with decision-making. I shuffled, fanned, and pulled a card that had an angel at the top who was looking down at a crowd of people. The people had their arms raised toward the angel in reverence.

Pepper moved closer to see. "Judgement. It signals an inner crossroads or awakening. Taking time to reflect on where you've been and where you're going will help you decide what you want to change in order to become your true self. This card also reminds you that the choices you've made in the past have affected the course of your life and that those choices may now be catching up with you."

I gave her a suspicious look. She knew my story. Silver handed me a thin book that explained the cards. The book agreed with Pepper.

Moon laid a hand on my shoulder. "Time to let go of the past so you can create a new present."

I felt spiritually ganged up on, but sometimes a hard shove worked better than a gentle nudge.

We said goodbye and told Pepper we'd see her at home later.

"You're looking a little stunned," Carly noted as we descended the porch steps.

"A little overwhelmed by magic, I guess."

"At least you're in the right place to deal with that." She stiffened when I didn't agree with her right away. "Aren't you?"

I put on a smile and assured her, "I'm not going anywhere, if that's what you're worried about." Especially not while Cricket was in potential danger. But if the danger followed me here . . . "We should move along. Who's next?"

CHAPTER 21

The building across from the apothecary was empty. We didn't need to stop at Tiny Togs because I'd already spoken with Miriam. We obviously didn't need to go to the diner. This left seventeen other stores. Nine of them were dark today. The owners either took Mondays off or were staying away because of the murder. Of the remaining eight, four owners insisted they didn't know anything before we'd finished saying what we were there for.

"Nothing suspicious about this at all," Carly muttered. "I understand if they're scared, but what could they be hiding?"

Stuart at the plant store, Earthly Delights, was happy to speak his mind.

"Yeah, I know the guy." He turned his collection of African violets, ensuring the opposite sides got time facing the window. "Kind of a pushy SOB."

"Was he trying to convince you to give him your store?" Carly asked.

Stuart stepped to his right to rearrange a display of pots. "Not this place. It's not good enough. He wanted one on the river side of the street. Your place in particular, Carly.

Personally, I didn't want the guy anywhere near me. It wouldn't have gone well." He paused and must have realized it sounded like he'd just made a threat against a man who had been murdered. "Obviously, it's horrible he was killed. I only meant if he had gotten a shop, I think he would have been constantly pushing the rules and making waves. He gave off that kind of vibe. Didn't you feel that?"

Carly agreed she did and after we left the plant shop explained, "Stuart is a total rule follower. Sort of has to be considering his profession. Plants have rules and won't bend to yours."

"Sounds like a quote."

"Something he told Nina. She brought home a sun-loving something-or-other but wanted to keep it in her bedroom window on the shady side of the house. Then she tried to blame Stuart for selling her a defective plant."

All of the stores in the mall used to be someone's home. Earthly Delights and Tiny Togs had been gutted to give a more open feel to the store. Waste Not Antiques used the individual rooms as staging areas for the old furniture and accessories. It sat on the river side of the mall, which meant Donna, the owner, had also heard from Beck.

"Oh, yes. He said the view of the river was exactly what he'd been hoping for. Serene and relaxing. Not sure what that has to do with selling groceries and kitchen equipment. I told him to take a hike. I mean, look at all this stuff." She swept a hand across the indeed packed store. "Moving and resetting everything would take months."

At Swank, the women's version of Tiny Togs two buildings closer to the diner, Celia echoed what the others had said. "Beck *really* wanted Comfort's Food because it faces the river, but after you and Comfort kicked him to the curb, he said this location would *suffice* for his vision. Not as well as the diner, mind you, but he could 'make it work.'" She looked offended. "All but used the term *sloppy seconds*. Way to woo me."

Grimoires & Gimlets was located across the park from the diner. It was literally half book store, half pub, and the vibe was fantastic. The walls in the book store half were painted a deep-forest-green color that made me want to curl up in a chair and read for hours. The bookshelves were all mismatched and filled with not only books but dried herb bundles, small crystal balls, scrying mirrors, small statuettes, gorgeous journals, and other ephemera for decorating.

On the pub side, light fixtures shaped like crescent moons and fifteen-point stars hung from the ceiling along with hundreds of lights that looked like Ping-Pong balls or tiny full moons. Pentacles were stained onto the wood floor throughout the building.

"This place is fantastic." Everywhere I looked, I saw something new.

"Isn't it?" Carly agreed. "People come from far away to shop here. And all the drinks are virgin, so it's family friendly."

We tracked down the owner, Tabitha, a pretty petite blond dressed like a nerdy librarian sorceress. "I heard what the others have said, but I think Ludo would have been a breath of fresh air. Far as I'm concerned, bend those rules right up to the breaking point if necessary. That leads to progress and positive changes."

"You mean Marilyn's rules," Carly interpreted.

Tabitha rolled her eyes. "You're lucky you own your building. Every time our lease renews, I ask her about a rent-to-own deal. Every time she refuses to discuss it. Fortunately, we've hit on a good thing with our theme and style, so she won't kick us out."

"What do you mean by that?" I asked. "She wouldn't evict you, would she?"

"Totally," Tabitha replied. "If she doesn't hear something positive or read a good review about you from at least one customer per week, you get a penalty point. Get too many points and she'll follow through with the Neighbors Helping Neighbors clause, which basically means my success helps your store succeed and vice versa. We all saw her use it against the juice bar."

"That's what was in the empty building across from Silver Moon," Carly explained.

"Real neighborly." I couldn't decide if I was more shocked or disgusted. "Thanks for talking with us, Tabitha. I will definitely be coming back here. You've got a children's book section, I assume. My granddaughter loves books."

"Oh, yes. We love wee witches here."

Our final stop was So Mote It Tea, the local teahouse, which also served coffee and light meals. After all that walking, talking, and absorbing information, I was ready for a pick-me-up. Outside, café tables stood in a line on the sidewalk. Inside, the shop had a more natural design. The wood floors were creaky, and the walls red and brown brick. Plants hung from the ceiling, stood in corners, and perched on countertops.

Behind the counter, a Black woman in a barista apron smiled at us. She had the most striking blue eyes. "Hey, Carly."

"Hi, Maggie. This is my cousin, Dusty."

"Pleasure. What can I get you, ladies?"

There were three chalkboard menus hanging above the order stand. One labeled *Nibbles* listed their lineup of simple sandwiches, soups, salads, and pastries. Another for *Joes* or coffees. The third was titled *Cuppas* or tea drinks.

Maggie smiled at the amused look on my face. "My daughter picked the name for the food menu. She was seven at the time and is twenty-two now, but the customers think it's cute, so we keep it. My husband chose the other two, and I named the shop."

"And there he is," Carly said of the man who walked out from the backroom.

"Carly. Glad to see Beau came to his senses and let you out."

"The credit for that goes to my cousin." She tilted her head at me and had a strange smile on her face.

He froze. "Dusty?"

"Russell?" I stared back at the guy we'd gone to high school with.

He stepped around the counter to give me a hug. Russell had always been a great hugger and a really nice guy. Except he jolted a little when we connected as though I'd given him a static shock. But instead of releasing me, he held on tighter.

Wait, was he reading me? Russell was a witch? I didn't know that. Or didn't remember.

After a few seconds, he said, "You've suffered a great deal lately." Then he let me go. "Sorry. That doesn't happen with people very often."

"Psychometry," Carly supplied.

The ability to sense something about objects or people by touching them. I could never decide if that would be something cool or annoying.

"I mostly get readings off of objects," he insisted, "which means I'm a great returner of lost items. Or knowing if a thing or place will be right for someone. Like this building. I knew within seconds it was the right place for us."

Okay, more cool than annoying.

"Until a few days ago, she was a lost thing," Carly volunteered and then asked Maggie for an iced dirty chai.

I didn't care for that comment. I was never lost.

"And for you, Dusty?" Maggie asked.

"A London Fog. But with oat milk, please."

"What's that?" Carly searched the board for my drink.

I rubbed my hands together in anticipation. "An Earl Gray latte with honey, lavender, and vanilla."

"Yum. I want that next time." While we waited for our drinks, Carly asked Russell and Maggie if they'd had any encounters with Ludo Beck.

Maggie shivered. "The man gave me the creeps. Not to speak ill of the dead."

"You're not the only one," Carly assured.

She handed Carly her chai. "He knew we've been here longer than many of the stores, so he'd come in every day, act all buddy-buddy with Russell, and ask for advice on how to get Marilyn to change her mind."

"Change her mind?" I repeated.

"That's how he disguised it." Russell shook his head. "He was trying to figure out how to bribe her."

"Marilyn?" Carly laughed. "No one changes Marilyn Kramer's mind once it's set. And she doesn't need money, so bribes won't work."

Russell pointed at her. "That's what I told Beck. The way I understand it, he came to check out the mall about a month ago. He went store to store and asked all sorts of questions about traffic through the mall, what the customer base was like, that kind of thing."

Maggie slid my tea across the counter, then went to clear tables.

"Sounds like standard questions," I noted, "for anyone wanting to open a business."

"Right," Russell agreed. "He asked me about your diner, and I told him it wasn't part of the mall properties managed by Marilyn. He said he'd fill out an application to get approval to open a store and work on getting the location he wanted while he waited."

Carly's jaw dropped. "He said that?"

Russell nodded.

I dabbed at the foam on top of my tea. "In other words, he'd try to convince whoever was in a building he wanted to vacate. That's what he was doing to Carly and Comfort."

Maggie came our way with a tray of mugs and plates. "I heard him talking to one of our customers one day. He must have been doing market research or something and told them about his grocery store. They said it sounded like a place they'd shop at and asked where it would be. He said the diner location was 'ideal,' but they should look for him on the river side of the mall."

Carly made a growling sound. "Even though none of those buildings were available. That man was just slimy."

"He put in his application about three weeks ago," Russell said, "and apparently Marilyn never gave him an answer."

"After three weeks?" I asked. "Is that normal?"

"Not when there's a building sitting empty," Maggie answered on her way to the kitchen. "Russell, the couple in the corner would like another Americano and an espresso."

Carly added to Maggie's answer. "How long Marilyn takes depends on whether she finds anything suspicious in her background checks. Marilyn can be a bit greedy, but she's a savvy businesswoman."

"She is." Russell started the new coffee orders. "Except for the slimy factor, I thought Beck's grocery store would be a good fit."

"Maybe she found something in Beck's background," I suggested.

"That's the only thing that makes sense to me," Russell agreed.

Maggie walked out of the backroom. "Or he did something to make her angry."

"A sure way to get rejected," Carly said. "Thanks for the drinks and the intel." She led me outside, where we sat in the shade to drink our teas and discuss something different. "Any thoughts on what you're going to do now that you're back?"

"As in a job?" I shook my head. "When I mentioned looking for something the other day, Gwynne reminded me there was plenty for me to do on the farm. They've had me floating around like they made us do when we were kids. I forgot how much I love being outside and working with plants."

"When we were at Silver Moon, you asked me if it's too late. To open our own store, you mean?"

Before I could answer, we heard, "Good afternoon, ladies."

We looked up to find Beau standing by our table.

"Beauregard." Carly's tone was laced with icy crispness. It would take a bit before she forgave him for jailing her.

"I heard that you two and Pepper were wandering around trying to dig up information on Beck." His attitude was as cold as hers and much stiffer than it had been at The Paddle Wheel Saturday night.

"*We've* been talking to some of the store owners," I corrected. "Pepper stayed at the apothecary."

Carly glared at him. "What's the matter, Officer? You seem upset."

He looked around—making sure no one was nearby?—and hissed, "You need to stay out of this."

"Out of what?" I asked. What was he so uptight about?

"This whole Ludo Beck situation. Carly is free and clear. Let me handle the rest."

"You told me at The Paddle Wheel if I heard anything—"

"Forget what I told you."

"What's going on, Beau?" Carly was more concerned than angry now.

He hesitated before saying, "There are dark sides and underbellies everywhere. Even here in simple little Blackwood Grove."

Winnie's words from the other night, that I was meant to be caretaker of the town as well as the aunts, sounded in my ears. Gooseflesh crawled over my shoulders.

"Be careful," he continued. "Please, do as I say."

"Do as you say?" Carly glared at him again.

He sighed. "That isn't a man to woman comment, Carly. It's cop to citizen." He looked directly at me and wiggled his fingers. "And don't manipulate anything."

"What is that supposed to mean?" She copied his finger wiggle.

"Your witchy stuff. Don't tell me it's a coincidence that June suddenly remembered details about the killer shortly before Carly's seventy-two-hour hold was up."

"That's offensive, Officer." Carly wiggled her fingers again.

His brow furrowed with confusion. "It wasn't intended to be. Just a clarifying gesture."

"Oh, so you wouldn't be offended if I limped around or used the word *gimp* to clarify your amputation?" She was really angry at him now. "Say *magic* and skip the hand gestures. And for the record, I would never use that word."

He clenched his jaw. "This has gone completely off the rails. Look, I'm trying to warn you that something is going on in this town. I don't know what Beck has to do with this, but this started when Beck came looking for a place to open his store about a month ago."

Right around the time Josie went missing.

"I can't stop you from asking questions," Beau continued, "that's your right, but for your own safety—"

"Got it," Carly snapped, but she'd deflated a little.

I assured him we'd tone it down, and when he walked away, I told my cousin, "He's only doing his job."

"Yeah, I know. Except he made me look like a criminal. Now the whole town thinks—"

"That you were innocent from the start. I haven't heard anyone say you're responsible for Beck's death."

We finished our drinks, decided to call it a day on investigating, and headed for home.

Still fuming, Carly asked, "What do you suppose he meant by something's going on?"

"I might know, but we need to be somewhere no one will hear us."

"That means the other side of the hedge." Carly led us to a spot between the main house and hers. "This is how the Ords get through when they want to buy something from the aunts. They're given a password, the hedge opens, and they follow the path down to that gate."

The path, worn down by so many feet it was nothing but dirt, went straight into the thorny hedge. "Looks like a lot of Ordies have come this way over the years."

"Shoppers go to Silver and Moon for remedies, and the townies come to the aunts. Hypocrites is what they are. Call us scary witches until they remember our ancestors were their ancestors' healers and midwives."

"Then those in power, usually a man, became intimidated because the witches knew too much."

"And sent those wise women to live at the edge of town on the other side of their hedge."

Those were the stories we heard around the fire when we were growing up. "Ever find it ironic that our hedge keeps them away from us?"

"Constantly."

"How do we get through?"

She cleared her throat. "Open, please."

The branches rustled and groaned, and an opening large enough for us to pass through without getting scratched appeared. It closed up again as soon as we were on the other side.

"That's the password? Open, please?"

"It is for us. The property knows Warren blood or those who live on the parcel. The Ords are given a new password every time, and the witch they're coming to visit lets the property know. Okay, what did you want to tell me?"

"The other night, when I was performing the spell to restore June's memory, Winnie caught me." I explained the exchange she and I had. "Have you felt anything odd going on around here?"

Carly thought and shook her head. "Not really. You have?"

"As soon as I got here. I've been gone for so long, though, I figured it was normal. You know how when you see something every day you don't notice that it's changing?"

"Yeah." She led us a little further into the orchard. "The Council seriously thinks someone is trying to take down the safe towns?"

"According to Winnie, yes. This could be what Beau is so worked up about."

"But he's not a witch. Even though he's lived here his entire life, the wards falling won't have any impact on him."

"Not the same as it would on us, but think about how conflicted he must be. The cops here treat witches and Ords the same. That's not true in Ordinary towns. If the wards fall and witches aren't protected by the safe towns anymore, where does that put cops like Beau? Do they defend lifelong friends or uphold their careers?"

Carly softened. "I understand."

"Obviously I don't know if any of this is true. I'm only saying what if."

Suddenly, I was immensely grateful that I was back here. Dad assured me the wards were still standing. *We* were safe, but I understood why someone needed to protect the town. I just didn't understand why that person was me. "Losing my job. My house burning down. Whatever is going on with Micah and Josie. The threat against Cricket. What if all those things are related to us being witches? And the timing of all that happening lines up with when Beck came here looking to open a store."

She nodded, letting all that sink in. "Micah and Josie are witches?"

"I'm not sure about Micah." I told her about the helicopter in his crib. "That was the only time I ever suspected he had powers. I saw Josie produce a toothbrush one time at my house, but I never talked to her about it. She's a lovely girl, and I like her very much, but I couldn't trust anyone with the truth of who and what I was. I'm sure she felt the same."

A look of empathy crossed Carly's face. "You had to suppress your true self."

"Completely."

"Was it worth it?"

I said what I always said when someone asked if I'd do it again regarding my scummy ex. "Yes, because I have Micah and Cricket."

"What we don't do for our family, hey?" Her frown turned into a tight smile. "Speaking of which, let's go check on the aunts and make a plan for tomorrow. You need to go talk to Marilyn Kramer."

CHAPTER 22

*C*arly insisted Marilyn was the best and possibly only
way we'd find out Ludo Beck's story. And by *we* she
meant *me*. The last thing I wanted to do was talk to Marilyn, but
I made a vow to take care of my family. Beck was murdered in
our diner which is concerning enough. When Comfort and I
watched that video, it looked to me like the killer was heading
for the kitchen and Beck either stopped him or got in the way.
Or he was the intended target all along. I needed to know more
about Beck. So I'd go to Marilyn's office by myself tomorrow
and ask if she'd found out anything helpful about him while
processing his application. And maybe confront her on her
threats from thirty years ago.

Carly texted her kids to come over for dinner. Pepper, who
was rejuvenated from spending most of the day with Silver and
Moon, was thrilled. All that time at the apothecary, she said,
made her think New Orleans, which meant another Cajun meal.
This time, she prepared a low-heat version of red beans and
rice, for those like Cricket who wanted less heat, as well as
shrimp étouffée, for those of us who liked a bit more kick.

Both dishes were fantastic, and dinner with the family was fun. There was no talk of accusations or wrongful imprisonment or murder. The kids were happy to have their mom home. Even Sebastian smiled and added a few thoughts to the conversation. And now that her daughter was free again, Comfort's baking was back on track. Her peach-ginger-honey pie turned out perfectly.

I couldn't help but think it felt like the calm before the storm.

At six fifteen, when I told Cricket we needed to go, she leaned against Emma. "I don't wanna go."

"But it's Monday. What happens on Monday night at six thirty?"

She thought, and then her eyes went wide. "Daddy!" She was halfway to the back door before I'd even gotten up from my chair. At the apartment, she kicked off her sandals in the entry, then scampered up the stairs. I found her staring open-mouthed at the kitchenette. "What happened to it?"

I was almost afraid to look. At the top of the stairs, I found that the checkerboard floor tiles had been replaced with the hardwood that covered the living area, and while the cabinets were still mid-century retro, they'd toned down from bright bubblegum to a soft baby pink. And anything that had been bright turquoise was now white. Thank heavens. The other version gave me a headache.

"Five minutes," I warned. "Grab your jammies and bring them to the bathroom."

This was our routine. While she talked first, I got her bath ready. When it was my turn, she jumped in the tub. That kept her busy so I could talk to my son and get and give updates.

"What does she mean you're living on a farm because the house burned?" Micah asked after Cricket handed me the phone.

"Hi, sweetheart."

"Yeah, hi. What's going on?"

I talked fast and told him about everything except the magic. That would require a phone call of its own. "We lost everything, but we got out safely. Not a scratch on either of us. Now we're living in Blackwood Grove with my family. My aunts are elderly and need a caretaker. We need a place to live. Win-win." I took a breath and checked the time. That took less than five minutes. I'd gotten very efficient with that retelling over the past five days. "We're seriously fine, so don't give it another thought. How are you?"

His heavy sigh broke off a bit of my heart. "I met with my lawyer this morning. No way I'm getting out. They say until they have proof of what happened to Josie, I'm staying right here."

"We'll get you out."

"How, Mom? The police have nothing. Not a shred of evidence to prove Josie is still alive." His voice broke on her name. "Her family is still insisting I did something to her."

"But they can't prove it."

"Right. No one can prove anything, but I'm still sitting in a cell."

"We'll figure it out, Micah. I know you didn't do this."

"If only they'd take my mother's word for it." Sarcasm weighed heavily in his voice today. On our last call, he was motivated, sure his lawyer would come up with something. What a difference a week made.

That truth spell worked so well on June. Who could I target to get Micah out— No. That spell worked because I knew the facts and all I had to do was ask for June's memory to be restored. The dream I'd had about Micah proved he was innocent, but I had no idea what had happened to Josie or who had her. Or, goddess forbid, where her body was. I had no facts. What kind of spell could I use in this situation?

"Mom?"

"Sorry, what did you say?"

"You're not even listening to me?"

"Micah, of course I am. I was thinking about alternate ways to prove you didn't do this."

"Like what?" There was the tiniest bit of hope in his voice.

"I'm not sure yet. A private investigator?"

"Can you afford that?"

I had no idea what one would cost. "I'll look into it, okay? Trust me. I am trying to get you out. Last week you told me you're safe. Is that still true?"

"Yeah. No one's bothering me."

Not sure I believed that, but I'd let it go. Maybe I could cast a protection spell.

"Is Cricket still having nightmares?"

"Not since our first night here. I've been putting lavender and mint sachets in her bath to calm her followed by an infusion—"

"Infusion? What exactly are you doing to her?"

"It's a tea, Micah, not an injection."

"Oh. That worked?"

"It did. She's been sleeping very soundly." And she's perfectly safe. Even at four years old, she must sense that nothing can hurt her here.

"Sorry if I sound like I'm doubting you, Mom. I'm not, I promise. It's just—"

"You're her father and should be the one caring for her. I understand, sweetheart."

"How can I ever repay you? You've done your time in the parenting trenches. You must have been thinking about retirement or life slowing down a little."

I thought of Pepper and how slow her life had become. "I was, but that wouldn't be anywhere near as rewarding as taking care of her until you can do it again. No payment required."

An automated voice announced that we had one minute left.

"How can I ever thank you, then?"

"Stay strong and trust me. Know that I will do whatever I can to help you." Whatever that meant. "Okay, little Cricket. It's time." I punched the speaker button.

"Are you there, Daddy?"

"I'm here. Are you there, Cricket?"

She giggled. "You know I am. You just heard my voice."

"Such a smart girl you are."

"Ready?" I asked, and she nodded. I counted down from three, and in unison we sang out, "I love you."

"With all my heart," she added.

"I love you more," he replied. "I'll talk to you in a week."

With that, the call disconnected, and my heart clenched. I turned away from the bathtub, closed my eyes, and took a shaky breath.

Please keep him safe until I figure out how to get him out of there.

Putting Cricket to bed after a phone call was always tough. And in the rush to get ready for the call, I'd forgotten the lavender-mint sachet. She sobbed when I tucked her in.

"I miss my daddy and mommy," she said through gasps. "Why can't I see them?"

What was I supposed to tell her? I wasn't about to say they'd be home soon. The truth was, despite my vow and intent, I had no idea if either of them would ever come home. She'd be better in the morning, she always was, but getting her to sleep was so hard when she was this upset. Finally, I crawled in with her, let her lay on top of me, and placed her ear over my heart.

"Can you hear it?" I asked, her tears soaking my T-shirt.

"Y-yes."

"What does it sound like."

"Boom-boom. Boom-boom."

"Right." I rubbed her back.

"Is that what Daddy's heart sounds like? And mommy's?"

"Exactly like that. Pretend you're listening to Daddy's heart. What is it saying to you?"

She looked up at me. "Hearts don't talk, Lola."

"Then why did you tell him you love him with all your heart? Your heart must have told you that. It must have whispered it inside your head."

She lay back down and listened. "It says it loves me."

"It sure does."

After a minute of listening and whispering *boom-boom, boom-boom*, Cricket grew still. Her breathing got slower and deeper. When I was sure she was asleep, I slipped out from beneath her, tucked the purple elephant under her arm and baba next to her, then pulled the blanket up over her.

I knelt by the side of her bed to make sure she stayed asleep and thought of Micah's comment about me retiring. My job as office manager had satisfied me only in that it provided me with a comfortable lifestyle. It hadn't fulfilled me in the least, and I wouldn't miss it. These past few days reminded me of how much I loved working with plants. Now was my chance to do the things I'd always wanted to do. Or try something completely different.

Earlier today, Carly and I flirted with whether it was too late to open our shop. Was she interested? We were only fifty, there was still plenty of time. Was Blackwood Grove the place to start over? Once Cricket was safe, of course. For now, I wasn't going anywhere.

I couldn't say how long I'd knelt there. Long enough that the sun had set, and my knees weren't happy. I groaned as I stood.

A hot shower washed away the day's grime from my body, but my brain still felt cluttered and not ready to settle down for the night. The sudden need for a walk and to breathe in fresh air overwhelmed me.

"Alarm, please," I told the apartment.

It responded with chirps.

"I'll be by the garden. Absolutely no further away than the pond on the far side."

Another chirp in reply.

The waxing crescent moon gave just enough light for me to see where I was walking. Solar lights along the pea-gravel pathway encircling the one-acre garden behind the carriage house provided a little more. In the silence of night, the gravel crunching beneath my feet sounded loud enough to wake the entire town, so I sidestepped to the grass. Then I pulled my sneakers off and reveled in the feeling of the cushiony turf and the blades between my toes.

While the darkness surrounded me like a hug, I walked a counterclockwise circle around the garden and thought of Micah. Was he a witch? If so, he must have been so confused. I'd never given him any guidance, ignored part of who he was, and figured if we didn't talk about it he'd be safe. So foolish.

What if Josie told him what she could do? I imagined them practicing together, him saying nothing to me for fear that I wouldn't accept him. What if one or both of them had performed spells and an Ordinary from our *not* safe town saw? Some Ordies outside the safe towns were fine with our magic. Others would drop whatever they were doing and go to the nearest police station and file a complaint. Every now and then, on the nightly news, there would be a story about a witch arrested for performing magic. Any kind of magic, no matter how minor. Neighborhood watch groups patrolled the streets at night and would look through windows. Some even used drones to look in windows above street level.

It was flat out wrong. Our choice was to be confined to a safe town or live in secrecy and fear.

Is that what happened to Josie? One of these groups caught her? Was Micah arrested by association? What did they do with the witches they arrested? Imprison them, but what did that mean? Micah said he was fine but . . . I shuddered to even think about it.

"I have to find out what happened to Josie. How do I do that?"

Ordinaries had the police. Witches had The Council, a balanced group established to work within the safe towns and address issues for both sides. For the last forty years, Dad was the witch representative for Blackwood Grove. Henry Kramer, Marilyn's husband, represented the Ordinaries. Yet another reason eighteen-year-old me took her threat seriously. She had some powerful backup behind her. I did, too, but hadn't seen it that way then.

The Council also had a legal team. Something I hadn't realized until Lucia Valentina appeared in the kitchen the other day. The Council had no power outside the safe towns, but maybe Lucia could help me with Micah. If she couldn't help directly, she might be able to point me in the right direction.

All of a sudden, something dark and low to the ground darted out of the garden in front of me. I leapt in surprise, my pulse racing.

Then the shadowy figure chattered at me. Pearl.

"Don't squirrels sleep at night?"

She dropped to the ground, mimicked sleeping, then hopped back to her feet.

"You were sleeping but came to help me with my dilemma." I sat on the grass, and she came closer. "I'm trying to figure out how to find Josie."

I told her the story and what I suspected could have happened to her. When I finished, Pearl climbed into my lap and then up my arm. She perched on my shoulder and pressed her tiny paw to my forehead. When I said I *was* thinking, she did it again.

"Not thinking . . . Oh! A vision."

She chirped happily.

"I can't force them . . . but there might be a spell to bring them on. If I can at least see where Josie is, that would be a start." I thought a little longer. "Carly used to be really good at scrying. Maybe between the two of us we can at least get a clue. Thanks. We forget that answers can be closer than we think."

Pearl slapped me a high five and then scurried off toward the orchard.

I'd still talk with Lucia but would also try to bring on a premonition or dream. The best place to start was the grimoire, of course. I stood and was about to go up to the attic when the back door opened, and someone stepped out. Down by the gate, a light flashed. Just like the other night. I'd been so lost in thought I hadn't even noticed. I dropped onto the grass and watched.

Flowing clothes and rounding forward of the shoulders. And the big giveaway, the long frizzy hair. And I saw her profile; it had to be Gwynne. Keeping my shoes off and taking care not to step on anything sharp, I followed her from a good fifteen yards back and only crept close enough to hear their exchange.

"You're sure this will work?" By the sound of the voice, it was a woman on the other side of the gate. They exchanged bags. Money for the spell, most likely. "I mean, I only get one shot. Right?"

"Correct, one shot." Gwynne sounded tired. She was usually in bed by this time. "Read the directions carefully. I suggest three times. And then follow them *exactly* as written. If you vary in any way, the spell won't work."

The woman thanked her and disappeared into the shadows.

Gwynne turned and shuffled back to the house but stopped and looked in my direction.

I froze. Had she heard me? Far as I knew, I hadn't made a sound, only feet on grass. Was I breathing too loudly? Did she see my shadow?

After a few seconds, she continued on. I stayed put until she entered the house and the porch light went out. Then I continued back to the apartment. But something on the second floor caught my eye. The light in Gwynne's room was on, and I swear I saw someone walking around in there. She couldn't possibly have gotten up there that quickly. Who was in her room?

CHAPTER 23

*D*espite my certainty that my aunt had lied to me, my excitement over possibly having a plan to help my son by bringing on a vision, and the dread of having to face Marilyn tomorrow, I slept well. I woke from a sound sleep, however, to something pushing on my cheek. And then my nose. And then my chin.

"Who's poking me?" I asked slowly. When she poked my nose again, I grabbed her hand, making Cricket squeal, and pulled her into bed with me.

"Your bed grew, Lola."

It had. As in, when I went to bed, it was a twin size. Now it was a full. And it was the perfect firmness. No wonder I slept well.

"Thank you," I told the apartment. I must have done something else right. Then I turned to the giggling girl next to me. "Why are you poking me?"

"'Cause I'm hungry."

"So am I." I pretended to gnaw on her neck and made her laugh even louder. "What would you like this morning? More pancakes?"

"No, oatmeal. Emma maked me some for lunch yesterday. It was so yummy."

That was new. "Oatmeal sounds delicious. Let's get dressed then we'll go see what's in the kitchen."

"I can dress myself."

She leapt off my bed and ran to her bedroom. Getting herself dressed. That was also new. And since my little bug preferred dresses, I didn't have to worry about colors or styles coordinating like I did with her father. "Oh, Micah. We need to get you and Josie home so you can watch your girl grow up."

We entered the kitchen a few minutes later, and Cricket told Pepper what she wanted. The elderly witch turned toward the stove and, within a minute, turned back with a bowl of steaming oatmeal in her hands.

After adding fresh diced peaches, a sprinkle of brown sugar and cinnamon, and a drizzle of milk to her bowl, I settled Cricket into her spot at the table.

"Gwynne," I asked my aunt, "can I talk to you for a minute?" I gestured toward the family room.

She groaned as she pushed up from the table and followed me. "What can I help you with, dear?"

"Let's start with the truth." I kept my tone serious but tried to not sound accusatory. "I followed you out to the gate last night."

"It wasn't me."

Exasperated, I said, "Gwynne, this isn't a big deal. I saw you take payment from whoever met you there and then give them a small bag. You told them to read the directions three times and follow them exactly."

She waited until I looked her in the eye, pushed her glasses up her nose, and said, "I know what you think you saw, but you didn't see *me*."

And then I understood. The rounded shoulders. Gwynne stood tall. The shuffling gait. Gwynne walked with confidence.

Gwynne and my mother were twins. I saw Mom last night. And two nights ago.

"She's here? Where? Has she been here this whole time?"

"I don't know, and that's the truth. She'll be here for days or weeks at a time, then she'll disappear for weeks or sometimes months. All we know is we rarely see her."

"But she was here last night." I headed for the stairs to the second floor and the bedroom she and Dad used.

"She's been staying in the attic lately," Gwynne called out.

In the attic? How had I not noticed that when I was up there the other night? Of course, there was so much stuff up there she could have been standing five feet away and I wouldn't have seen her. Was that the shuffling noise I heard? I thought it was Pearl but maybe it had been my mother.

I went back to Gwynne. "Why?"

"Again, I don't know. She told me years ago to stay out of her business. I'm honoring that request."

My arms hung like lead weights at my sides. "Do they ever see each other anymore? Mom and Dad, I mean."

Gwynne shook her head and shrugged at the same time. "On occasion, but not often. I think between Council business and birdwatching, his days are full. And she has pretty much disconnected from us."

Birds were more important than his family. Dad started pulling away when I was still here. He always insisted he loved Mom and her sisters, and he seemed to get along fine with Filip and Maks, but he'd never been able to handle a crowd, even if that crowd was his family. When I was six years old, he was offered that spot on The Council, and he jumped at it. They gave him a big quiet office, and whenever we asked where it was, he insisted the location of Council headquarters was top secret. He'd go there immediately after breakfast and come home late at night. Then he started staying away a night or two a week. Then three nights. Then four.

Mom was never bothered by it. They spent so much time apart, I wondered why they even stayed married. Although, when they were together, they seemed happy enough. Carly insisted she and Kyle had a great marriage and went weeks without seeing each other. Who was I to judge? I never had a real marriage.

"I should check the attic."

"If you want to." With a note of caution in her voice, Gwynne added, "Prepare yourself that she's different from the Griselle you knew thirty-two years ago."

I smiled. "You're all different than you were thirty-two years ago."

"Yes, but . . ." She cut herself off. "Go ahead. You'll see."

Gooseflesh raised on my arms and neck. I was almost scared now.

I charged up the stairs to the second floor, went straight to the attic door, and paused. *How* had she changed? What was Gwynne warning me about? I climbed the second set and stood right there at the top.

"Mom?" I waited, straining my ears to hear the softest shuffle, squinting to see the smallest movement. "It's Dusty, Mom. Are you up here?"

There was a light switch on the wall at the top of the stairs. I flipped it on and saw clearly all that had been in the shadows the other night. A twin-size bed was pushed up against the wall beneath the window that faced west. That window overlooked the gardens, the orchard in the distance, and the carriage house. She had a clear view of me and Cricket coming and going. Was she the shadowy figure I'd seen up here? Had she watched us? Did she know I was the woman staying in Apple Blossom Cottage? Did she care?

Along with the bed, there were dozens of books in stacks on the floor next to a large wood table about six feet square. On top of the table were various sizes of paper bags and small plastic bags just big enough to hold the ingredients for a spell. There was a journal almost as big as the grimoire filled with scribblings that might have been a register of the spells she assembled for Ordies over the years, but I couldn't decipher anything. It probably only made sense to her. There was also a basket filled with candles in various sizes and colors. A stamp, the kind for pressing a family crest into melted wax to seal an envelope, stood at the ready. She must seal the paper bags shut with candle wax. An armoire held some clothing and what appeared to be her private stash of dried plants. Next to it was a steamer trunk filled with cash, the bills seemingly tossed inside to stay where they landed.

I thought of her bedroom downstairs. It was big enough for two people to sleep in and store their clothes, but nowhere near big enough for the table, armoire, and all these supplies. Her staying in the attic made a little more sense now. What really upset me was the chaos of it all. My mother had never been an especially tidy person, but her surroundings never looked like this. Gwynne warned me her sister had changed. She wasn't exaggerating.

I'd seen enough. I didn't sense anyone up here with me this time, but just in case, I called, "You must know I'm back. I hope Dad has been keeping you up to date on me and my life. I wanted him to. Sorry if he didn't." My voice caught. "I'd really like to see you. You should meet your great-granddaughter. You'll absolutely love her."

I heard a scampering sound and turned to find Pearl and the long, tall gray cat with green eyes coming my way. Was he my mother's familiar? A gray cat for a gray witch? The color was an amusing coincidence. Mine was a black squirrel, after all.

The cat let out a scratchy, "*Mrow*" around a little rolled piece of paper in his mouth. I took the slightly damp scroll from him, unrolled it, and found two words written in the middle. *I'm sorry.*

Was this from my mom? What was she sorry for? Being on the same property for nearly a week and not giving me so much as a wave? Passing the gray witch curse on to me? Not contacting me even once in all those years? Never even acknowledging her grandson or great-granddaughter?

Of course, as the aunts and Carly pointed out, I never contacted her or anyone in the family during that time either. Never sent birth announcements. How hypocritical was it for me to whine about my parents' lack of interest?

I'm sorry could be an apology, but it could also be a forewarning. Was she trying to alert me to something?

Thoughts and questions tumbled around in my head all morning. And it turned out, I must have muttered most of them out loud, because when I looked up from weeding the herb garden, I found Cricket staring at me.

"Who are you talking to?" She had raspberries in her hand and juice on her chin.

"Myself." That happened a lot.

"Silly, Lola." She held a berry out to me and popped it into my mouth when I opened it.

"Were you helping Jett pick raspberries?"

"Uh-huh. They're sour."

"They are by themselves, but much better with other things."

"Jett said it's eleven thirty."

"Oh, heavens. I need to clean up, and then we get to go to the diner."

"Yay! Can I have ice cream?"

I'd created a sugar addict. "Let's worry about lunch first."

I showered and dressed in record time. Then Cricket and I hurried over to Comfort's Food. Emma had agreed to meet us there at noon and take Cricket so I could go talk to Marilyn. Carly had sent a text earlier saying she had information to share when I got there.

Carly cornered me the moment we walked in. "Let's talk."

"Let me get Cricket squared away."

"Emma will take care of Cricket. I only have a few minutes. Nina's handling the dining room, and as you can see, Mom is the only one in the kitchen." She led me to Comfort's office and closed the door. Not at all claustrophobia inducing. "Nash came in for breakfast, so I did a little pre-investigative investigating and asked about his parents. He isn't much of a talker, but I managed to find out that Marilyn makes Henry lunch every day at noon sharp. Then he goes back out to the fields or to the barn or whatever it is he does. I didn't ask for that much detail."

"I thought I'm supposed to talk to Marilyn. Why do I care what Henry's doing?"

"Once lunch is done, Marilyn goes to her office above the clothing store. Sometimes she stays there all afternoon. Other times she visits the stores and talks to the owners. You need to catch her at her office, so you should get over there and wait outside."

I blew out a long breath, still not happy with this plan. "Okay, I'm on it."

I gave Cricket a hug and told Emma she could have a small dessert, sugar-free pudding was best, if she ate all her lunch. Then I grabbed a pre-made turkey wrap and an iced tea to go.

CHAPTER 24

I sat on a bench in the park in front of Swank. Tuesdays understandably saw less traffic than the weekends, but this was *far* less. The longer it took to find the killer, the more nervous the townies were getting. I saw a few parents with kids at the playground, and Wayne, the homeless man, on his blanket with his small stack of possessions next to him. Some folks stopped and chatted with him. One woman handed him something. Money or food, I assumed.

At 12:23, according to the four-sided clock standing a few feet away—there were matching ones placed every hundred yards down the park walkway—Marilyn appeared. I knew her the moment I saw her, but at the same time, like everyone I used to know, she looked completely different from what I remembered. Her skin was weathered and wrinkled like her husband's. She wore her gray hair short but highly styled. I imagined her bathroom vanity was covered with hot rollers, curling irons, and plenty of hairspray. With her shirt tucked into her practical rather than fashionable jeans, the wide belt at her waist, and layers of necklaces in varying lengths, she gave off a trendy cowgirl vibe.

As she got close, I thought of her standing before me days after the accident, threatening me and my family. My mouth dried out, and I had to take a quick sip of iced tea in order to speak. "Hey, Marilyn."

The stern woman turned her gaze to me and froze. "Dusty Warren. I heard you were back."

Yeah, this was going to go well. I would correct her error on my last name another time. "Can I speak with you for a few minutes?"

She sorted through her keyring for her office key, I assumed. "I've got nothing to say to you."

"Said all you needed to three decades ago, hey?"

Her eyes narrowed, and she held my gaze. "I don't have time for whatever this is. I'm a busy woman, Dusty."

"I understand that." I stood and stepped toward her. "Just a few minutes, then I'll leave."

Deep lines encircled Marilyn's mouth as she pressed her lips together. She let out an inconvenienced sigh. "Fine. Come up to my office."

Feeling like I was being led to the lion's den, or lioness's in this case, I trailed behind her as she strode to a door on the side of the building that led to the second floor. That much was good. I'd worried I would have to follow her through the clothing store and then Celia would ask a ton of questions or spread rumors.

Marilyn's office was a wide-open loft space. Tall windows on every wall gave her a full view of the river and the mall. The sprayed black ceiling with exposed mechanicals, brick walls, and gleaming hardwood floor made a space that would fit right in among the trendiest areas in the trendiest towns. A nine-foot-long, freestanding, framed corkboard on wheels displayed a map of the mall. Every building, bench, and clock in the park was there, as was every piece of equipment in the playground. Comfort's Food Diner and Silver Moon Apothecary were drawn with gray ink where everything else was black. And interestingly, only a few buildings were permanently labeled with names—Grimoires and Gimlets, So Mote It Tea, and Swank. All the others had little handwritten tags pinned beneath them as though those businesses hadn't earned a permanent tag yet. The Neighbor Helping Neighbor clause was on full display here. Perform or get evicted.

Her spacious desk looked out over her queendom. Tufted leather chairs encircling a round coffee table created a comfortable sitting area for her guests. Or maybe *subjects* was the better word. She motioned for me to take a seat and poured a glass of water for herself but didn't offer me anything. I was definitely not a guest.

"What is the topic of discussion?" she asked.

"Ludo Beck," I said simply, matching her terse tone.

She let out a heavy sigh. "What about him?"

"You know he was killed in the diner?"

She gave a single short nod in reply.

"My family would like to know why, and Officer Balinski hasn't been able to find an answer yet."

"And why do you think I can help with that?" Marilyn inspected one of her necklaces.

"Out of everyone in town, you're the one who best understood who he was and what he was up to. He put in an application to open a specialty grocery store in the mall, right?"

"He did."

"That was three weeks ago, and you never gave him an answer."

"Like I said, I'm a busy woman with plenty of tasks on my to-do list. His application was only one of those things."

"But according to Russell and Maggie at the teahouse, you don't like buildings to sit empty for long and that one across from the apothecary has been empty for more than a month. I'd think filling it would be at the top of your list. Can't collect rent on an empty building. And empty buildings deliver the wrong message to shoppers."

She gave me a cold, slithery smile. "Back only a few days and think you're an expert on the community, hey?"

I wasn't going to let her rile me. "It's a small town. Doesn't take long."

"Longer than you'd think. For example, what makes you think I'm interested in helping you or your family?"

I jutted my chin toward the mall. "Because there's a killer in Blackwood Grove and business is down."

She didn't reply, but her lips pursed.

I thought of the security video and my fear that the killer planned to enter the kitchen. "There's a slight possibility that Beck's killer was after someone working in the diner that day. I'm concerned for my family's safety and the diner's employees. You want shoppers to come back. It's a win-win for us to work together on this."

She took her time drinking a bit of water, setting the glass on the table, and untangling her necklaces. Then she finally said, "Tell me what you know first."

I explained what we'd seen on the video and reiterated what the shop owners told Carly and me yesterday. When I reminded her about the stairs across from the diner and offered my theory about the easy access to the river, she leaned forward just a little.

"Was there something about Beck's proposal that concerned you? Were you worried that he might carry illegal inventory? Did you simply not like the guy? I mean, your buildings, your decision on who gets to use them, right?"

After a long pause, she replied, "Ludo Beck was arrogant, and in my opinion, he absolutely would have caused problems here. I've never had anyone push me for an answer the way he did. The thing is, the more someone pushes, the more I slow down. I told him I'd give him an answer when I was ready, but he wanted it now. 'Tomorrow is too late,' he told me, 'I'll go somewhere else.' I told him to go right ahead. Someone will be in that empty building eventually."

"Did you find anything concerning in your background check?"

Another pause. "There was something."

"Something illegal?" I asked.

"I can't discuss that with you. And I can't help you further. Plain and simple, I don't know why Mr. Beck is dead." She stood, signaling our time was up. "I know what the shop owners think and say about me. That I'm greedy and controlling, but if I wasn't, things wouldn't operate as smoothly as they do. Believe it or not, this town and the people who live here are of the utmost importance to me. I always put their interests and safety first. Have for the last thirty-two years." She paused to let that sink in. I got it. "That's why Mr. Beck was never going to get a store here and why I'm so choosey about who does. Now, I have work to do."

I got to the door when she stopped me.

"I told you there could be trouble for your family if you returned."

Stay in control. Don't let her make you angry. "Turns out that was something I should have done years ago. And the trouble with Mr. Beck and therefore my family happened before I got here." I reconsidered her words. "Or are you referring to something else?"

"You ruined my son's life, Dusty."

I was only surprised it took so long for her to go there. "I've seen Nash a couple of times since I got back. He's doing fine."

"Now, yes. You have no idea what he's been through because of you."

Looking her in the eye, I said, "I'd think dying from that boat crashing would have been far worse."

She met my gaze. "I guess that's something only you could know."

I turned the doorknob, preparing to leave before I did something I couldn't take back, but stopped before opening the door. "Someone is trying to take down the safe towns. Is that the trouble you mean?"

Her steps faltered, just for an instant, on her way to her desk, and she looked over her shoulder at me. "I have no idea what you're talking about."

I couldn't tell if she was being honest or covering her tracks.

I left Marilyn's office, feeling emotionally exhausted. Even though I'd been prepared, and it hadn't lasted long, being face to face with her was hard. I stopped at the diner.

"Did you get information?" Carly asked.

"A little. Want to come over later so I can tell you?"

She reviewed her schedule out loud. "There's still an hour before we close, then I need to get home and spend some time with Sebastian. We need to have a discussion about what he did at the Kramer farm."

Wincing, I admitted, "I heard about it. I was standing right there when Beau brought it up with Nina."

"He's a good kid," Carly insisted, "but he's thirteen and needs his dad. Fortunately, Kyle will be home soon. This afternoon, we'll spend some time together, and then I have to take him out to the Kribs' farm after dinner. He'll be helping Mason with some chores as part of his punishment. I'll come over after I drop him off. I can be there around six thirty?"

"Make it seven thirty. Cricket will be all tucked in and asleep by then. Speaking of which, anyone know where my bug is?"

"Emma said something about the playground." Nina tapped out a text to her sister. "Yep, still there. Should I tell her you're on the way?"

"Yes, please."

Knowing Emma would wait for me, I took my time walking

to the playground, happy for a couple of minutes to catch my breath. Josie, Micah, Cricket. My job, the house, the aunts. Carly. Beau and Nash. Ludo Beck. My brain was full of people and their troubles . . . and my troubles. It was getting harder to focus on one thing at a time. I couldn't even decide which was most important. Maybe because all of it was. I inhaled deeply and exhaled slowly. A few hours with my little bug would do me good.

Emma greeted me with a wave and a big happy smile that looked just like her mother's. "Hi, Dusty."

"I have thanked you for watching her, haven't I?"

"Every time. I like little kids, and she's easy. By the way, she ate every bite of her grilled cheese and sliced peaches. She says peaches are her 'favoritest' things in the world. I let her have a small scoop of ice cream. She picked green, which was pistachio, and then declared *that* was her favoritest thing."

I laughed. "How wonderful to have so many new experiences and find new favorite things every day." Sometimes being a grandma made me feel young. Other times, ancient.

Emma slung her backpack strap over her shoulder. "Did you need me anymore today?"

"No, I've got her from here. Thank you, sweetheart. Do you have any plans?"

"School starts in a week." She groaned, then shrugged it off. "I've got like three chapters left to read in the last book on my summer reading list. Fortunately, it's a good one. Oh, almost forgot. I saw Autumn Trainor and mentioned Cricket. She's got room in the preschool and is holding a spot for her. Just give her a call." She pulled a small scrap of paper out of her backpack pocket. "Here's her number and address."

She checked an item off my unexpectedly long to-do list. Such a small but also huge thing. I felt space open in my too-full brain. "Thank you, Emma. I'll call her."

I sat and listened to the sound of children laughing and

screaming with joy for a few minutes. Then Cricket saw me and skipped over to give me a hug.

"I was thinking we could do something fun," I told her.

"What fun?"

"I thought we could go explore the apple orchard. You can see how apples grow."

"Okay." She took my hand to pull me up from the bench, then let go again. "Wait. I have to say goodbye to my friends."

She made friends so easily. Just like her daddy always did.

At the apartment, we grabbed a snack—raisins for her, a handful of nuts for me—then filled two bottles with water. She decided the dancing bunny rain boots I bought her at Tiny Togs were perfect for walking through an orchard. Then we were off.

The orchard had apple trees of varying sizes and ages. I remembered that the full-size ones, at nearly thirty-feet-tall, produced an abundance of wonderful fruit but were so tall it was hard to harvest the apples. We had a few of the big beauties but opted mostly for smaller trees, which made picking easier for us and the community when we let them enter once a year during the Blackwood Grove Harvest Fest.

I picked Cricket up so she could get a closer look.

"They're so cute," she declared, cupping her hands around, but not touching, the closest one.

"Pretty soon you'll be able to pick and eat them."

"Apples are my favoritest."

I smiled and set her down. She ran from tree to tree and encouraged them by whispering "good job" while laying her hands on their trunks.

The deeper into the rows we wandered, the more I relaxed. Connecting with nature was always the answer for me. Without a doubt, the right job for me here would be to tend the gardens and these trees. And the aunties, of course.

"What's that?" Cricket called out.

"What?"

"That."

I knelt next to her, my knees crackling on the way down to the ground, and she pointed at a small shack.

"Oh, my stars." I let out a little gasp. "That is my and Carly's secret fort."

"A secret fort?" she whispered.

"It's not so secret. Pretty easy to see, isn't it?"

She giggled and agreed that it was.

"When Carly and I were little girls, we would come out here to read or listen to music or get away from our siblings."

Where were they? Brenda was completely MIA, but did Carly know where Etta and Benny were? I made a mental note to ask.

"Who's that?" She pointed again, and I squinted past the trees.

A woman in loose flowy clothes with long frizzy hair stepped out of the shack.

"Looks like Auntie Gwynne. Wonder what she's doing out here." Except, she would be working at The Apple Barn now. And the closer we got, the less this woman looked like my aunt. She was smaller, frailer. Her narrow shoulders rounded forward, and one sat significantly lower than the other. This woman's hair was completely gray, whereas Gwynne's still had a bit of blond in it.

Before I could stop her, Cricket went running over to the woman. "Auntie Gwynne!" She stopped in her tracks when the woman turned around.

The trees surrounding us blurred into a swash of brown, green, and red. My vision tunneled. I only saw my granddaughter in the foreground, the shack in the background, and this old hag of a woman between them. Her face held so many deep wrinkles I could barely make out any smooth skin. Huge bags hung beneath her exhausted, tortured-looking eyes.

This woman looked so broken I wasn't sure how she was standing upright.

"Mom?"

Cricket spun toward me, almost like she'd forgotten I was there, then ran to me and hid behind my legs.

Gwynne was right, she looked nothing like what I remembered. I would have guessed she was a hundred years old rather than seventy-eight.

"Hello, Dusty." Her voice sounded as dry as my name. "I knew we'd cross paths eventually."

"Cross paths? You've been here this whole time. You knew I was here and never bothered to even poke your head around a corner?"

"Of course I knew. Your father told me you were coming to help. That's a very good thing. Carly's been overwhelmed."

Her words were like an athame to my heart. *Carly's* been overwhelmed. Had Dad told her anything about my life? Well, he told her I was coming back. When was that? Immediately after we left the park, or had he been so sure he could manipulate me into this caretaker stuff that he told her before I'd even called him?

A horrifying thought whispered in my brain. *Did they burn down my house?*

Behind me, Cricket clutched my legs tighter. I scooped her up and held her tight. She wrapped her arms and legs around me. There was no need for Dad to manipulate me into returning. I had no choice. This precious child's life was in danger.

Still, the truth was, my parents *always* put their needs first. Brenda used to stomp around her room at least once a week and complain about how they never listened to her. "It's like they don't even care that they have daughters. Why do I even stay here?"

"For me," I wanted to answer but never did.

I always suspected they were the reason she left.

And now, Dad had known all along Mom was here on the farm? "Oh, she's around," he answered when I asked about her that morning in the park not quite a week ago. Everyone I asked said the same thing. They never knew when or for how long she'd be here.

"Dusty," Mom began like she was going to confess something.

"No," I cut her off, furious and overwhelmed. "Not now."

I turned and walked away, my heart racing. First my job, then the house, the note about Cricket, and now all this in six days. Maybe I just needed to catch my breath.

We'd been walking for a couple of minutes when Cricket tapped me on the shoulder like she'd been trying to get my attention. "Are we done in the orchard?"

I could make out the carriage house through the trees.

"Sorry, I didn't realize which way we were walking. Do you want to stay longer?"

She nodded. "I like seeing how apples grow."

I wasn't ready to leave the trees yet either, so I set her down and she immediately started talking about apples. She was once again my bubbly, happy little bug. Almost like she had no memory of her great-grandmother. Had my mother cast a spell on her? Just that fast? Or had she placed a spell on herself to make others forget her? Could that be why no one ever knew where she was? *I* hadn't forgotten her, though.

"Tell you what, we'll stay out here longer and play some games when we get back to the apartment."

"Hi Ho Cherry O." Her innocent eyes narrowed, and after a bit of pondering, she declared, "Lola, cherries are like baby apples."

I laughed so hard I almost cried.

CHAPTER 25

*C*arly arrived at precisely seven thirty and flopped down on my couch. "Ready to talk about suspects?"

I'd been so distracted by my mother and wondering if my family was lying to me about her, I forgot Carly was coming over. "First, tell me why no one told me my mother has been here for the past week."

She chewed her lip, like she used to do as a kid when she'd get caught fibbing about being done with her homework. Then she blurted, "I was incarcerated."

"You've been a free woman for more than two days."

"And during those two days, we've been investigating a murder and catching up on the last thirty-two years. And dealing with personal stuff."

Couldn't argue with that. "Any idea why the aunts didn't tell me?"

"Oh, lord, Dusty. If I could explain why they do the things they do, I wouldn't need your help. And that's not a brush-off." She paused. "I honestly don't know what's going on with Griselle. She'll hang around for days, seclude herself in her bedroom or up in the attic, skulk around like a ghost, and on rare occasions come down for dinner. Then weeks will pass, and we won't see even a hint of her. I have no idea where she goes during those times."

"You remember some things about her but not others."

Her brow furrowed with thought, then her expression brightened. "Yeah, there are holes in my memory. What are you thinking?"

"Do you suppose it's possible she put a spell on herself?" I told her what happened after we saw her in the orchard.

"I'd never considered that. Not even sure if it's even possible, but it would explain things."

A tornado of emotions swirled inside me. "She looks horrible."

Carly nodded. "She does. Consequences of all the gray spells."

I didn't want to feel empathy for my mother so let frustration move in instead. "It's obvious her body is breaking down. Why is she still casting? Why would she do that to herself?"

"I don't know, Dusty. It's like she's addicted."

"Addicted? To doing the wrong thing?"

"For the right reason. Those spells help people. If you really want to know, you'll have to ask her."

Addicted to restoring justice. That almost made sense. I sank back against the couch cushions. "Sorry for snapping at you."

"No worries. Don't know about you, but I would enjoy a glass of wine right now."

A bottle of Merlot and two wine glasses appeared on the coffee table.

I thanked the apartment, filled a glass half full, and handed it to her. "How was your afternoon with Sebastian?"

"You know, sometimes with kids it's like trying to solve a Rubik's Cube. Other times all you have to do is point out the obvious."

"Which time was this?"

"Thank the gods, today was easy. I pointed out that maybe he'd been so angry because his dad has been gone an extra-long time this trip, Alex is making goo-goo eyes at Savannah, and he's left with us girls."

"And?"

"He laughed so hard at me saying *goo-goo* he fell off the bed, then agreed he was pretty tired of girls. I had already talked to Mason, and he agreed to talk with him mano-a-mano or bro-to-bro or whatever. Bastian liked that idea and actually looked forward to serving his punishment tonight. Then on the way over there, he admitted he was scared they'd put me in prison and he'd never see me again." She put her hand to her heart and drank from her glass. "Darn kids. Just when you get yourself worked up into a good lather, they say something like that and you melt."

I held out my glass for a toast of solidarity, and she tapped hers against it.

"How did the phone call with Micah go last night?"

I loved that we were finally talking about personal things, like our kids. "Poor Cricket. She gets so excited to talk to him, then sobs herself to sleep once we hang up."

"My kids used to do the same thing when Kyle was on a trip. It tore my heart out, so we finally tried something different. Ask Micah to call just a little later if possible. Get Cricket all cozy and ready for bed and have him 'tuck her in' during the call."

"That's a good idea. We'll try that."

"Ready to make a suspect list?"

I retrieved the piece of paper the house had given me to take notes for getting Carly out of jail and flipped it to the clean side.

"Shouldn't we use a notebook or something?" she asked.

"How many investigations do you think we'll have to do?"

"True. All right, let's approach this logically. What did you learn from Marilyn?"

"Not a lot. She admitted she found something in Beck's background but wouldn't tell me what. She perked up when I told her my easy access to the river theory."

"Those two things could be related," Carly suggested. "Do they add up to murder, though? Did it seem like she was hiding anything?"

"As in did *she* kill him?" I considered that for a second, then remembered, "According to the security video the killer is a tall, thin man. It's possible Marilyn hired someone."

Carly leaned forward. "If we're focusing on one of the shop owners as the killer, that video helps a lot. There are twenty stores on the mall, one is empty, and sixteen of the owners are women. Your *hired someone* comment has potential, but otherwise, we're left with Stuart, Russell, and Eduardo."

"Both the plant store and the teahouse are on the wrong side of the mall," I noted. "Although, Maggie says Beck gave her the creeps and was in there harassing Russell daily."

"But only," Carly corrected, "to get an insider's opinion of how to manipulate Marilyn. Russell may have been annoyed by the guy, but I can't see him stabbing anyone due to annoyance."

I agreed. "I don't remember talking to an Eduardo. Which shop is his?"

"Dapper, the men's clothing store."

"That's right across from the playground on the river side. I noticed it yesterday."

"He's out of town. They took three days driving to his niece's wedding in New Mexico and then planned a week-long road trip on the way back."

I held out my wine glass so she could add a little more. "You need to be pretty close to stab a person, so not Eduardo."

For some reason, Carly found that so funny she nearly spit out her wine, then broke into a giggle fit. "Okay, I'm good. This means we don't need to spend any more time interviewing store owners. I wish we would have thought about the video sooner. I hate wasting time. I never have enough of it to begin with."

We sat in silence, trying to come up with more options.

"This guy is out there," I reasoned. "There's got to be a way to find him."

"There's always magic." She'd brightened with a thought. "What's your strongest power?"

"Gray magic."

My reply left her speechless.

"It's true. I can't actually bring on a dream or premonition. They just happen. While I don't understand how I do it, I make things happen with gray magic. That's my true power."

She waited until I looked her in the eye. "You need to talk to your mother."

"She's never helped me with my magic."

"Doesn't mean she won't now. I mean, if you think of the potential—"

"Potential?" My spine stiffened. "You think I want to develop this? You've seen what it's done to her. It scares the hell out of me."

"Would you rather risk another boat accident?"

I sat back and looked away from her. "That's cruel."

"It wasn't meant to be. You didn't stop the boat on purpose, which is my point. If you don't learn how to control it, something else bad is sure to happen."

"Can we focus on finding the killer, please?"

"Sure. What I meant is that there's got to be a way to bring on dreams or premonitions." She set her glass on the coffee table and stood. "I'm going to go get the grimoire."

"I'll go with you. It's not supposed to leave the attic."

"That's what they told us to keep us from taking it to school. I'll be right back."

While she was gone, I fumed and paced the room and got steadily angrier at her comment. She knew how the accident had nearly destroyed not only the lives of everyone on the boat that day, but my life too. How could she use it against me like that?

But she hadn't meant it to hurt me. And she was right, the power wasn't going anywhere. Like Gwynne said, it was a natural part of me. I could either continue to live in denial or accept my true self and learn how to control and use the gray magic.

"I forget how big this thing is," Carly said a few minutes later when she got to the top of the stairs. "Are you done being mad at me?"

"Yes, I understand what you meant."

"Okay, good. I'm sorry my comment upset you." She plunked the book down on the coffee table and murmured, "A spell that will bring on premonitions." As she flipped through the pages, I saw something I hadn't the other night. "I don't remember all those blank pages."

"They've always been here," she dismissed and continued flipping.

"No, there weren't any when I was looking for a memory spell. Hang on." I opened the book to the middle like I had the other night. "Show me a spell to return a lost memory."

The pages flipped on their own and stopped on a blank page.

"Interesting," I noted.

"What is?" Carly asked.

"The page is blank." I glanced at my cousin. "Suppose that's because it's a gray spell?"

"And the book won't reveal it because a non-gray witch is looking? Makes sense to me." She followed my lead and asked for a premonition spell. The pages began flipping again. "Here we go. Literally titled 'How to Bring on Prophetic Dreams and Premonitions.'"

"Very helpful. What does it say?"

"There are all sorts of things you can try. A dream pillow or bath sachet with chamomile, yarrow, and mugwort. Those three are starred. You could also add passionflower, bay leaves, cinquefoil, or calendula. Or you can try sleeping beneath a black walnut tree."

I thought of the property. "Do we have any black walnut trees?"

"I've never seen any." She ran her finger down the page. "You can also place mandrake beneath your pillow or marigold under your bed, burn jasmine in your bedroom, or drink a rosebud infusion at bedtime."

"What's this one?" I pointed at a drawing of an apothecary bottle. "Oh, a witch bottle. Put dried mugwort, lavender, and an amethyst crystal in a bottle, stopper it, and seal it with wax." I read a little more. "It says those same things—mugwort, lavender, and amethyst—will also work for scrying. You could try scrying for the killer."

"I haven't needed to scry in a while. Of course, I've been too busy to practice." She smiled. "The reason is awful, but it's exciting to use my magic again. Let's go get the supplies."

"Cricket alarm, please. We'll be in the main house."

The alarm chirped, and we rushed down the stairs and across the courtyard. While I pulled the necessary bottles of dried herbs and flowers out of the pantry cabinet, Carly ran up to the armoire in the attic where the aunts kept the crystals and stones.

I wondered briefly if my mother was up there.

"Goodness, dear," Pepper said, surprising me when she showed up in the kitchen. She produced a sturdy basket and indicated the lineup of bottles on the counter. "Use this to carry all that."

I loved that she didn't ask why I was raiding the pantry at nearly nine in the evening.

"Thank you." I explained what we were doing.

"Add a pinch of pink salt to your dream pillow and bottle. And to the rosebud tea. It will help open your third eye."

"Thanks, Pepper." I took the bottle of salt too. "I'll note that in the grimoire."

"Here's the amethyst," Carly announced and placed two small purple crystals in the basket. "Have you got it all?"

"Just need lavender." I scanned the shelves. "Can't find it."

"Um." Pepper gestured at the island. "That's because I used it all. I made lemon-lavender shortbread cookies. They're quite tasty if I do say so myself."

"We're out of lavender?" Carly asked. "We've never run out of lavender."

"I must have forgotten to put it on the list," Pepper answered. "There's plenty in the garden."

Carly shook her head. "We need dried."

"Guess I'm going back to the apothecary tomorrow."

CHAPTER 26

At breakfast, while Cricket ate her oatmeal with peaches and a sprinkle of brown sugar, and rain pattered on the windowpanes, I told the aunts I'd seen my mother. I figured they'd react with a little embarrassment for not telling me she was here, but they'd become immune to her comings and goings over the years. Basically, nothing regarding Griselle Warren fazed them anymore. I'd stop pulling that thread now.

Instead, I moved on to my decision regarding my position within the family business. "I'm happiest in the gardens and out in the orchard. That's what I want to do."

Jett celebrated my announcement by leaping out of her chair and kissing me on the cheek. "Caring for the animals goes with the job. I enjoy it, but it's up to you if you want to take that on as well or hire someone to do it. Your apprenticeship will begin today."

"Count on me tomorrow. I've got a project today." I explained the spells that would help bring on dreams, visions, and enhance Carly's scrying. "Except someone used all the lavender."

I winked at Pepper, who asked, "Did you try the rosebud infusion?"

"I did, and yes, I added a pinch of pink salt. Can't say anything prophetic came to me last night, but I did dream. Just don't remember what I dreamed."

"Keep a journal next to your bed," Gwynne instructed. "First thing in the morning or if you wake in the night, write down your thoughts."

A piece of paper and a pen appeared on the table in front of me.

"Thanks," I told the house, "but I feel like a dream journal should actually be a journal. I'll find one when Cricket and I run over to the apothecary."

The page disappeared, and the sound of paper ripping filled the kitchen.

"I didn't mean to offend you," I apologized.

"Don't mind the house," Gwynne said. "Like with my knees, rain makes its bones ache, and it gets crabby."

"Maybe we should smudge it," I suggested. A lemon-lavender shortbread cookie appeared on the table in front of me where the paper had been. A reward.

"Good idea." Pepper went to the pantry cabinet. "I'll make a moon water, red Hawaiian salt, and rainbow pepper infusion and spritz the house today."

Cricket and I put on rain jackets, gifts from the property, and followed Jett out to the coop to collect the morning eggs. While Cricket performed her duties, Jett gave me a short lesson on caring for the chickens.

"Think I'll pick up two journals. I can already tell there will be a lot to learn." I hadn't decided on whether I wanted to take care of the goats, chickens, and bees as well as the gardens and orchards, but I needed to at least know how. Thankfully Jett wasn't going anywhere, so I had time to learn it all. At least I hoped she wasn't going anywhere. I'd become rather fond of the woman over the past week.

When it was time for Cricket and me to go, the rain was falling harder, so we added rain boots and umbrellas along with our jackets and trudged the two hundred yards to the apothecary.

As we approached the emerald-green hut, I thought of taking over for Jett and where that could lead me. I could hear the whispers of my and Carly's old dreams calling to me. *It's not too late*, they seemed to be saying, answering the question both Carly and I had asked.

"You're back!" Silver greeted when we entered the store.

"It is moving." Cricket whispered in awe. I'd told her about the ceiling and walls. Cool as that was, her attention quickly turned elsewhere. "Kitties!"

Two cats strolled through the store. One was a gray striped tabby with blue-green eyes. The other was orange with amber eyes and ears that folded forward.

"This is Dawn," Moon said of the orange one, "and that's Dusk. You must be Cricket."

My girl eyed her suspiciously. "How do you know my name?"

"Miss Pepper told us about you yesterday," Silver said. "What can we help you find today?"

Cricket giggled. "Not me. Lola needs help."

"In more ways than the obvious," I joked. "We're completely out of lavender, and I need some for a spell. A couple of spells actually." This was the first time I'd even mentioned casting a spell to someone other than a family member, or my friend Vic, in more than thirty years.

"Not a problem. We've got plenty." Moon filled a big bag for me, and I took two small bottles with stoppers from the shelf. "Anything else?"

"Yes, I need two journals."

Moon pointed out a table near the front of the store. "We restocked everything yesterday, so we've got a nice supply of those too."

While I spent way too long choosing my journals, Cricket played quietly with the cats. Like she had a few days ago in the family room, she almost appeared to be conversing with them. She was telling them something about the familiars at the farm, and they sat as though fascinated by her.

"Can she communicate with them?" Silver asked.

I smiled. "I've been wondering the same thing." Thinking back to her following the frog into the viburnum bush, and her devotion to the farm animals and familiars, the signs were there.

"So cool if she can," Silver said with a hint of envy in her voice. "A wee Dolittle."

"All set?" Moon asked when I set my three items on the counter.

"Yep . . . Wait. I need to buy a gift. Do you know Emma?

"Carly's girl? Sure."

"She's been watching Cricket for me, and I want to give her a thank you gift."

Moon thought for a moment and then brightened. "I think I know just the thing." She led me to a case loaded with necklaces, earrings, bracelets, and rings made from various stones and crystals. She pulled a tray of rings from inside the case and pointed out a silver ring with a yellow stone. "Citrine symbolizes thanks and gratitude."

"You think a ring instead of a necklace?"

"She always comments on mine," Silver offered, wiggling her fingers full of rings, "but never comments on my necklaces so . . ."

"Okay, then." I took four rings from the tray and placed them in my palm. Within a few seconds, a simple silver one with a small round citrine grew warm. "This is the one."

Moon rang up my items and took my credit card. "Tell Emma to stop in if the ring needs sizing. We can help with that."

I thanked them, and as we left Cricket hollered, "Good bye! See you later."

I was pretty sure she meant the cats.

"You were such a good girl while Lola shopped." I looked to the sky. "The rain has stopped for now. Would you like to play on the playground for a while?"

She gave me a sly smile. "Can I splash in the puddles?"

Such a negotiator. What were knee-high rain boots good for if not splashing in puddles? "Okay but try not to get too wet."

While she played, I looked around the mostly empty park. It seemed the rain and a murderer on the loose were keeping people home.

A little way down the park, Wayne was shaking the rain off his tent. His sleeping bag was strapped to the top of his backpack. A water bottle, a blue hat, a pair of flip-flops, and other necessities hung off loops on the sides. All of the man's possessions fit in a backpack.

As I watched him pack up, I thought of his comment to Beau, that he didn't see anyone going into the diner before or leaving after the approximate death window. That didn't sit right with me. What if he had seen someone but, like some of the shop owners were, he was afraid to tell a cop because he was also freaked out by whatever was going on in this town? He didn't know me, but maybe I could get him to open up to me.

I took a couple of steps toward him when Cricket appeared in front of me.

"It's raining again, Lola." She held her arms over her head, blocking the drops.

I laughed. She had both a hood on her rain jacket and an umbrella but opted for her arms as protection from the rain. I opened her umbrella and handed it to her. "I think it's going to rain all day. Let's go home and I'll turn on a movie."

I'd come back and talk to Wayne later.

ONCE CRICKET HAD CHANGED into a clean, dry outfit, I made her some hot cocoa and let her pick a movie. Within minutes she and her array of stuffed animal friends were lost in an animated world.

In the kitchenette, I gathered all the ingredients to assemble witch balls and a sleep pillow, my intent being to bring on a dream or premonition about the killer. The process made me think of the last time I had mixed plants. Micah had been in middle school and caught a cold with a nasty cough. I made a simple cough syrup of one part each licorice root, mullein leaf, and wild cherry bark steeped in a cup of water, reduced to a half cup, and then I added a bit of honey.

The spells in the grimoire read like recipes, except the instructions weren't very specific. A pinch of this, two pinches of that. How big was a pinch? What if I put in too much of something or not enough? I was probably overthinking this. At least the spells I was casting indicated quantities. Others in the grimoire simply said *mix the following herbs together* with no quantities specified. Very helpful, dear relative.

With everything laid out before me, I drank some more rosebud and pink salt tea and got a clear image of Beck in my mind. Or as clear as possible. I never saw the man's face. Once all the proper number of pinches were in the little sachet bag/sleep pillow, I pulled the strings and tied it shut. Then I added mugwort, lavender, and amethyst to one of the jars I bought at the apothecary, inserted the cork stopper, and dripped wax over it.

As the wax slowly sealed the stopper into place, I thought

about talking to Wayne. He must have seen something the day Beck died. I'd get back over to the park and talk to him as soon as I could.

Thinking about Wayne made me think about seeing him at The Paddle Wheel which made me think about Henry Kramer. Of all the things Henry said to me, one statement really bothered me. *If you think you know all there is to know about your family now, you've grown into a stupid woman.* At the time, I figured he was just causing trouble, poking the bear. Now I knew that my family had been keeping things from me, either purposely or unintentionally. What else didn't I know?

A bit of wax dripped onto my finger, jolting me back to the present. I'd put more than enough on the stopper. I considered making one for Carly, but she should make her own and infuse it with her intent. Instead, I put the ingredients she'd need, the second empty bottle, and a candle in a paper bag. Then I put the bottles from the pantry cabinet back into the basket Pepper gave me and set it aside with the grimoire to return when we went over for dinner.

When I brought the witch jar and journals to my bedroom, I found curtains on the sliding glass doors to the balcony. They had some stains, were hung crooked, and were sheerer than I preferred, but at least I wouldn't feel quite so exposed now.

"Thanks," I told the apartment. "I'm not sure what's going on around here anymore, but I really am doing my best."

Dinner was simple. Pepper served pork chops and potato chunks with mushroom gravy and applesauce. A comforting meal for a rainy night. It was just me and Cricket, Pepper, Gwynne, and Jett. Granny Sadie hovered in the background. I felt like they were all watching me, and I couldn't help but wonder if every sideways glance or pause before speaking meant they were hiding something new.

When we got back to the apartment, I found a message on my cell phone from Vic.

"Hey, girl. It's been a week, so I'm checking in to see how you're doing. I did some research on your charming little town. I'm still thinking about a day trip to see you and do some shopping because your mall looks promising. I could stay overnight, and we'll have dinner and drinks. Let me know when that would work for you."

My first thought was, why was he so interested in coming here? I liked Vic, he'd been a good friend, but he had a voyeuristic side. We were people, not a sideshow. My second thought was that by *it's been a week*, he didn't mean it had been a stressful one for him. Today was Wednesday. One week ago, almost to the minute, my house caught fire.

I WOKE WITH A START, my sheets damp with sweat that had nothing to do with a hot flash. The rosebud tea must have kicked in. Or maybe it was the witch ball or dream pillow. Or a combination of all three. I grabbed the journal I'd designated for dream use and started scribbling.

Shop owners and people from town, both witches and Ordies, had gathered in a large group in the middle of the park. One by one, people vanished from the group like popcorn popping in reverse. In seconds, only those that Carly and I originally identified as possible suspects were left. Then they vanished as well, one by one, slowly as though being swallowed by a mist. Before disappearing completely, they each pointed in the same direction. At Wayne. He was the last one remaining.

Suddenly the background changed from the park to in front of the diner. Wayne put a hand over his eyes and walked into the diner. He was wearing a Milwaukee Brewers baseball cap and a baggy flannel shirt.

That's when I woke up.

I grabbed my phone from the wobbly bedside table and was

about to dial Carly's number, but it was four o'clock in the morning.

When Cricket woke at six, I urged her to get dressed so we could go have breakfast. Not that I was interested in eating. Naturally, this was the day she "wasn't hungry" and wanted to play. Fortunately, she liked the idea of playing with the familiars.

"Since she's chief egg gatherer, can you watch her for a bit?" I asked Jett. "I won't be gone long."

She agreed and reminded me that my internship was to start today.

I squeezed through the hedge, darted through the park, and saw Beau walking into the teashop just as I spotted Wayne getting ready to clean up his space. Good to know Beau was close. I debated about calling him over, but Wayne might not talk if he saw a cop.

I called out to Wayne. He looked up and gave a half-smile, probably trying to remember if he knew me.

"Glad I caught you." I couldn't help but notice the flannel shirt tied around his waist. "I wanted to ask you a couple of questions."

"Me?" His smile had faded by this point. "What's this about? And who are you?"

"Sorry. My name is Dusty. I'm related to Comfort, Carly, and Nina at the diner."

Those names he knew, but he was still wary. "Okay. What did you want to ask?"

"I'm sure you know about the murder that happened last week. A man was found dead inside the diner."

"Yeah, that was real sad."

"Officer Balinski told me he'd talked to you about it and said you told him you hadn't seen anyone go into or leave the diner. I've been doing my own investigation, and it seems like people are afraid to talk about this. So I was wondering if you were, too, and that's why you didn't talk to the officer."

He returned to packing his things. "Don't know what you're talking about."

I glanced at the teahouse. Beau hadn't left yet. I needed to come at this from a different angle. Compassion. "I heard that you've been here for a while. You must like Blackwood Grove."

"I do. The people are real friendly. They make sure I get enough to eat, and the cops don't care if I pitch my tent here in the park long as I'm cleaned up by the time the shops open."

As he talked more about how friendly the town was, his words slowly faded away, and sorrow or perhaps fear slid in where the smile had been.

I felt bad for him. "You know what happened at the diner, don't you, Wayne?"

He shook his head, attention focused on attaching a Brewers cap to his backpack. "I told that cop I didn't see anyone go in there."

Beau should hear this. "You didn't see anyone go in because you couldn't have *seen* yourself entering the diner. Could you?"

He froze.

"You killed Ludo Beck. Didn't you?"

Wayne sat back on his heels. After a *long* pause he said, "They asked me to do it."

"Who did? Someone in town? People Beck was doing business with?"

Wayne shook his head. "I can't tell you. Seriously. They'll kill me if I even say their name."

And he really seemed to believe that.

Who were these people? Folks Beck had gotten tangled up with? Was that the thing in his background Marilyn found? Or . . . were they the same ones who had threatened Cricket and set my house on fire? Maybe Wayne carried out his assignment too early on Thursday. Was he supposed to go after me or

Cricket and finish what the fire was meant to do? Or had his target been other members of my family?

And according to what Beau told us outside the teashop, Beck first came to Blackwood Grove at almost the same time Josie went missing. All of this was connected. It had to be.

I took a step away from Wayne as my mind spun. "Did they offer to pay you?"

"Not exactly." He was shoving things into his backpack faster now. He was going to run.

"What does that mean?"

He paused again, then released a sigh that seemed to come from his toes. "They said they'd give me a legit job if I did it, but looks like they lied 'cause now they won't even talk to me."

"You'll go to prison for murder, you know. If you turn them in, they'll go to prison."

"Lady, you don't get it. People like that, they know people. I'd live the rest of my life looking over my shoulder, waiting for someone to shank me. At least this way I'll have a bed every night and three meals a day."

It broke my heart that prison was the better option for him. Then I blurted, "I can help you."

"You can't help me."

"I'm a witch, Wayne. I can cast memory spells. Whoever you're scared of, I can cast a spell to make them forget it was you."

What the hell was I doing? My mother's wrinkled face, frizzled hair, and scrawny crooked frame flashed in my eyes. Was this what she did? Cast gray spells for random people? Wrong thing, right reason. Wayne had been promised a better life. Except, he killed a man in cold blood. There was no right reason behind this wrong thing. He wasn't worth the consequences of a gray spell. Was he?

And why did I suddenly believe I had the right to decide who was worthy and who wasn't?

"Thanks for the concern, lady, but I'll take my chances. Go get the cops if you want. I'm tired of living my life this way."

The teahouse was just a few yards away. I'd been facing it the whole time and hadn't seen Beau leave. It would take less than a minute for me to run over there and get him. But if Wayne ran . . .

I pulled my cell phone out of my back pocket, looked up the number for So Mote It Tea, and dialed. Russell answered on the fourth ring.

"So Mote It Tea, can you hold, please?"

"Russell, it's Dusty. I'm right outside in the park. Would you send Beau over please? It's an emergency."

The moment Wayne saw Beau exit the teahouse, he grabbed his backpack and ran.

Beau held his hands up in a *what's going on* gesture. I pointed at Wayne and shouted, "He's the one. Get him."

Beau took off after him, and while he ran faster than I expected with his prosthetic leg, Wayne was faster.

Without thinking, I raised my hand . . . and froze. What was I doing? I felt the magic tingling in the tips of my fingers, ready to burst free and stop Wayne. But there were other people in the park. What if my long unused magic hit one of them? I'd nearly killed ten of my classmates last time. I couldn't risk hurting anyone again.

Fortunately, other townies heard me, saw Beau taking chase, and tackled Wayne.

The next thing I knew, Carly was at my side. "What's going on? Officer Chapman was in the diner to pick up breakfast. We all heard Beau's call for help over her radio."

I explained my dream and what Wayne had told me. Carly's mouth dropped open with shock. By that time, Beau had come over to me while Officer Chapman took Wayne to the jail. I told him what Wayne had said to me. He shook his head, sad for the homeless man.

"Do you know the rest of the story?" I asked him. "Do you know why Beck was killed?"

He hemmed and hawed and eventually said, "It's all going to come out soon. Keep it quiet until we make this public."

We promised we would.

"You were right about Beck wanting access to the river, but not for reasons you probably thought. He wasn't doing anything illegal. He had a questionable past but has been clean for a good ten years. That's likely why Marilyn wouldn't approve his application."

"Did he really want to open a grocery store?" Carly asked.

"He did. A specialty store like you'd heard."

"What could be questionable about that?" I asked.

Beau replied, "Do you know what the number-one shoplifted item from grocery stores worldwide is?"

"Liquor?" Carly guessed. "Meat?"

He shook his head. "Cheese. Ironic, considering we live in Wisconsin and it's pretty much our state food. I kid you not, cheese theft is a thing. International cheese heists, worth tens of thousands of dollars per heist, have been a problem for decades. The same is true in the US. Beck wanted to open a shop where his delivery people would be safe. He figured having shipments come in from the river instead of trucks driving down the highway would be the safer option."

"How do you know this?" Carly asked. "Was he right? Would his plan have kept delivery folks safer?"

"I know this because I'm good at my job. Would they have been safer? He died, so I'll say no."

Unless Beck wasn't the real target.

Beau continued, "I'd like to thank you two for your help with this, but then it'll sound like I condone you potentially putting yourselves in danger. Please don't do that again."

"Do you expect there will be opportunity for us to *help* again?" Carly asked him.

She had to be referring to the discussion I'd had with Winnie the other night. About the safe towns being in danger.

Beau looked between us. "I wish I could say this was only related to Beck, but . . ."

"Beau, what's going on in this town?" I asked. "I feel like this is bigger than cheese theft."

"Another very good question I wish I knew the answer to."

CHAPTER 27

*L*ater that night, Carly came over after she'd had dinner with her kids. There was still an hour before bath time, so she and I wandered around the farm with Cricket, who wanted to say goodnight to the chickens, goats, and bees, her entourage of familiars trailing after her.

"You're quiet tonight," Carly noted. "Is it the Wayne thing or is something else going on?"

"It's a lot of things, actually." I took a breath. "I can trust you, right?"

She stared at me before answering, "Not sure if that question surprises or offends me. Of course you can. What's going on?"

"Henry made a comment to me—"

"Don't listen to Henry."

"No, seriously, it's eating at me. He started by saying I was a stupid kid when I left here and didn't know anything about anything—"

"Jackass," she muttered.

"No doubt, but that's not the part that got to me. He said, 'if you think you know all there is to know about your family now, you've grown into a stupid woman.'"

"Wow. And what are you thinking about that?"

"That it feels like the truth. For my first eighteen years, my relationship with my parents was rocky at best. Since then, it's been pretty much nonexistent. I spoke to Dad for two minutes every six months. He didn't tell you guys anything about me, but he never told me anything about you either. I have no idea what happened to my sister. Something is wrong with my mother, and no one seems to care. Dad never comes over, and no one cares about that either. I feel like my part of the family has been erased. Maybe that's why Cricket and I can't stay in the house."

When she was sure my rant was over, Carly replied, "Keep in mind that you haven't been here for the last thirty-two years. To you, sure, it feels like all of this happened recently, but we've been dealing with it the whole time. We've tried *many* times to help Griselle. The wrinkles, the blank-eyed not fully connected to reality appearance, it's part of the consequences, and there isn't a reversal spell. You can't do something good to balance out your karma after casting a gray spell. We've tried to convince her to stop casting and focus on selling spells at the gate. She refuses. Like I said yesterday, I think she's addicted and can't stop. As for your dad, of course we care about him. This being away from the family thing started before you left. Remember? He comes over every few months and is always welcome. And as for why you can't stay in the house? The property is mad at you."

"Like you all are. Because I left to keep you safe."

"Because you left without a word or even a damn postcard, Dusty. You could have sent a freaking carrier pigeon or set off smoke signals. Anything. Yes, your dad could have said something, but when you didn't hear anything regarding us, *you* should have done something. That's why we're all upset with you. And can *you* trust *me*? I should be asking you that question."

I nodded, humbled but not backing down. "I understand, agree with, and appreciate every word you said. I'm sorry that my question upset you, but the truth is I don't know who I can trust anymore. Josie went missing, Micah was arrested for it, I lost my job and my house, and someone threatened my granddaughter. All those things happened within the last month, and I don't believe it's all coincidental. Someone did this to me and my kids. Winnie told me The Council wants me to protect this town. What if Dad knew the only way to get me back here was for it to be my only possible option, and he set me up? What if The Council set my house on fire? With me and Cricket inside!" I swallowed the emotions growing in me. "I know how paranoid that makes me sound, but what if? I need one person I know I can trust without hesitation, and I really want that person to be you."

She nodded, and I could tell by the look in her eyes that she understood. "I told you before, I can't do all this by myself. If you can promise me you're not going to bail on me again and be honest with me about everything, then we're golden."

My eyes stung with threatening tears. "There were a few speed bumps this week, but I feel like I'm in the right place. I want to be here and am beyond grateful I'm getting another chance. You've got the diner. I told Jett I want to take over the farm."

She smiled, genuine and warm. "Nina wants the diner. I actually want The Apple Barn. Since it looks like we won't be getting that specialty grocery store, I've got some thoughts for expanding the Barn's food section."

We stared at each other, both surely thinking the same thing. *We can still make our dream of running a business together come true.*

"So what's next?" she asked.

"I need help finding Josie so I can get Micah out of prison. I know Cricket is safe inside the hedge, but it's a concern if she goes to Autumn Trainor's preschool. And I want to keep proving my loyalty to you all."

"Getting me out of jail and catching the killer brought you a long way with that last one."

I placed my hand over my heart in thanks. "What about the aunts? What are we supposed to do for them?"

"I think it's time for them to slow down. Past time. Mom can't maintain her current pace at the diner. I'll talk with Nina about that. Same with Gwynne. I'll talk with her about me taking over the shop."

"And Jett has already started my apprenticeship on the farm."

"We're going to have to find someone to take care of the house. Sooner than later."

"You don't think Pepper can handle it? The house seems in good order to me."

Carly arched an eyebrow and asked, "How much actual cooking have you seen her do this week?"

I thought back. "She taught Cricket how to make pancakes one morning, and I think she made the rice and beans and shrimp étouffée Monday night." That's all I came up with. "I guess everything else did appear really fast." A little stab of pain, like a needle into a voodoo doll, pierced my heart at the revelation. "The house has been doing it. It's good that Moon and Silver want her help."

"It is."

"So, if the others work less at their jobs, maybe the four of them can take care of the house?"

Carly's eyes went wide. "Witches gone wild. What could possibly go wrong? Guess we can give it a try." She didn't seem convinced. Then she yawned, which made me yawn. "Are we good?"

"Good goddess, I hope so. I've missed you so much, and I'm so sorry—"

"You don't have to apologize anymore. I understand why

you did what you did. I'm just glad to have my Dust Bunny back."

Tears filled my eyes as I hugged my best friend.

"Okay." She pulled away and blinked repeatedly. "I need to get home. Kyle is coming home tonight." She waggled her eyebrows at me. "Should be here soon."

"Go, woman. Why are you hanging out with me?"

"Oh, I've got time. I won't get him until the kids are done talking his ear off. See you tomorrow."

I loved that we could say that.

"Come on, Cricket. Time for your bath." I caught her climbing the fence to the goat pen. "No, no, little miss. Those goats love you too much. You'll be surrounded in seconds."

I pulled her in and nuzzled her neck, making her squeal with laughter.

We got to the carriage house and couldn't get in. The door was locked. I pounded and called, "Let us in. I don't have a key."

A note shot out from beneath the door.

"What does it say, Lola?"

"We're supposed to go to the house." Another note appeared. "To the front door."

So we crossed the courtyard and followed the driveway to a sidewalk that led us around to the front. When we entered the foyer, all the aunties, Granny Sadie, Maks, and Freddie were waiting for us.

"This way, please." Maks held out his left elbow to me and his right hand to Cricket. We went through the foyer, and instead of going into the family room and turning left to go to the kitchen, we took a right down a short hallway. The first door on our right was closed, but the second was open to reveal Cricket's room.

"It's my bedroom," she exclaimed. "Exactly like the other one. How did it get here?"

"It seems," Comfort began, "that the house decided it was time for all of us to be together."

In other words, it was done being mad at me too. I hoped. I hadn't seen where I was meant to sleep yet.

"I love being with everybody," Cricket declared. It helped that she didn't have to get used to yet another new bedroom.

"Would you like to see your room?" Gwynne asked.

"Of course. Did my room move over here too?"

"It gave you a little more than that," Pepper said with a wink.

Jett opened the double doors to the room we'd walked past, and my mouth dropped open.

What used to be the sitting room was now the most beautiful British Colonial style bedroom I'd ever seen. The beams in the coffered ceiling were stained deep brown, and the same color wood floor was covered in a soft bamboo mat. The bed—oh, the bed!—was a queen-size four-post bamboo beauty with a mosquito netting scarf draped from each post. The walls were a soothing soft yellow and all the doors and trim a glossy black brown. There was a small sitting area with chairs, matching ottomans, and a television. Tall potted palm trees stood in each corner. There was a fireplace, a private bathroom, and an amazing view of the river and bluffs beyond.

Honestly, I'd never considered the style before, but since it screamed *safari* like my wardrobe, I loved everything about it. When I turned to let my family know how pleased I was to be closer to them, I found they'd shut the door to give me a few minutes of privacy.

Instead, I went to test out the bed—it looked wonderfully soft—and found an envelope with my name written on the front. Inside, was a note.

THE COUNCIL DECLARES THE OUTSTANDING LOAN BALANCE TO DUSTY WARREN HOTTE PAID IN FULL.

A witch's knot pendant on a gold chain lay on the bed too.

Thus began my change of life. Again. My Judgement, according to that tarot card. It was time to expand my horizons. I laughed. It appeared expanding my horizons meant returning to where I'd started. And although I still had a lot of questions surrounding my family and Blackwood Grove, things could be worse.

ABOUT THE AUTHOR

Mystery and fantasy author Shawn McGuire loves creating characters and places her fans want to return to again and again. She started writing after seeing the first Star Wars movie (that's episode IV) as a kid. She couldn't wait for the next installment to come out so wrote her own. Sadly, those notebooks are long lost, but her desire to tell a tale is as strong now as it was then. She lives in Wisconsin near the beautiful Mississippi River and when not writing or reading, she might be baking, gardening, crafting, going for a long walk, or nibbling really dark chocolate.

Printed in Great Britain
by Amazon

49500804R00158